Force
of
Habit

ALICE LOWEECEY

A FALCONE & DRISCOLL INVESTIGATION

FORCE
OF
HABIT

MIDNIGHT INK
WOODBURY, MINNESOTA

First Edition
First Printing, 2011

Book design and format by Donna Burch
Cover design by Ellen Lawson
Cover art © Ray Laskowitz/Purestock/PunchStock
Editing by Brett Fechheimer

Midnight Ink, an imprint of Llewellyn Worldwide Ltd.

This is a work of fiction. Names, characters, places, and incidents are either the product of the author's imagination or are used fictitiously, and any resemblance to actual persons, living or dead, business establishments, events, or locales is entirely coincidental.

The Holy Bible, New International Version®, NIV® Copyright © 1973, 1978, 1984, 2010 by Biblica, Inc.™ Used by permission. All rights reserved worldwide.

Library of Congress Cataloging-in-Publication Data
Loweecey, Alice.
  Force of habit / Alice Loweecey. — 1st ed.
      p.   cm. — (A Falcone & Driscoll investigation ; no. 1)
  ISBN 978-0-7387-2322-8
  1. Rich people—Fiction. 2. Ex-nuns—Fiction. 3. Ex-police
officers—Fiction. 4. Private investigators—Fiction.
5. Intimidation—Fiction. I. Title.
  PS3612.O8865F67 2011
  813'.6—dc22
                                    2010036430

Midnight Ink
A Division of Llewellyn Worldwide Ltd.
2143 Woodale Drive
Woodbury, MN 55125-2989
www.midnightinkbooks.com

Printed in the United States of America

For Mom and Dad

ONE

Giulia Falcone—formerly Sister Mary Regina Coelis—
popped a tangerine Life Saver in her mouth to stifle a curse.

No wonder the client was desperate. She would be too if a
stalker had sent her notes that escalated from adoring to obsessive.
Given the choice, she'd rather be chased by a rabid Doberman.

The office door squeaked, letting in the aroma of fresh coffee.
Giulia looked up. Light from the hallway glinted off the title on
the frosted glass: Driscoll Investigations.

Frank Driscoll stood in the doorway, a steaming cup in each
hand. "Any ideas?"

"I enjoy having a boss who looks like Nick Charles bring me
coffee." Giulia tilted her head to one side. "If you put on the suit
jacket, you'd be the image of that classic detective."

Frank's blue shirt, gray shadow-striped tie, and charcoal trousers sat well on his muscled, six-foot-tall body. Very well.

Stop it, Giulia. He's the boss.

She pushed the notes away. "This is one sick broad. Why couldn't you need help with a nicer case? Like someone looking for their long-lost twin sister."

"You figured out the messages?" Frank kicked the door closed and set a sleeved paper cup next to her. "I apologize for the cup, but Common Grounds doesn't have espresso-sized paper."

"I worship you." She removed the lid, inhaled, and sipped. "I take it back. I worship their espresso."

"Women are fickle."

She swallowed a smart remark after a glance at the challenge in his grinning, freckled face. "As your dutiful assistant, I'll graciously overlook that."

Frank went into his office and rolled his chair next to her. "Tell me what the letters mean."

"They mean that this woman needs to learn the true nature of love. Stalking her ex with the Song of Solomon is wrong on so many levels."

"What makes that wrong? What's the Song of Solomon?"

"Heathen. Ever hear of the Bible? The Song of Solomon is probably the most beautiful love poem ever written." She sipped espresso. "It's also filled with euphemisms for men's and women's naughty bits."

He picked up one of the messages. "Really? I don't see that in here."

"She's leading up to it. The first one was innocuous. But think about the second one: 'Your love is more delightful than wine. Pleasing is the fragrance of your perfumes. Take me away with you—let us hurry!'"

Frank slurped from his own paper cup. "I wouldn't mind a woman writing that about me."

Men. All ego and appetite. "You would if she sent your fiancée a message that says, 'Tremble, you complacent woman; shudder, you who feel secure! Beat your breasts, for you will be completely forsaken.'"

"That's part of the greatest love poem?"

"No. It's from one of the Prophets, I think."

"You don't know? I'm shocked. Didn't you teach this stuff when you were Sister Mary-whatever-you-were?"

"I tried not to rub the kids' noses in the R-rated parts." Giulia tilted the cup to get the last intense mouthful. "What about you? Didn't the nuns teach you anything in school? You come from a good Irish Catholic family."

"My brothers gave me all their hoarded cheat sheets." Frank leaned back in the chair and scooted away. "I'll go to Confession on Saturday." He stood and opened the window. The early June breeze filled the room with fresh air and the smell of frying sausage from the pizza place across the street.

The phone rang.

"Good afternoon, Driscoll Investigations." Giulia aimed her empty cup at the trash while listening. "One moment, please." She hit the *Hold* button. "It's Mr. Parker. Want to take it in your office?"

"Nah." Frank rolled back to her desk, hand extended. She hit *Hold* again.

"Frank here, Blake . . . Already? . . . What was in the box? . . . Okay." He made a "gimme" gesture, and Giulia handed him pen and paper.

"Calm down." He held the phone between his ear and shoulder and scribbled. "Here's what I need you to do. Bring me the package and a list of everyone you've dated in the past three years . . .

Of course, names, addresses, and phone numbers . . . See you at six."

He lobbed the phone at Giulia and she hung it up.

"More letters?"

"The Golden Boy of Cottonwood, Pennsylvania, is not happy. New deliveries to him and the Perfect Fiancée."

"Creepier than the others?"

"Hers was. A dissected snake in a jewelry box. His was a pair of lovebirds."

"Dead?"

"No—they came in a box that had air holes drilled in it." He shook his head. "She dyed them pink and blue."

Giulia laughed. "Sorry. Good heavens. How does this woman sleep at night?"

He stacked the letters and tapped their edges on the desk. "You sure these are all quotes from the Bible?"

"I'll check the Old Testament for the 'tremble and shudder' quote tonight."

———

Giulia jogged past St. Thomas Church as the electric carillon finished "O Sanctissima" and the Angelus bell rang. That meant it was six o'clock. The Latin words looped in her head as she finished her last half-mile.

Oh, come on. It was high time she dragged herself into the twenty-first century and jogged to Metallica or Queen. She could stretch the budget to cover an iPod Shuffle, even though she'd already pawned the plain gold "wedding ring" she received the day she took final vows and became a "bride of Christ."

She flexed her bare left hand. After she left the convent she'd kept the ring as a reminder of the mystical union she'd once shared with God Himself. But money got tight when she lost the waitressing job in the Mexican place after dropping an entire stack of enchilada-filled plates. The pawnbroker gave her seventy-five dollars for the ring, and peanut butter on cheap white bread had never tasted so good.

Her stomach growled and she picked up her pace. Around the block, past the dollar store, down to the gas station. She smiled and waved at the evening mechanic as he locked up.

"You got yer mace, lady?" he called.

Giulia pulled the mace-sprayer necklace out of her T-shirt, and he gave her the thumbs-up. When she turned the corner, he was at his nondescript van making his first sale of the day. Perhaps it was another mace necklace or a hand-dyed shirt . . . or pot in a small bag labeled *All-Natural Herbal Tea*. She wondered if the gas station's owner turned a blind eye to that part of the van's supplies. She really hoped the mechanic was supporting an invalid mother with the drug money, but even she knew that thought was painfully naïve.

St. Thomas' carillon changed to "Panis Angelicus," and she grimaced. Even country-western on a portable radio would be better than moldy Latin hymns.

You'd never have said that in the convent, Falcone. Thought it maybe, but never let it pass your lips. Maybe Sister Mary Fabian was right and you really are going to Hell.

Then at least she'd arrive in good shape. She laughed and started an extra lap around the block.

———

Giulia had surrounded herself with most of the papers from the corner filing cabinet when Frank walked in at nine the next morning.

"Frank, did your last assistant ever update the computer files?" She waved a handful of manila folders at him.

"Good morning to you, too." He stopped short, setting down a lumpy, translucent package on her desk. "Why is everything on the floor?"

"Because it's the only way to see what's been stuffed in here." She groped on the cabinet top for her breakfast peanut-butter sandwich. "Don't worry." She swallowed a bite. "It'll be back together by five. I'll start transferring everything to the hard drive tomorrow."

"Forget about the files for now. I want you to do something else." He pushed her chair toward her. "Sit down."

Her stomach fluttered. Had she screwed up? Maybe he loved old-fashioned filing. Or hated Windows. Why had she waited an entire month if he didn't like her methods? He knew she hadn't much experience with "regular" jobs. Few other twenty-nine-year-olds had a résumé that jumped from bagging groceries in high school to pouring coffee ten years later. Some Catholic school systems treated the habit and veil as instant teacher qualification. Six weeks of Methods and eight years' experience didn't count anywhere else, though. She needed this job. For the first time in nine months, her checking account had a buffer.

"What?" She sat.

He unwrapped more than a dozen layers of plastic wrap from the package to reveal a long, flat jewelry box. "This is the snake received by Pamela van Alstyne, Blake's fiancée."

She opened it and coughed. "Nasty."

"I'll open the window. Car exhaust is better than that smell." He walked two steps to the outer wall and pushed up the bottom sash.

Giulia unfolded the paper stuck in the lid. "'Go down, sit in the dust. No more will you be called tender or delicate. Your nakedness will be exposed and your shame uncovered.'" She studied the ex-grass snake. Its peeled skin stuck to the bloody cotton wadding beneath it. "Does the fiancée actually have any deep, dark secrets?"

"I ran a background check on her. Your life in the convent was more exciting." He took out two envelopes from the same pocket and gave her a folded pink paper from the top one. "This came with the birds. That's 'Passion' you smell. My last girlfriend liked to douse herself in it. Every time we kissed, I sneezed."

She snickered and opened it. "'Awake, north wind, and come, south wind! Blow on my garden, that its fragrance may spread abroad. Let my lover come into his garden and taste its choice fruits.'"

She held the note in two fingers to hand it back, resisting the urge to say, *Just tell me what you want, Frank.* "Phew. Cloying. See what I meant about those euphemisms?"

He nodded. "Even I got that last one." He set the note on the desk and held out the second envelope. "I want you to interview Blake's last five girlfriends."

Her jaw dropped. "Me?" She shut her mouth with a click.

"People talk to you. Here's your cover story: Pamela's mother hired you to see how Blake treats his women, because he seems too good to be true. You can also hint that her mom wouldn't object to busting up the happy pair."

"But . . . I mean . . ." She sat straighter. "That'd be lying."

"Spare me." Frank slid off the desk and pushed the window higher. "This is the real world, Giulia. I lie all the time when I deliver subpoenas. Nobody'd open the door for me otherwise."

No, no, no. She took this job for peace and quiet. Routine. No surprises. "I'm just an administrative assistant."

"And you were a teacher for eight years. You can talk to strangers." He appraised her while a passing fire-engine siren faded. "You got a decent suit?"

She glanced at her jeans and button-down striped shirt. "My job interview suit."

"That navy blue one? Good. Blake only dates women with money or status, so you have to blend in with that crowd."

Giulia scrambled for a way out. Detectives pried. Dug under people's skin. Exposed them. That was okay for Frank—he liked people who zipped their mouths shut. Thought they were a challenge. And he used what he learned only for doing good. But she'd had too much of prying in the convent.

"Frank—"

"I need you, Giulia." He set down the envelope and paced from the window to the filing cabinets and back. "These women won't give me the time of day. I'm the social equivalent of their pool cleaner." He leaned both arms on the desk, facing her. "But they'll dish dirt to another woman."

She took out the list. "This one's on the north side—that's ten miles from here. This one, too. The last one's in Pittsburgh. I don't own a car."

"That's what Enterprise is for. You can drive, right?"

She nodded.

"Thought so. By the time you go home and change, they'll have a car waiting outside your apartment." He stared at her. "What?"

8

He didn't understand. She needed to be invisible. From people. From God. The dissected snake lay right in front of her. One of these five women probably disemboweled it. They'd look at her like that. God looked at her like that. *Stop. Don't bring your baggage to work.*

One more—businesslike—try. "I have no idea how to collect the information you need. I am completely green on interviewing techniques. I—"

He turned his back to her and walked into his office. His old desk drawer rattled and banged. He returned a moment later and slapped a Day-Timer into her hands.

"Never used. The precinct guys got it for me when I opened. There's a pen inside." He squatted in front of her and looked up into her eyes. "Giulia, I get the feeling this is my big break. The case that'll get me word-of-mouth rep. I need to crack this."

Blast. He treated her like more than a typing and filing grunt. And he sure knew how to make big, green Bambi eyes. Could she say no to a legitimate employer request? Hey—if she did this for him, and he got more cases, he could hire a real assistant and she could go back to anonymity.

"Will they be home at this hour?"

He grinned and bounced up. "Guaranteed. They're society types. The only way they'd be out is if they're doing charity work. No big fundraisers are happening till the August Children with Cancer auction."

"All right. I'll call them from home. Give me half an hour before you send the car."

"Tell me how to thank you."

Never ask me to do this again. "How about hiring someone to clean the bathroom?"

"Does it need cleaning?" He looked genuinely puzzled.

She rolled her eyes. "Not today, because I scrubbed it yesterday." As she opened the door, she said, "Can you print out directions to the Pittsburgh address? I'll pick them up on my way to the first girlfriend's."

TWO

GIULIA SAT IN THE sedate maroon Impala listening to the engine cool. The house of Blake's most recent ex, three doors to her left, wasn't as intimidating as she'd feared: a shingled Cape Cod in a not-quite-rundown neighborhood, one street over from the perfectly landscaped McMansion section.

If Blake Parker only dated money, she'd bet Sandra Falke never brought him home to meet the folks. Wrong income bracket.

Now or never. Her interview after this one started in forty-five minutes.

Keys in her jacket, dinky purse in the glove compartment. She took a deep breath, crossed herself, and got out of the car. Blouse tucked in, jacket buttoned, hair . . . well, nothing would make that sedate. Day-Timer under one arm, she stepped onto the curb and snagged the heel of her pump. Arms flailing, she caught herself before her knee hit the cement and ruined her only pair of pantyhose. A robin hopped past and cocked its head at her. She blew it a raspberry.

A poodle in the adjacent backyard yipped and tried to bounce over the fence when she rang the bell.

Give it up, dog. My mother had cats bigger than you.

The door opened. "Yes?"

Audrey Hepburn would look drab next to tall, blonde, slim, manicured Sandra Falke. Giulia's clothes instantly became frumpy and ill-fitting.

"Uh . . . good morning."

"Thank you, but I don't require a copy of *The Watchtower.*" She started to close the door.

"Wait, Ms. Falke! I called earlier. I'm with Driscoll Investigations. We're looking for information on Blake Parker." She stifled her conscience and with a smile plunged into the lie. "His fiancée's family is naturally concerned that Ms. van Alstyne makes the right choice for herself and the family name." Her ears heated up. "They've asked us to make inquiries. Part of this investigation includes his treatment of women."

The delicately tinted eyebrows lifted.

"May I come in?" Giulia's armpits felt damp. Had she put on enough deodorant? Was any amount enough to cover this kind of flop sweat?

Sandra opened the door. "As I said on the phone, I have an eleven o'clock appointment. I'll only be able to give you fifteen minutes."

Giulia stepped carefully over the threshold—now would really be the wrong time to trip—and followed her through a cream-and-gold parlor into a small sewing room. Sandra sat in the only chair. To gain a moment, Giulia unzipped the Day-Timer.

"Oh, no," Sandra said. "I would prefer not to be quoted."

"Sure, uh, no problem." The zipper stuck on the top corner. *Leave it.* When she looked up, Sandra hid a smirk a long second too late.

"Would you like me to summarize, dear? You seem new at this."

Giulia stomped on her pride and attempted a sincere yet professional smile. "It's my first time in the field." Was that the right word? She'd heard it on TV. "I'm hoping to get promoted." Lie number two. She could hear her former Superior General now.

"How nice." Sandra crossed her legs and ticked off points on her salon-perfect fingernails. "Blake will be on the Board of Directors of the company he works for before he's forty. He's sharp, ambitious, knows the right thing to say and the right time to say it. He's building a network of business contacts. My guess is they're using him exactly the way he's using them." She gave a half-smile. "Am I going too fast for you, dear?"

"No, you're fine." Giulia cringed every time Sandra sneered. If she'd ever treated an erring student like this, karma was biting her in the butt.

"Oh, good. I'm sure with a little practice you'll be able to remember the important points." Sandra straightened her silk cuffs. "Blake likes his women to look good and act submissive, yet to be cool and assured in a social setting." She met Giulia's eyes. "Did you require information on how he is in bed?"

Dear Lord, get me out of here. "We, uh . . . no, no thank you."

"Blake always treated me with courtesy in public, but he liked complete control in public and private. I ended our relationship because of that. He also thought it was cute to call me 'Sandy.' He said I was his life-sized Barbie doll." One hand clenched just for a moment. "You can see why the relationship failed. He focused only on the benefits he offered me. He refused to treat me as I deserved

13

to be treated." She glanced at her gold-rimmed watch and stood. "I'm afraid I have to end our interview. I hope it will help the future Mrs. Parker."

Giulia aimed hurry-up thoughts at Sandra as she preceded her through the living room. When Sandra opened the door, a tall young man stood there with a key poised to enter the lock.

"Sandra. I didn't know you had company." The strength in his hard voice belied his tall, thin body.

"Don, you're five minutes early."

"You're not dressed, Sandra." He indicated his tight black T-shirt and black jeans.

"I'm dressed for my ten-forty appointment." Sandra looked from the young man to Giulia.

Giulia took the cue and held out her hand. "Thank you for your time and trouble."

The Vision in Black took it. "My sister hasn't introduced us. You are?"

She swallowed. "Giulia Falcone."

"Ju-li-a." He stretched out each syllable like he was tasting her name.

Sandra turned on her mechanical smile. "I hope you get that promotion, dear. Are you ready, Don?"

Don looked Giulia up and down. "You're not staying? Too bad."

His eyes gave Giulia shivers—they were compelling and eerie at the same time. She pulled back on her hand and was not at all disappointed when he released it.

The door closed behind them as she stepped carefully onto the sidewalk.

They're not watching you. Don't turn around. Use the nun walk—smooth and controlled. Like you're gliding.

Safe inside the car, she yanked the stuck zipper and the pen flew onto the dashboard.

"Argh!" She grabbed it and scribbled Sandra's list of Blake's qualities. As she wrote, an image of Sandra's dusty-rose nails superimposed itself on Giulia's short, practical, unpainted ones. Her pen stopped as she wrote a description of the house. *Her nails matched the roses on her couch. Good Lord.*

What would the other four be like? If Frank thought he was out of their social league, she was no more than a kitchen maid.

She reread the three pages of notes she'd just written. Had she forgotten anything important? This taking-notes idea wasn't going to work. What if the others were worse? She punched the radio's *ON* button and surfed till she found a New Agey station. Lutes and ocean waves filled the car, and she leaned her head on the steering wheel.

A tape recorder. Her high school students sometimes brought them to final-exam reviews. No. She understood their open use, but she'd have to hide it in the Day-Timer. If Sandra hadn't wanted her to write verbatim responses, guaranteed the others wouldn't want to be taped.

How else was she going to do this job? It wasn't like she'd post the transcripts on the Web.

No. She remembered reading an official-type printout in one of the filing cabinets. Something about two-party consent to record a phone call. It probably applied to face-to-face conversations, too. Anyway, she couldn't do it. Not after living through ten years of her mail being read and her phone calls being monitored. She was not about to turn into Sister Mary Hezekiah. The way that woman used to sneak around corners . . .

But someone was sending Blake Parker and Pamela van Alstyne borderline-psycho letters and packages. She didn't know which was worse—the clinging vows of passion or the veiled threats of scandal. All the signs pointed to an ex-lover on the edge. Most likely one of the five on her list. What if Ms. Scorned decided to prove the truism of Hell and fury?

A mellow DJ announced the next song, and birdsongs with harp arpeggios began.

Giulia banged her hand on the dashboard. *Suck it up. You have a good memory. Focus on what they say and ignore the attitude.*

Her mouth twisted. She would ignore it. Fourteen nuns and one priest couldn't beat her into submission with attitude her last year in the convent. Half-hour interviews with five society queens were nothing.

She worked the zipper around the sticky corner and back again. She certainly wouldn't try to exploit this snippet of authority like Father Mitchell did.

The zipper jerked too hard and stuck again. *Get over it, Giulia. It happened more than a year ago. You're past it.*

She eased the zipper pull over the bent tooth. And she was over it. Really. Until the memory surfaced and she'd see herself weeping in the face-to-face side of the claustrophobic Confessional, trying to explain why she thought doubting her vocation was a sin. Father Mitchell scooted his cushioned chair closer to her uncushioned one and rubbed her back. Then he crowded both of them onto the wooden floor and held her. So comforting. So kind. Until he pushed her against the wall and her veil slid sideways and his mouth crushed hers so hard that her lips were swollen for three days.

She sneered at her reflection in the windshield. She'd bitten through his bottom lip and escaped, but she hadn't even tried to report him. Everyone loved Father Mitchell. He was on the fast track to Monsignor. They'd say substitute-teaching censored Sex Ed classes had warped her.

If the snide notes in her mail slot were any indication, no one missed her after she walked out of Queen of Martyrs Convent, released from vows and still a virgin. Thank God.

A commercial for Super Summer School replaced the harp-and-bird song.

Of course. Mnemonics. She'd taught them to review classes every June. They were just what she needed for the rest of the exes.

11:10. Twenty minutes to the second interview. She popped the glove compartment, found the keys, and started the car. The mall was only five miles south, and her third interview wasn't till 12:30. The five dollars in her wallet would cover a cheap lunch at the food court.

She sniffed her armpits. More deodorant wouldn't hurt, either.

THREE

"Good afternoon. I'm Giulia Falcone, and—"

"Oh, yes. You called this morning." Isabel Groesbeck—another tall, slim blonde—pulled her inside and shut the door to the pillared veranda. "Please don't look at the mess. My sister is getting married in August, and the seamstress is fitting us for bridesmaid gowns today."

She led Giulia past a formal sitting room. Four girls stood on ottomans while two women with measuring tapes crawled around them.

"Would you mind terribly if we talked in the breakfast nook? The maid just started to clean the lunch things from the dining-room table."

"That'd be fine." She followed Isabel through a twisting hall covered with carpet so thick her heels turned with every other step. What would happen if she kicked off her shoes and let her hot, pinched feet sink into the rug?

"Here we are." Isabel pushed a swinging door and they entered a room as big as Giulia's entire apartment. A bow window gave her a clear view of the pool, hot tub, and tennis courts beyond. The table could seat twenty—forty if they were all dieting. The chair she sat in could practically hold her and Isabel side by side.

Nook. Right.

Giulia set her purse on the table and unzipped the Day-Timer. "Would you rather I didn't take notes?"

The geniality left Isabel's smile. "I'd certainly prefer it. I don't wish to feel that I'm being interrogated."

Giulia smiled and zipped it back up. "Not a problem."

Isabel rested her hands on the blue linen tablecloth. "Would you like a cup of coffee or tea?"

"Thank you, no." Mnemonics worked best with no distractions.

She settled her hands in her lap. Before her conscience launched another enraged sermon, she began, "The van Alstynes are anxious that their daughter makes the right marriage decision for herself and the family . . ."

———

Four down, one to go. She finished the Groesbeck notes and tucked them in the glove compartment with the rest. Keeping all the interviews under half an hour hadn't overloaded her brain yet.

Unzipping the Day-Timer before the first question had worked every time. The tall blonde sophisticates had shuddered at its newspaper-reporter image and then became almost confidential when she zipped it closed. Not quite, though. Giulia might have been wearing a neon sign on her lapel: *Social Inferior.*

So she worked for a living. Life was rough. She looked in the rearview mirror. Hair and makeup still passable; lipstick could use a retouch. And she needed a bathroom.

Pittsburgh next. She opened Frank's directions. Half an hour from the office . . . that'd make it forty minutes from her current location. The library was on the way; she could use their bathrooms. The appointment wasn't till 5:30. Plenty of time.

Her conscience poked and pinched her. *Sister Mary Hypocrite! What a Confession you'll have this Saturday!*

She turned on the radio. More waves crashing on some shore accompanied by mellow guitars. She pressed *SEEK* and found "Bohemian Rhapsody." Cranking the volume, she rolled down the window and headed north, singing as loud as possible.

It didn't drown out her conscience.

————

"I apologize for squeezing us both into my car, Ms. Falcone, but AtlanticEdge has one of those open office floor plans. Not a door in sight." Camille Osborn smiled at Giulia.

Giulia wasn't taken in. Camille's weekly paycheck wouldn't cover the price of her suit, let alone her shoes. Giulia lusted after those shoes.

This is about stalking, not Jimmy Choos. Wake up.

"So Blake's charmed another one? Let me guess: she's dripping with both money and status." Camille drummed her fingers on the gearshift. "I'll bet he's still using the organizational charts I created for him. He only got that promotion because I taught him efficiency."

"I see."

"If he'd stayed with me, he'd be climbing higher, faster." The smile grew brittle. "I'm different from his other women: I work for a living. They're living off their family's money."

Giulia glanced at those shoes again. She couldn't help it.

"Gifts from one's family are another thing completely." Camille crossed her ankles. "I hope his fiancée is Martha Stewart and Stephen Covey and Jenna Jameson all rolled into one. She'll need to be."

This is the best one yet. All I have to do is listen.

———

Common Grounds, the coffee shop below Driscoll Investigations, opened at six. Giulia met Mingmei, the barista, at the door the next morning.

"What're you doing here, Giulia?" Mingmei flicked on the lights and headed behind the counter. "I thought you worked human hours now."

Giulia yawned. "I have a ton of transcribing."

"Hope you're getting OT." She opened a vacuum-sealed bag an inch from Giulia's nose. "Crème brulée flavor. You know you want it."

"Of course I do. Extra-large, please. And no, I'm not getting OT."

Mingmei shook her long black hair. "Come on, you know better. You can't make rent by giving your time away. That job at the Marquee pays only ten bucks a show."

Giulia inhaled the rich, sweet scent as the coffee started brewing. "Twenty, and I met Frank in that pretentious orchestra pit, so it has its perks." Her eyes focused on the trays of baked goods. "May I have a cinnamon-apple muffin, too?"

"Good choice. You remember what's worth eating from your servitude to the cappuccino gods."

"It wasn't that bad here. I like early hours."

"Strange woman. I thought you met Frank here over coffee, not there over your flute and his cello."

"That was just serendipity. He took the office upstairs, and lo and behold, here I was behind the counter."

"And the rest is history." Mingmei's hand hovered over the paper cups and plucked an extra-large when Giulia nodded.

———

Armed with her coffee and two muffins, she booted the office computer and pulled out the notes and her new iPod.

She waved hello when Frank walked in, but stayed at her keyboard.

"How'd it go yesterday?" he asked, peering at the screen.

"Fine. Go away. I'm transcribing." She paused *Classic Reels and Jigs* and pulled out one earbud. "I'll get the phone when it rings."

———

At 4:30 she spread a stack of manila folders on his desk.

"In alphabetical order, Margaret Bischoff, Sandra Falke, Isabel Groesbeck, Elaine Moreton, Camille Osborn. All blonde, slim, and tall. Not all as polite as they could be."

He opened the top folder. "Wow." He opened the second. "*Iontach.*"

Giulia gave him her "mouthy student" glare.

Frank laughed. "That was just G-rated Irish. It slipped out. We had cousins from Galway visit last month, and I decided to dredge up all the Irish my grandmother taught me when I was a kid. My cousins taught me some interesting new expressions." He grinned. "Which I will keep from your proper ears, ma'am. Now, about these reports. What made you think of folders?"

"They're the most efficient way to collate the information. Look." She opened all the folders and set them in a row. "Personal characteristics. Neighborhood. Description of home. Family members I happened to see. For Osborn, the inside of her car. She's the only one who has a real job."

"Wow." He shook his head. "Let me think. Anyone stick out?"

"My clothes weren't good enough to touch Falke's furniture, and she showed it. Bischoff and Groesbeck almost treated me like a regular human being. Osborn was all business, an android from a sci-fi movie. Moreton acted like I'd stepped in dog poop and was dragging it through her house."

She pointed to a column in the middle of the Osborn report. "Blake has one habit they all hated. He gave them nicknames. Cammy. Ellie. Mags. Every one of them boiled when they told me that."

Frank picked up two folders like a kid who couldn't choose which candy bar to try first. "How did you remember all this?"

"Mnemonics."

"Huh?"

"Mental tricks to help remember details."

"Sure. Good thing you didn't tape them. It's illegal in Pennsylvania. We couldn't have used any of this in court, if it ever came to that." He jogged the folders into a neat stack. "You did good. You did great, actually. These women would never have told me about their cutesy nicknames. I wouldn't have gotten one-tenth the information you did." He smiled at her. "Above and beyond the assistant's call of duty. Super-nun!"

Shut up, conscience. Little lies that might save the client were a good thing. I didn't hurt the exes. I didn't invade their privacy.

She attempted to return his smile. "Ex-nun."

"And glad I am for it." He looked at the clock over the filing cabinets. "It's nearly five. Let's call it a day. I'll take these home tonight and pretend they're as interesting as Yvonne."

"Yvonne?"

"My newest admirer." He grinned. "She saw me in the orchestra pit last Friday."

"You have a groupie?" She covered a laugh. He almost distracted her from her raging guilt.

"I beg your pardon. I have swept a discerning cello enthusiast off her feet. She says I have great hands."

"Uh-huh. And she likes musical comedy."

"Sometimes. Her younger brother plays the hero's sidekick. She's coming again Friday night. I'll introduce you after the show. We're planning an intimate post-theater supper." He wagged his eyebrows. "Want me to see if she has an older brother?"

"No!" Her voice leapt up an octave. She swallowed. "No, thanks. I'm not ready to date."

"Giulia, you . . . what is that phrase you used . . . you stopped being a nun nearly a year ago."

"Jumped the wall." Privacy fence, actually. The face the world saw had changed since the thirteenth century. The real face, when the mask came off, remained medieval.

Frank snapped his fingers. "Right. Great image. So get back into the swing of things. The next time Evelyn comes to inspect her coffee shop downstairs, ask her to fix you up."

She shut down the computer and gave him half a smile. "She already tried. When I was her barista she introduced me to two of her nephews."

"And?"

"Please shoot me before I try that again. One had way too many hands for a human being. The other one wouldn't come within a foot of me. Said I had a 'nun aura.'"

Frank guffawed. "I'm not touching that one. All right, go spend another night with Godzilla."

"We're very happy together. He understands what I need."

He opened the outer door. "And that is?"

"Escape." She locked it behind them.

FOUR

"PARTNER?" GIULIA STARED UP at Frank, her morning coffee cooling on her desk.

"Not right away," Frank said. "It's more like partner-in-training. You need three years' documented experience working for a PI before you can apply for your own license."

She closed her mouth, sure she looked like a deer caught in headlights. "Why?"

He held up yesterday's girlfriend folders. "Are you kidding? You have the touch. Not only do people talk to you like you're their Father Confessor, but you classify data like a born geek."

"That just makes me a decent assistant." Boring. Invisible. The perfect job.

"You're wasted as an assistant. I can get anyone in here to answer phones and type letters. This—" he flapped the folders at her, "this proves you're just what Driscoll Investigations needs."

He sat on the corner of her desk, his herringbone blazer opening to a white polo tucked into crisp jeans. "I was up till midnight working out all the possibilities these showed me. For instance," he opened the file labeled *Osborn*, "she still works for the same company as Blake. She knows his schedule, she could get to his car, she resents that he just got a promotion—even though she doesn't need the money and she's only working a nine-to-five job to show her friends she's not a rich parasite like they are. She said it here—" he flipped over a page. "'They're parasites on their families' wealth.'"

"She tried to convince me she and I were equals. Her hairstyle cost more than my interview suit."

He cocked his head. "Did she say that?"

"Of course not. I could tell."

"Oh. Okay." He set another file on top of Osborn's. "And Bischoff. She didn't treat you like dirt, but the way she described Blake dumping her tells me he should avoid crossing the street if she's driving her car through the same intersection."

"Oh, yeah. I got a similar impression."

"Exactly."

The phone rang. When Giulia put it on hold, she said, "Captain Hogarth."

"I'll take it in there." He scooped up the files. "Think about it, okay? It's a great idea. It means a raise, too."

Giulia stared at his closed door until her Godzilla screen saver roared and made her jump. Her coffee was lukewarm now, but she gulped a third of it anyway.

Frank had just offered her a promotion and a raise for abusing the trust of five strangers.

She'd lain awake most of Wednesday night wrestling with guilt and shame. Remembering all the years she'd spent fighting the unchecked power of her Superiors. All the resentment she let fester in her every time another already slit envelope arrived in her mail slot. Seething every time a delayed click on the phone meant the Superior was doing a random conversation check.

And what had she done? Continued the legacy.

When she wasn't flogging herself with guilt, reason sneaked in and explained that she was really doing the opposite of the years of eavesdropping. She was no power-hungry local Superior looking to shine in the eyes of higher authority, ratting out underlings under the guise of spiritual growth. She was gathering private data—information she would keep like her own secrets—to prevent a disturbing situation from getting genuinely scary.

And her conscience sneered and called it sophism, and she'd be back to self-flagellation.

Around two a.m. she had wondered if the nuns in the Middle Ages had it right, and actual self-flagellation—with one's own three-knot cord—made repentance tangible to oneself and the entire Community. You couldn't argue with blood.

At least she had the common sense to know thoughts like that came from a punchy, overtired brain. She dragged out Carlyle's *French Revolution,* and, as always, it put her to sleep.

———

Godzilla battled Mothra on her screen as she sipped her coffee again. Cold.

She dumped the rest in the bathroom sink, closed the door behind her, and replaced the empty paper towel roll.

Private investigator. Too public, no pun intended. But if Frank needed help, she could be his stage crew. Smooth the details behind the scenes to let the actor concentrate on wowing the audience.

She stared into the bathroom mirror. Yike, dark circles. And her moustache needed plucking.

Stop distracting yourself.

She'd keep all information she gathered private, of course. And she could refuse to spy on cheating spouses or get involved with similarly grubby cases.

Not for the first time, she wished she had someone to talk to. Aunt Carmela out in Phoenix was the only family member who still spoke to her now that she'd "spit on the Cross." Uncle Vincenzo had surpassed himself in the only letter he'd written her. If he was right, her parents were weeping in the courts of Heaven, and not a single one of their blessed tears would cool her sinful forehead when she finally burned in Hell.

She'd ripped his letter into confetti and gone to LaRocca's for garlic pizza, where she'd drunk two—well, one and a half—glasses of red wine. She didn't think she was as depraved a sinner as all that. And whether or not she fried in Hell was up to God, not Uncle Vincenzo.

She splashed cold water on her face, patting it dry to protect her makeup. She could help people in trouble lots better as a PI than just as an administrative assistant. More than she could in the convent, too: no habit to scare people off. If her conscience turned shrewish again, she'd deal with it on a case-by-case basis.

Case by case. Maybe she'd do okay. She knew some of the jargon.

Giulia opened the bathroom door, walked past her desk, and knocked on Frank's door.

"Yeah."

Frank looked up when she opened it, and raised his eyebrows. She sat in the client chair and smiled.

"Define 'raise.'"

FIVE

"I HATE LEGALESE." GIULIA frowned at the multi-page Pennsylvania Private Detective Act. The noon lunch crowd swirled around them as she and Frank celebrated her promotion over cheeseburgers and onion rings.

June didn't get any better than this. A handful of fluffy clouds in a brilliant blue sky, and sunshine cascading over everything in sight. Little kids squealed as they splashed in the fountained wading pool in the park next to the restaurant. Every table under the awning and on the Pig-Out's patio was filled. Cottonwood might be one of Pittsburgh's biggest suburbs, but on days like this it resembled a popular resort rather than a steel-and-asphalt town with a population of more than 60,000.

She sucked iced tea through a straw without picking up the glass and turned a page.

"This is pretty clear once you get used to the language," Frank said. "I highlighted the parts you need to know. Just start logging your hours, beginning with all the Wednesday interviews." He inserted a whole onion ring into his mouth and followed it with several gulps of root beer. "My old captain will sign your second certificate of approval. I partnered with his son for five years, before the idiot who T-boned our squad car ruined my promising police career." He pointed to the page in front of Giulia. "You'll need two certificates, but that's three years away. How much do you know about guns?"

She swallowed a bite of cheeseburger. "Only what I've seen in movies."

"I'll take you to the shooting range this week, and we'll get you started."

"Started with what?"

"Practice. You need to learn to shoot a gun before you can get a license."

She hadn't thought about weapons. "Is that necessary?"

"You have to know how to defend yourself."

"Violence begets violence, Frank."

He coughed on a mouthful of root beer. "You sound like my grandmother."

"Just because I'm not in habit doesn't mean I've abandoned Franciscan principles."

"Giulia, it's the twenty-first century. Save all the homeless animals you want—Saint Francis was the animal guy, right?—but eventually you'll end up serving a subpoena on a loser with a .45."

"But—"

"And he won't think you're a cute gal who's kind to kids and dogs. He'll think you're the enemy, and you'd better be prepared for it." He wagged his straw at her. "You took this job. It involves some things you might not like."

She picked a sesame seed off her bun. This morning she'd thought she'd made the right decision.

He finished his burger and frowned at her. "What kind of shape are you in?"

The kosher pickle in her hand froze halfway to her mouth. "I beg your pardon?"

"I'm not coming on to you." A moment later he laughed. "Are you blushing?"

She chomped the pickle. "No."

"You should get out more. I meant, do you run or lift weights or anything?"

"Oh." Maybe she should get out more. "I run two miles a day—usually."

"Not enough. Make a fist."

"There are people here." Her ears pulsed. They had to be fire-engine red.

"Who cares?"

"You're not going to feel my arm."

"Just let me—"

"Back off, Frank. I don't like to be touched."

He sat back, eyes wide, then narrowing. "Sorry."

Pound pound pound. She breathed deep and slow to calm her heartbeat. What was her problem? Frank wasn't going to grope her like Evelyn's nephew did. Just because her first contact with men after ten years had been fodder for bad bar jokes . . . She forced a smile. "Sorry, too. You're trying to say I need to lift weights for the job?" She sucked more iced tea through her straw.

Frank's eyebrows looked like a sandy brown caterpillar over his nose.

Was that pity in his face? Oh, no. Not for her. She wasn't some emotional cripple. She had a few . . . quirks, that's all. And Frank wasn't going to jump the gap from professional to personal. She was sure he knew better. Everyone knew office romances were a disaster waiting to happen.

"Frank."

He blinked. "Yeah."

"I need to get in shape in case someone goes postal on me. Is that what you mean?"

"Yeah . . . yeah. I work out at the Y. It has a good weight room. I play basketball with the guys from the precinct once a week, too."

She probably couldn't afford the Y membership, but he didn't need to know that. "I'll figure something out."

Time to get distance between them before he tried some psychobabble on her about dealing with past issues. And get him off the gun subject for now. "Anything else I have to do besides increase muscle mass?"

He gulped the last of his root beer and crunched an ice cube. "Nothing important. If you, uh, want to keep fixing the files, that'd be great. I'll call the temp agency about a part-time receptionist."

She grinned. "So, it's a promotion in name only."

"No—no—honest. We just have to—"

"I'm kidding, Frank. Lighten up."

He smiled like he was thinking of something else. She paid attention to the last bites of the pickle and her remaining onion rings.

He crunched his last two ice cubes. "I have to pick up some equipment. You done? We'll stop on the way back."

———

Giulia held the wireless security camera in her hand while Frank checked the receiver settings.

"I had no idea they made these things this small now."

"Yeah. Great, aren't they? Motion sensitive, color, night vision, and small enough to hide next to the mailbox." He pressed a button. "Smile."

"How's that?"

"Good. Plug this cable into that port on the back. Yes, that one. Just let me plug the other end into my tower." He crouched under his desk. "Go into Explorer and open the E drive." His voice was muffled.

"All set."

He backed out and stood. "This should give us a close-up of your face." He double-clicked and a window opened, flashed a logo, and there she was, fish-eyed in the screen.

"Lovely." Her nose looked like a glob of modeling clay.

"You bet. Look at the clarity. It's almost this good at night, too." He closed the window and pulled the cable out of the camera. "Now the other one."

"If Pamela's so rich, doesn't her house already have security?"

"House? Try estate." Frank grinned into the second camera and plugged in the cable. "Sure, but we're hampered by Blake's paranoia."

"He's afraid of his exes?"

"No, of his CEO. Apparently a VP back in the nineties got caught in a massage-parlor sting and the company lost some huge clients. Blake's worried that any trouble, even trouble that's not his fault, will deep-six his promotion chances." He deleted the photo of himself and unplugged the cable from the three-inch camera. "So he doesn't want me contacting Pamela's security company to view their footage. That's why we're going to Blake's to set up one camera, and he's going to plant the one at Pamela's house."

"This is where I say, 'Whatever makes the client happy,' right?"

Frank set the cameras on his desk and shook her hand.

"Congratulations, Ms. Falcone. You've just passed the first rung on the ladder to success."

SIX

THE FINALE AT LAST. Giulia waited for her cue, flute in her lap.

This run of *The Music Man* appeared to be making a profit. The leads were just a mite too talented to stay in community theater. She'd heard "Marian" and "Marcellus" at rehearsals talking about the grind of trying to make it in New York. They had both tried and given up, and agreed that not having to land a part to pay the rent was infinitely better.

"Zaneeta" and "Tommy" opened their mouths and chewed the scenery. The Marquee Theater had enthusiasm going for it, if nothing else.

The Second Violin had great pecs. She could watch his bowing technique all night. The light on his music stand illuminated him from beneath at the perfect angle.

Admiring men from a distance again. How safe. He'd brought an equally buff friend to the opening-night party. So she was probably admiring a gay man from a distance. Even safer.

"Professor Harold Hill" raised his shackled arms, and the baby brothers of seven cast members put fake band instruments to their lips.

Giulia played Beethoven's "Minuet in G" a third lower than originally written. The Clarinet played it a fourth higher, the Saxophone in a different key. The kids tried not to giggle as they earned large *aww*s from the audience. Just like every performance.

———

Frank caught her on her way to the exit. "You have to meet Yvonne."

She'd forgotten. "Right. Your groupie."

"Ssh! I'm not too sure about her sense of humor yet."

A leggy brunette with an off-center blonde streak waited in the second row. *Now that's a miniskirt.* Gold lace on the hem and a blouse to match. A flower tattoo on her cleavage—Giulia didn't look close enough to see what kind of flower.

And here she stood in basic black jeans and T-shirt.

"Yvonne, this is Giulia, my new partner."

Yvonne's tiny smile revealed tiny, perfect teeth. "Um, hi. I thought you were Frank's admin."

"Just got promoted. Nice to meet you." That certainly wasn't jealousy in Yvonne's eyes. Just how frumpy did she look? "Gotta catch the ten-twelve bus. See you tomorrow night, Frank."

———

Denver and the Mile High Orchestra's latest CD drowned out Giulia's carpet sweeper. DMHO was her secret addiction, even though they weren't Catholic. Her hardcore relatives wouldn't approve, which made DMHO's music the perfect complement: her hardcore relatives hadn't approved of her since last August.

Ten a.m. and all four rooms finished. *Who said scandalous women couldn't keep a clean house and a clean conscience? Stuff that in your white gloves, Aunt Assunta. I even dusted the top of the fridge.*

She carried a pitcher of water to the potted plants by the living-room window. "Hey, tomatoes. Nice flowers. Have a drink. Hey, basil, you're limp. You have all the sun you need. Look at the parsley and oregano. They're laughing behind your back. Shape up or you won't make it into my next batch of sauce."

Time for coffee. Kona-macadamia blend sounded good today. *Gotta love those three-for-a-dollar samples.* The mail should be here by now, and the new issue of *Cosmo* was due any day. Every issue drove home the fact that she had so much to learn.

As she walked down the first-floor hall back to her apartment, she shuffled through the envelopes. Junk, credit-card offer—*as if*, pizza coupon, cellophane-window envelope with *Second Notice* in the bottom corner. Oh, no. Did she forget to pay a bill?

She closed her door and shut off the coffee. Pulling out a butter knife, she slit the bill.

Other than her address and several brown smears, the paper was blank. And smelly. She put one of the smears up to her nose and sniffed. Excrement.

"Ugh!" She dropped it on the counter. "What a sick joke." Shielding her fingers with a napkin, she picked up the paper and envelope and threw them into the trash, then tied the bag in a knot.

The twins on the second floor. This was just the kind of prank they'd pull. She still checked her mailbox before sticking in her hand after the spider incident last fall. The landlord never repaired the wall dents from Mr. Dachert's squashing marathon. Good thing the boys hadn't been in Dachert's range.

Scalding hot water and soap took care of her hands and the counter, then she dumped the rest of the mail into the recycle bin. If the twins had been her students . . .

———

After she'd jogged a mile, the annoyance faded. No real harm done. Just a serious gross-out.

St. Thomas' steeple loomed up on her right. Saturday—Confession. The elegant Gothic-style church intimidated her as she jogged in place by its statue of Thomas kneeling before the resurrected Christ. She shouldn't feel this way about a church. She'd been "on the inside" for years. Ten short months shouldn't have changed her that much.

Don't kid yourself. You changed the minute you formally petitioned the Superior General to release you from vows. You're an outsider now.

Those beautiful, carved wooden doors were closed in spirit if not in fact. Anyway, she couldn't go in like this. Father Carlos would have a stroke. Besides, she had to jog an extra mile to build stamina to fight the bad guys.

Cranking the volume on her iPod, she ran past church, statue, and grounds. Confession didn't end till two. Plenty of time to shower, change, and walk there in respectful clothes.

———

The bouncing theme to one of Margaret Rutherford's Miss Marple movies started on the tiny living-room TV as she scrambled eggs for a midnight supper.

"Wait for me!" Giulia sprinkled cheese in the pan and buttered a wheat bagel.

The credits ended as she set the dishes on the coffee table and plopped on the couch.

A perfect June Saturday. A clean apartment, hours at the library, groceries for the week for less than forty dollars, and an enthusiastic theater audience.

But no Confession.

Her forkful of eggs stuck to her tongue.

She'd skipped it. After her jog, she took a different route to the library so she wouldn't pass the church. Confession would've been pointless anyway. She couldn't promise Father Carlos she'd sin no more, because lying was part of her new job description. Probably.

She swallowed the eggs. Maybe next week.

———

"A reading from the Holy Gospel according to Luke."

"Glory to You, Lord." Giulia stood with the rest of the Sunday-morning congregation—all twenty-seven of them. Mostly little old ladies and men with late tee times came for 8:30 Mass.

Father Carlos removed his glasses after the Gospel reading and stepped out to the center of the nave. "I'd like to talk to you today about vocations."

Giulia shriveled in her corner of the next-to-last pew. If inanimate objects heard prayers, the floor would open up and swallow her right . . . about . . . now. When the scuffed wood ignored her, she peeked between her curls to see how many eyes stared at her.

41

None, of course—they didn't know what she used to be. She reached up automatically to fix the bottom corner of her veil, the one that always slipped forward.

Dolt. You haven't worn a veil since last August.

The ceiling fans stirred her hair, and a breeze tickled her exposed neck.

Father Carlos described the five-step process of discerning God's call.

God never called you. She never deserved to wear the habit. He only wants the humble, the holy, the steadfast—

Her conscience jeered at her right up to Communion. The faithful edged from the pews and lined up in the center aisle. But she couldn't receive the Host with sin on her soul.

Before anyone returned to their places, she slipped out the back door.

SEVEN

"Giulia, wait!"

Mingmei held the coffee shop door open with one foot and reached back inside with the opposite arm. The 8:30 a.m. bus fogged them with diesel as it roared away.

"This was on the doorstep next to the newspapers." She handed Giulia a box the size of a bakery box.

"Thanks. I love the hair."

Mingmei fluffed her short black hair streaked all over with bright purple. "It's a shameless grab for attention. I went over to my boyfriend's, and he and his buddies had the last three *Sports Illustrated* swimsuit issues spread out on the kitchen table."

"They saved the old ones?"

"Some of the photos had drool marks on them." Mingmei put a finger partway down her throat and made gagging noises. "I took a long, hard look in the mirror and saw 'bland.' Yesterday I told my hairdresser to go to town on me."

"What did your boyfriend say?"

"He hasn't seen it yet. We're going to the retro-punk dance bar tonight. Come inside for a second."

Giulia followed Mingmei into Common Grounds and inhaled to the bottom of her lungs. Fresh coffee, almond danish, Earl Grey tea. All the faux-Tiffany lights over the bistro tables were lit, their 60-watt bulbs geared not to startle the pre-caffeine customers.

Mingmei closed the door and beckoned Giulia behind the counter. Her head and shoulders just cleared its four-foot height. "I need your honest opinion, girl to girl." She put her hands under her small breasts and jiggled them. "Should I get one of those push-up bras?"

Giulia averted her eyes. "I think you're proportioned just fine."

"Not compared to the swimsuit babes. Look at you." Mingmei stood beside Giulia. "We're the same height, but you have hips and shoulders and boobs. Yours stick out at least two inches farther than mine. I need to enhance nature."

The bell over the door rang, and the owner of the copy shop two doors down dragged himself to the counter. "I need intravenous espresso, Mingmei." He yawned, stretching the grapevine tattoo around his jaw. "Hi, Giulia."

"Good morning, Quinn. Late DJ gig?"

"No. The baby's on his second ear infection this month."

"And nobody slept."

He yawned and nodded simultaneously.

Mingmei giggled and poured an extra-large regular, added three creams, and popped on a lid. "You're interrupting girl-talk, Quinn."

"I swear I didn't hear a thing." He twisted the lid to open the sipping hole and drank. "Ambrosia." He placed two dollars on the counter and waved. "Please continue. I gotta open the store."

After he left, Mingmei poked Giulia's box. "Want to tell me all about this secret admirer? I love romance."

Giulia laughed. "Nothing to tell. This must be something Frank ordered for the office."

"In your name?"

She shrugged. "He's kind of informal."

"Uh-uh." Mingmei shook her head, the purple streaks disappearing and reappearing. "Office romances are bad news. Don't do it."

"There's no romance. I promise."

Like she'd jeopardize her job. Like she wanted any man to touch her. Ex-nuns needed their own version of *Cosmo*. Maybe called *Baggage*.

"Good." Mingmei gestured to the display case. "Extra-large black? Muffin?"

"Just a small French roast."

"Miser."

"Frugal, thank you."

"Apple-filled croissants tomorrow."

Giulia's mouth started to water. "Ooh, you know I can't resist those."

"We got more cinnamon syrup for the coffee, too."

"You are murder on my budget. I'm leaving before I succumb to the lure of a danish."

Giulia turned the box over as she walked upstairs.

Sent from an illegible Cottonwood street name. Didn't people know that magic marker bleeds into brown paper? This felt like a grocery bag, too: the coarsest kind of brown paper.

She unlocked the office door and flipped the light switch. Sipping the French roast, she set her purse and the box on her desk, booted the computer, and opened the windows.

Pre-coffee surprises on a Monday. Not her idea of a great start to the workweek. She logged in and checked e-mail. The box hovered at the edge of her vision. Nobody would send her a gift. And if she had a secret admirer—right—why here and not to her apartment?

She deleted the last of the spam as Frank walked in. Today was one of his Sam Spade days. Fedora, pinstripe suit, paisley tie. Circles under his eyes, too. Could Yvonne have spent the night?

You can't get jealous, Giulia. He's the boss. And you can't make moral judgments. A thirty-five-year-old adult has perfect freedom to sleep around if he chooses.

"Good morning." She checked the clock above the door. "You're early. It's only eight forty-five."

He set a bakery-size box on her desk. "Blake called me yesterday at seven a.m. Pamela found this in her mailbox on Saturday. He brought me the camera, too. Let's see who left the latest gift."

Giulia hovered over his shoulder as his computer fired up, and he attached the cable to the camera.

"Come on, load. Piece of junk." Frank yawned. "Should've had more than one cup of coffee this morning." He drummed his fingers on the desk until his log-in window appeared. "Finally. Let's see. E drive, SpyEyes program, open file . . . there."

They squinted at the first photo. A crisp image of a mailbox, a bush trimmed to impeccable right angles, and a furry puff of something in the bottom corner of the frame.

"Squirrel must've set off the sensor. Date and time stamp works. Five fifty-three a.m." Frank clicked on the *Next* button. "Stupid squirrels." Again. "There."

The mailbox, the bush, and three slim fingers.

"A woman's hand." Giulia leaned in. "How often will it take a picture?"

"I set it for five-second intervals after the first sensor trip."

The mailbox, the bush, and a side shot of someone in a long, black coat bending over.

"What's she doing?" Frank enlarged the window, but the photo lost clarity. "Bad idea." He moused to the *Preferences* tab and reset the window to 100 percent.

The lens went black.

"Damn! Sorry, Giulia. I'll get it back." He clicked. Nothing. Another click. Still nothing. "Where are the rest of them? We put in new batteries yesterday."

"Could the squirrel have knocked it over?"

"Maybe. I don't know. I'll have Blake hide it in a different spot tonight." He closed the black window and detached the camera.

"Let's look at something solid." Giulia went through the doorway to her desk. "What did she leave?"

Frank stopped with his hands on the lid. "It's not pretty."

"Not more dead animals." She moved her coffee mug to the opposite side of the monitor. "Go ahead." He set the lid on the desk and unfolded layers of waxed paper.

"Gross—" She covered her nose and mouth and stared into the box. An actively rotting pomegranate half nestled in more waxed paper. Green and white mold fuzzed the brownish seeds and speckled the skin. The waxed paper was there to stop leaks, she supposed.

Frank handed her a folded square of plain white paper. "Careful when you open it. It got slimed."

Good thing she hadn't eaten breakfast yet. The paper smelled almost as foul as Saturday's prank bill. She opened it with fingertips only.

"Hard to read the first sentence . . . 'Your temples behind your veil are like the halves of a pomegranate.' Looks like she ran it through with a permanent red marker. 'All who honored her despise her . . . Her filthiness . . .' Can't read this part. '. . . she did not consider her future.'" Giulia set it on the box lid. "Frank, can't the police do anything with this? Whoever she is, she's headed over the edge."

He shook his head. "When I was still on the force, every so often we'd get stalker complaints. These letters, even the snake and this"—he grimaced and replaced the lid—"are nothing more than extreme pranks in the eyes of the police. They won't waste time on mild stuff when there are rapes and murders being committed."

She wouldn't call disemboweled snakes and hate mail "pranks." But Giulia could hear Frank's words in the mouth of an overworked officer. Along with "We have to use our limited manpower where it will do the most good."

"Did Blake get a delivery? What about his camera?"

Frank snorted. "Apples and raisins in a heart-shaped box. He's bringing the camera here later. This came in the box." He took a lace-edged paper out of his jacket pocket. "'Strengthen me with raisins, refresh me with apples, for I am faint with love.'"

Giulia sighed. "That woman is ruining a beautiful poem."

He tossed the paper on her desk. "Tell me again why she's using this Bible poem to mess with Blake and Pamela."

"She's using the Prophets on Pamela. I told you that. Scaring her with death, doom, and despair. But she's flattering Blake. Comparing him with Solomon: rich, virile, powerful."

"That's the way to his heart. Stroke his ego. He always dated the sycophants in high school."

She raised her eyebrows. "You went to high school together?"

"Yeah." A wry smile. "He started center mid on Varsity soccer. I played defense. The goat if they scored on me, blinded by the glare of Blake's triumphs otherwise. He went to the prom with the principal's daughter."

"Let me guess. Tall, blonde, and dressed like a magazine fashion spread."

Frank didn't laugh. "What else?"

"Did you and your prom date have a good time anyway?" *And why did he care more than seventeen years later?*

"Kind of. All the girls wanted Blake. Made the rest of us feel like leftover cabbage."

Mothra screeched an e-mail alert. She ignored it. "This is more than a big case, then." She stared out the window at the top of the *!PIZZA!* sign across the street. "It's another competition. Only he's on the bench, and you have to save the game for him." Where did she find these sports metaphors? She never watched sports.

A grin split his face. "Giulia, I'm Jesus Christ come down from Heaven. I'm smarter and more clever than him, and he knows it. I'm also discreet. He's desperate to make this marriage come off. Pamela has money, status, class—everything he's drooled over since we were freshmen. Each woman he's dated has been one step higher on the social monkey bars."

Giulia clenched her hand under her desk. She knew Blake's mother must have raised him not to take the Lord's name in vain, but she kept her mouth shut about the blasphemy. "And?"

"And he needs me to grab the prize. The skinny sweeper who stopped dozens but didn't score a single goal in two years on Varsity."

"Shouldn't you have some professional detachment, Frank?"

He chuckled and sat on the corner of her desk, bumping the box. "I am the soul of professionalism."

She raised an eyebrow.

"Honest. I know where the line is. Blake will get the very best from Driscoll Investigations. Think about it. When we return his life to the idyll of cutthroat business deals and social climbing it once was, all the business circles he moves in will hear my name. 'Need information before you close a big deal? Call Frank Driscoll. I use him exclusively.'"

"You've got dollar signs in your eyes."

"You bet. Blake can pretend he's patronizing me all he wants— we'll both know I saved his shallow butt."

She clicked the e-mail. Spam. "Frank, that other box by your hip must be yours and not mine. Did you order supplies in my name so the e-mails would get sent to me?"

"I didn't order anything. Where's it from?"

"Can't read the return address. Someplace local." She batted her eyes. "You're a detective, aren't you?"

He glared. "I'll get you for that. It's probably a gift from the Second Violin."

"I have no idea what—"

"I've seen you sizing him up. Why do women always fall for muscles? You're all alike."

"Frank—" She stopped, sure the heat in her cheeks wasn't from the breezeless, muggy day. Was she that obvious? Hadn't she learned anything from *Cosmo*?

He leaned forward, an evil grin on his face. "I dare you to open it in front of me."

It was probably nothing. A sample from a new office-supply store. No one would send her presents. Her birthday wasn't till March anyway.

She slit the tape with her letter opener and popped off the lid. Unfolding a sheet of waxed paper, she said, "Bet it's free memo pads from—"

A moldy pomegranate half stared up at her.

EIGHT

GIULIA'S MOUTH OPENED AND shut, but nothing came out.

Fuzzy, white mold splashed the fruit's sides. Green and brown slime puddled on the seeds. And the stench—

A piece of paper began to unfold from the inside of the lid and she jumped.

"Holy shit," Frank said.

She didn't *tsk* at the oath. She was thinking the same thing.

"What's the note say?"

Get a grip. Be a professional. It must be a misdelivery meant for one of the other ex-girlfriends.

Her fingers shook the tiniest bit when she opened it. "Uh—this one didn't get anything on it. 'This is your plague: Your flesh will rot while you are still standing on your feet, your eyes will rot in their sockets, and your tongue will rot in your mouth.'"

Wrong. No one was going to threaten her with the Bible. "If only I could read the return address. There's a verse from Revelation I'd like to send her." She handed him the note.

He smoothed it out on the desk and placed the note sent to Pamela next to it. "Same handwriting. Same paper. Why's she targeting you? Did any of them follow you after you left?"

"I don't remember. But I'm no threat. Wrong looks, wrong family, wrong bank balance. According to you, not Blake Parker's type."

"Not a romantic threat, no . . ."

Good thing she wasn't vain. The way Frank still had his eyes on the notes, he had no clue how that sounded. Plain Giulia and her plain life. At least that meant he wasn't about to consider her as anything other than an employee.

Too bad, a Cinderella voice in her head whispered. *You'd love him to.* She scowled into the psychedelic mold. *Stuff a glass slipper in it, voice.*

"Maybe you're a threat to her plan. You know, because your story made them think you're working to keep Pamela and Blake engaged."

"So this pomegranate is really a neon sign saying 'Back off'? Why couldn't she have used sour milk? Milk is a frequent metaphor in the Song of Songs."

He looked up from the notes. "What's the difference?"

"Because I like pomegranates."

Two quick raps and the door burst open.

"Frank, you have to do something now!"

The Perfect Male stood in the doorway. Wavy blond hair, broad shoulders, muscular arms and legs obvious even under the impeccably tailored suit. If he'd been smiling, Giulia wouldn't have been surprised at a cartoony gleam from his front teeth.

Frank stood and pulled his jacket straight. "Blake, we are doing something. Did anything else happen?"

Of course. The apparition could be no one but Blake Parker. Even stressed and panicky like this he would turn every female head in his office.

"Pamela called me an hour ago. She's not eating, she's not sleeping, and she hasn't been able to continue with the wedding plans." He rubbed his hands over his face. "You promised you'd help us, Frank. When are you going to stop this?"

Frank's hands came down on Mr. Perfect's shoulders. "I told you I'd eliminate your problem and I will. Did you bring the camera?"

"Yeah. Here." He pulled it from his suit jacket. "There was mud all over it. Didn't rain that much last night. Besides, I thought the spot we picked would've protected it."

Giulia's eyes met Frank's. The ex was smarter than they'd given her credit for.

"Come in here, Blake. We'll see if it caught anything before the mud."

Giulia looked away from Blake's blondness and saw both boxes. She'd better hide the extra pomegranate.

Opening her top drawer, she slid the wrapping and note from her delivery inside. With silent footsteps, she opened the third drawer of the nearest filing cabinet and set her box in the back. If he didn't leave soon, she'd have to wash the drawer with undiluted disinfectant.

She carried a manila folder back to the desk. A faceless grunt doing her faceless job.

"Time stamp says 4:42. All I see is . . . an arm in a long sleeve?" Blake's voice from Frank's office.

"If she moves just two inches to the right, we'll see her face in the next shot." Frank, in his detached, concentrating voice.

"What the—where'd the picture go?"

"Blake, don't touch the camera."

"The connection must be broken." A rattle and a metallic knock.

"She covered the camera with mud, Blake. That's why there's no picture."

"What? How'd she know it was there?"

"She looked for it. She's no dummy."

"Now what do we do?" If that had come from a child's mouth, Giulia would've labeled it a wail.

"You take Pamela's camera back and hide it . . . let's see . . . behind that embroidered pillow in the wrought-iron chair on the front porch. Make sure the lens has a clear line of sight to the mailbox."

"Fine. What about the one at my place?" Footsteps and Blake's voice coming closer.

"We'll bring it out this afternoon." Frank passed Giulia's desk, Blake following.

"We? Who else have you told?" Blake grabbed the shoulder of Frank's jacket. "Don't you understand confidentiality?"

"Of course I do." Frank smiled the way that made Giulia unable to stay mad at him. "I have a partner. Ms. Giulia Falcone, let me introduce Blake Parker."

Stand. Smile. Look him in the eye. "Pleased to meet you." She grasped his hand. Clammy. His, not hers. Better that way. Gave her an air of competence.

"Same here." His eyes traveled from her lived-in sandals and cotton skirt up to her plain, yellow camp shirt.

Yes, she shopped at Goodwill. No, she wasn't tall, thin, or blonde. And yet—he was giving her a "Hey, babe" smile. Good

Lord, was it possible for any male to be that convinced of his universal appeal? Apparently.

Frank tapped the monitor. "She's the organized half. I'm the deducer."

"Are you sure she can keep her mouth shut? It's bad enough there's some psychotic bitch after me and Pamela. I don't need more women screwing up our lives."

Don't react. You're invisible. Let Frank stroke this arrogant pretty boy.

Frank's smile clenched, then relaxed. "Blake, you hired me because you trust my skill and judgment. I know that trust extends to every part of my investigation." He shifted his balance, and his stance became at once assured and easy.

Blake waved a hand in Giulia's direction. "Fine. Whatever it takes to get us out of this mess." He sniffed; his eyes found the original pomegranate on her desk. He pointed with a slightly crooked finger. "That—disgusting thing. Are you positive someone I dated is doing all this?"

"'Fraid so."

Blake spread his hands, the picture of ingenuousness. "They all took the breakup so well."

Giulia nearly laughed, but her speakers screeched. Saved by the e-mail bell. She swiveled to the screen as Frank walked Blake over to the window, talking.

Blake interrupted Frank's soothing report, leaning out the window and muttering about the stink.

Poor baby—he really should do something about that whine. It distorts his modulated voice.

Frank planted his elbows next to Blake's on the wide sill. "We're on top of it. These things don't resolve overnight. We're collecting the data we need to close this."

Another impatient whine.

Frank stood. "It's just like in high school—I got your back."

Blake drew his head inside and poked his crooked finger into Frank's lapel. "Just do it quietly. No cops." Poke. "If word gets to upper management that I'm involved in anything to do with the law, my promotion is out the window." Poke. "It doesn't matter that I'm the victim. They want squeaky-clean execs."

Frank pushed the finger aside. "I got it."

Blake ran his hands over his blond waves and adjusted his Mondrian-pattern tie. "I'll tell Pamela we have complete confidence in you. The camera'll be back there tonight."

He closed the door much more quietly than he'd opened it.

Giulia deleted the e-mail. "Well."

Frank banged the edge of his fist several times on her desk. "Someday I'm going to re-break his finger."

"You showed commendable restraint. My teeth might've found that top finger joint, if he deigned to notice my humble presence enough to point it at me."

Frank sat on her desk and chuckled. "Good thing I learned to keep my temper in check when I was a cop. We never knew when somebody might be hiding a gun. Hey—" he scanned her desk, squatted and looked beneath it, then around the room. "Where's the other box?"

"Stinking up a filing cabinet." She retrieved it and set it on the windowsill. "These aren't evidence or anything, are they? Can't we throw them out?"

"I want to try to get a fingerprint off the wax paper first. Bring that one into my office, would you? The letters, too." He carried the one from her desk at arm's length and set it on the floor next to his filing cabinet. "Now bring me some paper from the printer."

"Yes, sir, Mr. Boss, sir."

He took the twenty-plus sheets from her with one hand as the other rummaged in a bottom drawer of the filing cabinets. "Close the door behind you so there's no breeze to disturb the powder."

Three more e-mails waited for her attention. She deleted the one offering low-cost drugs and answered the others before upping the spam filter.

Why was the stalker targeting her? Giulia hadn't done anything except interview her. Whichever her it was. Had the cover story been that thin? Had she been that bad at it?

And who sent the box? Bubbly Isabel, secretly furious that she wasn't planning her own wedding to Blake? Perfectly matched Sandra looking for the perfectly matched husband? Efficient Camille determined to rectify the inefficient breakup?

Yesterday Giulia would've said her only enemy was herself. If she didn't count all the relatives who blamed her now that there wasn't a nun or priest in this generation of Falcones. And maybe the Community's Bursar General.

She chewed the inside of her cheek to prevent a smile. There'd been a moment in their final meeting when she thought the woman simply couldn't bring herself to sign the check returning her dowry. All three hundred dollars of it. But she didn't think Sister Mary Beatrice would send her a rotten pomegranate at the exact same time an ex-girlfriend of Blake Parker sent one to his fiancée. If nothing else, Sister Mary Beatrice wouldn't waste perfectly good food.

The stalker knew she wasn't a threat. This definitely was a "stay out of my business" message. Nothing more.

"Sorry, whichever one you are. The job comes first." She glanced at Frank's closed door. "Gotta stop talking to myself at work."

She got the disinfectant from the bathroom closet and sprayed the file drawer. Meh. But better bleachy chemicals than rotten fruit. With a grunt, she shoved up the bottom half of the window another foot. Diesel fuel and hazelnut coffee blew in on the breeze. The city hall clock tower struck at ten a.m., but she wasn't hungry.

"Yes!" Frank's voice through the closed door. A moment later he opened it, waving one of the letters in a rubber-gloved hand.

"Fingerprints."

NINE

"Whose?" Giulia shook her head. "Never mind. Stupid question. On what?"

"Pamela's letter. Index and thumb. Half a thumb on yours."

"I'd applaud you, but what are we going to do with them?"

He collapsed against the door frame. "O ye of little faith." His face scrunched. "Did I quote that right?"

"Yes, you sinner." She hoped she didn't look old-ladyish. She had to drag herself out of Catholic high-school teacher mode. "Why do we need her fingerprints?"

"They're insurance. If we ever have to bring in the police—God forbid, Blake will have a cow—we'll plug these into the criminal database." He wiped his other gloved hand on his trousers and left a black smear across the pinstripes. "Shoot. I have to clean up the mess I just made. Be right out."

Rattles and sneezes. "Giulia, in the filing cabinet behind the door should be a box of those clear sheet protectors. Third drawer, maybe?"

She opened the drawer. Nothing. She tried the second. A cock-eyed hanging folder stuck to the back of the cabinet. She worked her fingers into it, felt thin cardboard, and yanked. With a rip, the box popped out and she barked her knuckles on the bottom of the drawer above.

"Got it."

Blowing on the scrape, she opened the top of a plastic protector and held it out as Frank slipped in a letter. The black-outlined prints showed up as dark as the bloody red line through the first sentence.

"Why does she think stalking him with the Bible is going to make him come back to her?" She held the wastebasket while he slid in the brown paper wrappings. "Rhetorical question. Don't answer." When he raised his eyebrows, she said, "I don't know if I want to get into her head to find out."

He peeled off the gloves. "Giulia, do you see why you need to learn to defend yourself?"

She stared down at him. "Just because someone says 'boo' doesn't mean I'm going to scream."

"That wasn't some bored-teenager prank. It sent Pamela into hysterics." He crumpled the paper in his hands and slam-dunked it into the basket.

Excess powder poofed up her nose and she sneezed. "Pamela's led a sheltered life."

"And you're a woman of the world?"

"I'm quite sure I have more experience than she does. I did teach high school for eight years." The basket plunked on the floor next to his desk.

"Convent years don't count. You might be thirty—"

"Twenty-nine."

"Okay, twenty-nine, but sometimes you're as naïve as a sheltered Catholic-school kid. And did you know you talk like my grandmother?" Sitting on his heels, he replaced the fingerprint-kit components into their slots.

"It's the training. We were supposed to be a placid example at all times, and that includes how nuns walk and talk." She pulled out his client chair and sat. "Don't change the subject. Why are you so upset over this? It was creepy but inherently harmless."

He closed the box and set the kit into the bottom drawer. Then he closed his eyes instead of answering her question.

Was he counting to ten?

Frank's eyes opened. Green and almost luminous in the shadow of the desk, they made it difficult to look away.

"Let me put it this way." He went to his own chair and sat facing her. "You agreed to be my partner. That carries certain responsibilities. One of them is to get your head out of your butt."

Who was he to— Why did he think he could—

"And before you go all righteous anger on me, let me tell you about Karen Reed. A sweet lady who found true love at age twenty-five. Except her true love liked to own things. Like girlfriends and knives."

The phone rang.

"Let the machine get it."

"I—fine."

"When True Love showed his possessive side, Karen ended the relationship. Then the phone calls started. Twice a day. Four times. Letters in her mailbox. Then special delivery. She thought it would stop as soon as he found another girl. When he started to drive behind her after work and park outside her apartment for hours, she called the police."

62

He picked up a pencil by the middle and tapped both ends like a seesaw on the desk. "You are paying attention, right?"

"Yes." Better keep it short, or she'd say something she'd regret.

"Good. A rookie cop named Driscoll tagged along with his partner to interview Karen. Because True Love hadn't actually done anything, all the police could tell her was to be careful and let them know if things changed."

He stopped tapping the pencil.

"A week later the letters got simpler: 'We'll be together forever.' Accompanied by photos of both of them with a dripping heart around their faces. The hearts were drawn in blood. She called us. A judge issued a restraining order."

"Fine. That's exactly what restraining orders are for."

"Oh, God. Grow up. Three days later her boss called us. She hadn't shown up to work, and her neighbors hadn't seen her. Rookie Driscoll got the key from her landlady, opened her door, and puked his guts up a minute later. True Love knew how to use those knives. Karen lay on the kitchen floor surrounded by a heart. Made from her own guts. We found her actual heart on the wall in True Love's apartment. Two other hearts next to it had already shriveled. True Love came after Driscoll's partner with one of the knives, and Driscoll shot True Love's leg out from under him."

Giulia's heart contracted. "That poor girl. But if he was that misguided, could anything really have stopped him?"

"Misguided?" The pencil snapped in two. "Do you have a brain under all those curls? He was a twisted killer, and she died because we didn't take him seriously till it was too late."

"No one is irredeemable—"

Frank slapped both hands on the desk. "Listen to me. Forget the crap you fed your students. You want this job, you drag yourself out of the nunnery and onto the streets. I don't care if you get on your knees every night to pray for whoever is stalking Blake, as long as you know this is not a game."

"I am quite aware of that." She recognized her tone of voice. The last time she sounded like this, her Superior was lecturing her about her lack of decorum.

"Then act like it. Have you started a spreadsheet of Blake's and Pamela's notes and packages received?"

"Of course."

"Add a tab for yourself. We'll hope this is a fluke, but it absolutely has to be catalogued."

Giulia counted to ten this time. "Frank, it can't be anything other than a one-off. I'm no threat. Am I rich? Tall? Blonde? Do I come from the right background? Please."

He drummed his fingers. "Jealous women—"

"Even our jealous and obsessive stalker picked the appropriate target: Blake's new tall, blonde, rich, Barbie doll." She waved the folder in front of her face. "Why is it so hot in here?"

"I closed the window so the fingerprint powder wouldn't blow all over the room." He felt the back of his neck. "I didn't notice the temperature."

Giulia went to the window and shoved it up. Pretending to adjust the screen bought her a minute. *What a pig-headed, arrogant know-it-all.* She inhaled mingled coffee, baking bread, and the overflowing dumpster between the buildings before she turned around. "Your advice has been noted and filed. Please dismiss the idea that I take any of this lightly."

Damn him for that look on his face—puzzled and frustrated and . . . charming. Damn him for making her curse. Damn her for losing her objectivity.

"I'm taking an early lunch. Should I take the pomegranates to the dumpster?"

"Uh . . . no, not yet. I want to study them some more."

"All the spreadsheets will be updated and in the shared directory by the end of the day."

She managed not to slam the outer door.

TEN

"Tomorrow night, seven to eight-thirty, Master Class Karate Studio on Euclid Avenue." Frank ripped a page from the *Cottonwood Community News* and held it in front of Giulia until she took it.

"'Learn self-defense from a Master.'" She rolled her eyes. "Frank, I thought we—"

"We did not. We left the conversation unfinished." He folded the rest of the tabloid-sized paper and dropped it in her trash can. "Before lunch you said you took this job seriously. That means, of course, you'll be at this class tomorrow night."

He opened his door but stopped in the doorway. "It's twenty-five dollars. Do you need to expense it?"

That stung. "I'm not destitute."

"Good." He closed the door between them.

Giulia propped her elbows on her desk, the spreadsheet as unimportant as yesterday's weather.

She gave him too much lip earlier. He was the boss. She couldn't forget that. She needed to—oh, no—sit down, shut up, and obey. A noise came from her throat that actually sounded like a growl.

He wasn't the Superior General. She wasn't under vows to him. Only employee-employer agreements. She had to do what he said at work, but he didn't own her, body and soul, 24/7. That was the difference. She was free in every way that mattered.

She picked up the phone and dialed. A deep male voice answered on the second ring. She still didn't want to do this, but . . . "I'd like to register for your self-defense class tomorrow night . . . Do you prefer cash or debit card? . . . Sweats and a T-shirt, fine . . . What bus line are you on? . . . Thanks."

———

Twelve women in sweats including Giulia, seven female and five male instructors wearing those white karate uniforms . . . what were they called . . . and thick cloth belts. Nine brown and three black.

Giulia tapped the shoulder of the older woman next to her. "Brown and black belts are for the most experienced students, aren't they?" she whispered. "I've never done anything like this."

The woman smiled. "Don't worry. My sister took this class last month. All the instructors are trained to be extra-controlled around us weenies."

Before Giulia could reply, the school's owner began his soft-sell pitch. The fees for twice-weekly regular instruction were astronomical and the bus transfer times inconvenient. Giulia pasted politeness on her face and squinted at the Japanese characters painted above the mirrored wall. The translation was too small to see from her back corner. During the skills demonstration, every time the owner and his instructors executed kicks and spins, a disinfectant-laden breeze wafted over her head. The frayed gym-mat corner tickled her bare foot, and she crossed her legs instead.

The demonstration lasted fifteen minutes, and left Giulia in awe of their collective strength. Those loose uniforms hid some impressive muscles.

"Every hold has a weak point." The owner of the school held up his arms and grasped his own wrist. "Watch my thumb and index finger. Pressure applied to this opening is the key to breaking this hold." He pushed against his fingers, and his trapped wrist slid out.

He toweled the sweat from his graying crew cut and arranged Giulia and the rest of the class in pairs to practice. Giulia held out her hand to her linebacker-sized partner. He bowed. She dropped her hand and returned the bow.

Great. Not only had she forgotten karate etiquette already, but now a strange man got to touch her. She'd never remember these lessons. Too obsessed about getting over ten years of "your body is Christ's temple and no human man should ever touch it."

Thanks, Postulant and Novice Mistresses. And thank you, Frank, for guilting me into this.

"Now you'll learn to do the unexpected." The owner beckoned to one of the female black-belt instructors and gripped her fore-arm. "When an attacker grabs you, what is your instinctive reaction?"

The instructor planted her feet and yanked her arm. Giulia would've done the same.

The owner answered his rhetorical question. "To pull away. As-suming the attacker is taller and stronger than you, this gives him an even bigger advantage. Watch." With little effort, he flexed his bicep and pulled the resisting instructor tight against his chest. "Now you're in his power."

He released the instructor, and she backed away one step.

"But if you move into his hold—" This time she stepped forward when he clutched her wrist, bending their arms double between them. "For a few seconds you have the element of surprise. Go for his most vulnerable spots. Crush his instep." The instructor raised her foot a fraction and stopped it just above the owner's.

"Put all your weight behind this and you can cause enough pain to loosen his grip and run. This move also works if an attacker grabs you from behind."

The instructor faced away from him, and he put one arm around her waist and covered her mouth with his hand. Before Giulia counted one—two—the instructor's heel hovered over the owner's foot, ready to smash. The owner released her, and she returned to her starting position.

"You might think the obvious response to a frontal attack is to knee him in the groin."

Several giggles from the class. The owner smiled.

"Every man everywhere expects this." He grabbed the instructor's arm. She raised her knee, and he turned away from the attack, locking his arm around her throat at the same time. "Do not put yourself in this situation." He released her, and they faced each other again. "The most vulnerable spot on the body is the nose. Watch."

He pulled the instructor in, and she pushed the heel of her hand under his nose and up. He moved his head back with her motion until he stared at the ceiling. "Done correctly, this can break his nose." He and the instructor bowed to each other, and she returned to her spot next to the woman on Giulia's right.

Giulia's partner, the linebacker with a shy smile, took her wrist as she tried not to flinch.

"Evening, ma'am, I'm Larry. Sensei would never say this, but you can sum up everything you learn here as 'Hurt the bastard and run like hell.'"

She smiled. Nice of him to try to alleviate her nerves. She must be radiating stress.

"Aim with the heel of your hand. Keep your arm straight and hit from your shoulder."

That worked. She clenched her teeth and practiced the correct angles for nose-breaking and foot-smashing over and over.

After fifteen minutes, the owner and the same instructor moved to the center of the mirrored wall again.

"Now that you have mastered the simple defenses, I will show you a skilled counterattack before we move on to basic throws."

He held the instructor's wrist. "Remember the nose." He pulled her toward him, and her other hand whipped out and "chopped" his nose.

Giulia jumped.

"Again, the nose is a delicate structure. Even the weakest of you will be able to cause enough pain and blood to escape a would-be attacker."

Giulia and Larry both laughed at Giulia's first attempts.

"Ma'am, try this." He pushed her fingers together and straight. "This edge of your hand is stronger than you think. Move it short and sharp. Like this."

He backed away a step and brought his arm to her face. She flung up her hands, and his chop touched her knuckles.

"I'm not going to hurt you, ma'am. Why don't you take my wrist and watch my movements so you can imitate them."

Giulia held his left wrist with her right hand. He took a quick step in, and his hand stopped just beside her nose.

"I almost got it," she said. "Would you do it again?" She grabbed him. He twisted in toward her and his arm came up.

Stars exploded in her head. Blood gushed from her nose. Pain whooshed through her face, and her breath became little gasps.

"Oh my God—ma'am! Are you okay? Somebody get a towel! I'm sorry—I didn't stop in time."

"What—I'm bleeding—" Giulia's ears rang like Easter bells. She inhaled and choked on a mouthful of blood.

Larry shoved a handful of paper towels in her face, and she clutched them to her nose and mouth. She blinked, but everything stayed blurry. Her nose throbbed. She coughed and it throbbed worse.

"Let me help you." A younger woman's voice. A hand took hers and led her along the wall—Giulia bumped it twice—and through a door. "Here. Sit down and let me look."

Giulia squeezed her eyes shut and opened them again. The bathroom. The instructor who'd demonstrated the moves for the class stood at a sink and held fresh towels under the tap.

"Let's check the bleeding." She tugged at Giulia's hand. "Still flowing. Press this hard on your nose."

Giulia gulped another glob of blood. Larry opened the door and hovered.

"Larry, get out of the women's bathroom." The instructor pushed him back and closed the door again. "Memorizes katas faster than anyone, but useless at the sight of blood." She frowned at Giulia. "The towels aren't quite as red now. Looks like the flash flood's over." She switched the damp towels for fresh and dumped the stained ones in the trash.

Giulia's face throbbed. The bathroom light shot through her eyes and sparked a jackhammer headache in both temples.

The instructor stopped in front of the sink and stared at her hands. "Um . . . you don't have AIDS, do you?"

Giulia laughed and coughed and laughed again. "Ow. No." She couldn't think of a short answer to explain why the question was funny.

The instructor smiled and shrugged. "Sorry, but these days you have to be careful. Let me clean your face."

Giulia closed her eyes while cool, damp paper caressed her nose, cheeks, and chin.

"There. Much better. I'll just stuff a piece of towel into your nose . . . there. Are you okay to wash your hands?"

"Sure." Giulia wobbled to her feet and flung an arm out to the sink. "You didn't see that."

"Of course not." The instructor patted Giulia on the back.

The soap frothed red; it took two complete scrubbings to clean her hands and nails. Then she saw the bloody tie-dye on her T-shirt and sweats. "They're ruined."

"Maybe not." The instructor squatted and felt the material. "Lots of cold water and soap as soon as you get home, then club soda."

"Home." Giulia blinked several times, and the blurriness finally disappeared. Now she could see her helper's deep brown eyes and the laugh lines around her mouth. "I don't know how to thank you."

"No trouble at all. I've got three kids. Minor catastrophes and mopping up body fluids are old news in my house."

"Then I thank your kids for their childhood injuries. Wait. That didn't sound right."

The instructor laughed. "I know what you meant."

"Do you have the time?"

The instructor stood and cracked open the door. "8:10."

"I have to leave. The next bus comes in seventeen minutes." Giulia touched the bridge of her nose. It kicked back. "This is going to be purple tomorrow."

"It sure is. Don't overdo the makeup for the next few days. That'll just make it worse. I'll get you some ice for the ride."

Giulia followed her to the door. *Deep breath. Everyone'll be staring at you. Suck it up.*

The self-defense students were twisting out of the instructors' choke holds. Giulia hugged the back wall and smiled beneath the towel plug. Larry broke away from his conversation with the school's owner and intercepted her beneath the exit sign.

"Ma'am, I'm sorry. A black belt should know better. I have no excuse."

Giulia put up her hands. "It's all right. No real harm done. I'll be fine tomorrow."

"Ms. Falcone." The owner handed Giulia her purse. "Please accept my apologies. Of course we'll be refunding the course fee to your account."

The instructor who'd cleaned Giulia up walked over with an ice-filled plastic bag. "When everyone asks, remember to say, 'You should see the other guy.'"

Giulia groaned. "That hurt worse than my face does." She held out her free hand to the owner. "Thank you."

Larry opened the front door for her. "Do you need an escort to your car?"

She shook her head and pain stabbed her sinuses. "Thank you, no. I'm just going to the corner bus stop." She looked behind her at the clock. "It's coming in eight minutes. I should get out there."

———

Giulia fumbled her deadbolt into its slot and tossed her purse at the kitchen table. The ice had melted by 8:45, and the bells at St. Thomas were striking nine o'clock when she got off the bus. She aimed the water-filled bag at the sink, where it hit with a splat.

The bathroom mirror lights stabbed through her eyes into her brain. She peeled off her clothes and scrubbed them in the tub. When she wrung out the T-shirt, she pressed the cool, soft cloth to her face.

She pushed aside the aspirin; it'd just make her bleed more. There. Acetaminophen. She swallowed four and stuffed a new Kleenex plug into her left nostril. The soothing darkness when she switched off the light was a touch of paradise.

She felt her way around the corner from the bathroom to the bedroom. Without thinking, she flicked the bedroom wall switch and the standing lamp right above her eye slapped her with sixty watts of torture.

She pushed the switch down. *Ahh.* She could navigate her own room in the dark. Closet to her left, bed four steps straight ahead. She'd never been so grateful her nightstand was on the other side of the bed—nothing for her to trip over. Hooray for summer, too, because she didn't need to leave the plant lights on for the herbs.

Her knee bumped the bed before her questing hands did. She pulled down the comforter and eased onto the sheets, spreading a hand towel from the bathroom over her pillow just in case. Pillows were never quite the same after washing and drying.

Oh, those cool sheets felt good.

More ice? Too tired . . . should say my nightly rosary . . .

ELEVEN

Giulia, I'm delivering subpoenas all morning, read the note taped to the frosted glass, below the word INVESTIGATIONS. *The new admin will be here at 9. See you at lunch.*

"Nine? Where's she—he—going to sit? Where am I going to sit?" Her key turned in the lock. "I thought he wasn't going to hire someone till next week. At least I got the new PC configured."

She flicked on the light and stopped one step in. Two desks now sat kitty-corner in the main office. Her chair backed against the dividing wall, and her desk faced the opposite wall instead of the door. The new desk beneath the window faced Frank's door.

"Nice chair." She ran a hand over the chair back and the desk-top. Used but good.

A sticky note on the new desk's monitor read *Giulia*. She squatted beneath the desk and booted the hard drive.

"Hello? Anybody here? I'm early."

Giulia jerked up. "Hi."

A stick bug stood in the doorway. Brown pants, brown shirt, brown hair, brown messenger bag, two brown Common Grounds coffee cups in her hands.

"I'm Sidney Thomas. Are you Ms. Falcone? You must be. Mr. Driscoll said you'd be training me." She held out one cup. "The lady downstairs said you liked cinnamon syrup in your coffee."

When Giulia got within three feet of the cups, Sidney nearly dropped them. "Whoa! What happened to your face?"

Giulia winced, which hurt, and winced again. "Karate chop."

"Wow. On purpose? Do you have a first-aid kit here? Ice pack, you know?"

"It happened last night. Most of the swelling's down already."

"But your cheeks are purple and blue and—wow—your eyes have all these little red veins in them. Ice'll help that. My trainers always nagged us to keep icing a day or two after an injury. Depends on what kind of injury, natch. But you want ice. Your nose looks like, looks like . . ." Sidney wagged a finger in the air like she was flipping through an air Rolodex. "An old movie actor. Hated kids. I thought he was nasty, but my dad watched him all the time."

"W.C. Fields." Giulia picked up her cup. "You didn't have to bribe me with coffee. I'll yell at Mingmei later for making you think you had to propitiate me."

Sidney's smile almost vanished. "I didn't mean to get her into trouble. I was just trying to be friendly, you know? Our senior guidance counselors told us to smile when you meet new co-workers. That way they'll think you're on their team right from the start."

And Giulia thought *she* was insecure. "I'm sure you'll work out fine, Sidney. Let me check your desk. My stuff might still be in it."

She opened the side drawer. "Yup. It'll just take me a minute to clean this out."

"No prob. I need to use the bathroom anyway." She looked left and right. "Which door?"

Giulia pointed. "Left. Right is Frank's office."

"Be right back."

Giulia moved her iPod and her Godzilla coffee mug to her new desk. Sidney must've been on the swim team. She hadn't seen her breathe between sentences yet. At least she'd have a human to talk to instead of her monitor. She grinned.

"I opened the window in there—it was really stuffy. Is that okay? I don't want to overstep my bounds or trespass on your job description."

Giulia grinned wider. "You work here too, Sidney." She finally tried the coffee. "This is excellent. Thank you."

"Oh, good. It was nothing, you know? I mean, it's something because it's kind of a gift, but it wasn't like a real expensive gift. Mine's green tea. You know about all the antioxidants in green tea, right? And detoxing? Coffee's okay, but your body can get addicted to caffeine, just like a drug." She gulped from the paper cup. "This is my first real job out of college, so I'm a little nervous."

Giulia kept a perfectly straight face. "Just let me log in and I'll set you up." She dumped her things in the drawer. "Spell your first name."

"S-i-d-n-e-y."

"Not with two *Y*s?"

"No, spelled like the guy's version. My parents expected me to be a boy. They planned to use me to suck up to a rich uncle. When I came out they named me after Uncle Sid anyway."

"Did it make him happy?"

"Not when it counted. He left all his money to the PETA crazies. Mom had a major cow. Dad ended up talking her down instead of venting like they wanted to. It turned out okay, because I got into college on a swimming scholarship." She unbuckled her bag and took out a bobblehead in a Penn State swimsuit and a swim cap.

"What do you want for a password? Letters and numbers."

"I don't know . . . How about *big10relay*, um, all lowercase? That was my senior team. We kicked major butt in the Big Ten championships." Her face scrunched. "Um, sorry, everyone says I kinda babble when I'm nervous."

Giulia smiled as she tapped several keys. "Don't be nervous. You'll do fine. There. You can boot up now. Your tower's beneath the printer cart."

Sidney opened each drawer and rifled the contents until her computer beeped. "What's my username?"

"Your first name."

A few taps on the keys. "It works. Oh, wow, a real job in a real office. I've been working full-time on the family alpaca farm since I graduated, but they're like the only animals on the planet I don't get along with. Plus spinning yarn from their wool throws my back out every year. You don't know how much I look forward to my summer job—I coach swimming for the Y. No spinning, no straw, no bagging alpaca poop—if you're a gardener, Ms. Falcone, I can tell you about that part later." She tapped a few more keys. "This is so cool. What are you going to teach me first?"

"The C drive is your own. E is shared between all of us. Click on it, and you'll see the correspondence folders."

———

Thump. Thump.

Giulia looked up at the rattling door. "Sounds like a foot."

"I'll get it, it's my job." Sidney hopped up and opened it on Frank, arms piled with three foam containers and extra-large cups in a gray cardboard holder.

"Lunch. Told you I'd be back. Giulia, can you grab the pop before I lose my balance? What happened to your face?"

"Self-defense class." She plucked the pop holder from the top of the tower and set it on Sidney's desk.

"What? How? Hi, Sidney."

"Hi, Mr. Driscoll. Let me take those."

"Top one's yours, middle one should be Giulia's, bottom one mine. You're vegetarian, right?"

"That's right, wow, thanks for remembering that from the interview." She headed into his office with the bottom container.

"No, leave it here. I'll use the windowsill. I need to stretch after this morning."

"Why?" Giulia handed out paper towels from the bathroom to use as napkins.

"My legs hate being cramped up in the car for hours. I drove all over town. The last subpoena was the worst. The guy hadn't paid child support for more than a year, and he knew his ex was after him. I had to break out the old 'Neighborhood Watch' ploy. When he signed the fake petition, I pretended I couldn't read his name. When he said it, I handed him a fake brochure. When he opened it and saw the subpoena, I was at the street before he had time to question my parentage."

Giulia blushed, and hated herself for it. Sidney laughed through a mouthful of spinach and feta calzone.

"Why subpoenas, Mr. Driscoll? I thought you found missing persons and spied on cheating husbands and all that."

"Extra money, Sidney. The rent's not high here, but now that I have two employees, I have to make payroll." He winked at Giulia. "How's the spaghetti parm?"

Giulia sucked the mouthful off her fork and swallowed. "Not bad. The sauce is homemade."

"And you would know."

"My grandmother would spin in her grave if I let bottled sauce pass my lips."

"I figured. Mine is that way about soda bread. Now tell me about that double shiner. You know you look like a psychedelic raccoon."

"Your sympathy is overwhelming. At least the guy who did this had the grace to apologize. More than once." She took a long drink of lemonade. "As a preface, I'll remind a certain person in this room that he required me to take the class to—ahem—protect myself."

Frank laughed so hard when Giulia reached the "You don't have AIDS, do you?" part of the story that he slipped off the windowsill and stamped like a horse. Sidney looked from one to the other and, like a student, raised her hand just to shoulder level.

"Ms. Falcone, why is that so funny? Everyone's at risk for AIDS once you've slept with someone. You know you're sleeping with everyone they've ever slept with—"

Frank pounded the wall and clutched his stomach. Giulia held up a hand to stop Sidney.

"You—you're such a fast mover, right, Giulia?" Frank wiped streaming eyes with a paper towel. "You've racked up half a dozen conquests since last summer, right? Oh, my stomach."

Giulia stuck the tip of her tongue out at Frank and smiled at Sidney.

"Up until last August, I was a Sister of Saint Francis for ten years."

Sidney's eyes got big. "You used to be a nun? Wow. I've never known a real nun before. Did you wear that long black dress and the headscarf? No, wait, that's a different religion. Was it anything like *The Sound of Music*? Julie Andrews is so cute. Did you sing that 'Dominique' song? No, wait, isn't that another movie?"

Giulia sighed. "Why does everyone ask that? No and no." She smiled at Sidney's embarrassment. "Although I do play guitar."

Frank hiccupped and tossed his trash into Sidney's basket. "Never laugh like that while drinking pop. Sidney, I have a stack of papers for you to sign. Giulia, now that we've established your HIV-negative status, what are you up to?"

"I need to run over to Quinn's, but it'll only take about half an hour."

————

Quinn refilled the 11 x 17 paper tray while Giulia waited. When he inserted her copy counter, he said, "Giulia, ask me how my day started."

"Only if you turn your back so you don't see what I'm enlarging. It's confidential."

"Deal." His left arm's elaborate tattoo of the Headless Horseman galloping after Ichabod Crane hovered just at her eye level.

"How did your day start, Quinn?" She hit the *Start* button.

"Discussing vaginal pH with my teenage brother."

"What?"

"I drive him to school because it's on my way here and I open at seven-thirty. I asked him about Homecoming, and he informed me that the expectation at school is that there'll be one pregnancy after the Homecoming dance, one after the junior prom, and one after the senior prom."

"Good heavens."

"You know it. As I'm *argh*ing at him, he said, 'Yeah, I know, use a condom.' I said, 'No—keep it in your pants!' Trouble is, what with our father getting his chippie pregnant, I'm pretty much the only discipline he has now."

"What about your mother?"

"She's still dealing with dad's affair and the divorce. That's why I drive Wes, so he gets some male role model time."

"But vaginal pH?" Giulia jogged her copies into a neat stack.

"Then he came out with, 'But they say there's a pretty safe time to have sex.' Of course I told him there isn't."

"He thinks it's right after a woman finished her period, I bet."

"Yeah. Dope."

"Italian grandmothers used to tell women to eat broccoli if they wanted to have a boy."

"Can I turn around now?"

"Oh, yes. I've covered everything up."

He pulled out the copy counter. "Come to the register, and I'll cash you out. I used that exact same example—my wife's Italian. Then I explained how broccoli alters a woman's vaginal pH, how some women are naturally more acid or more basic . . ." He keyed the totals into the cash register. "Or more hostile or receptive to sperm. I topped that off with the tidbit that some women have very receptive fluids and the sperm can wait in there until ovulation, and then, even if they haven't just had sex, wham! Fertilization."

"Tell him that some women ovulate on penetration, too."

"Good God. I didn't know that."

"One of the perks of teaching Sex Ed."

"I'll spring that one on him at the next opportunity. That'll be four bucks for the enlargements."

"Your day's been more interesting than mine, and thank you for not commenting on my face."

He practically whimpered. "It's killing me not to. You're always so quiet and nondescript. Wait—I didn't mean that the way it sounded. I mean, uh, that you, uh . . ."

She wanted to wince, but the thought of the lurking pain stopped her. "Don't worry. I know I'm not going to be the next Victoria's Secret model. I took a self-defense class last night and my partner didn't pull his punch."

"Man. I hope you got your money back."

"I did. But I'm avoiding mirrors for a few days."

"At least you weren't discussing vaginal fluids at seven-fifteen this morning."

TWELVE

"GIULIA?"

She looked around the filing cabinets. "Hey, Mingmei. What brings you up here?"

"A messenger or something left this for you before lunch. We got busy, and I must've just missed seeing him. Or her. I couldn't get it up to you till now."

Giulia took the brown-wrapped shoebox from Mingmei's hands. "Did you know the new chef's aprons would look so good with your purple hair?" She made a complete circle around Mingmei. "And do I point out that they're—ahem—coffee-colored?"

Sidney giggled. "Well, duh, Ms. Falcone." Her mouth shut with a click of teeth. "Oh—I didn't mean to sound rude. I'm sorry. It sounded like a joke—I apologize."

"Sidney, relax." Giulia smiled. "It was a joke. You're fine." Sidney's brown eyes returned to their normal wide-eyed state.

Mingmei snorted. "A lame joke, too."

"You have no appreciation of subtle humor. If you'd only read something besides *MAD* magazine—"

"Which is a classic of the comedic art."

"Let's stop before we come to blows and Sidney has to separate us." Giulia hefted the shoebox. Weighed about a pound. "I wonder why the messenger didn't deliver this to me?"

Mingmei shrugged. "Maybe they didn't see your nameplate next to the door. We had ours propped open because it got wicked hot. I thought I heard a voice asking for Driscoll's, but I was behind the counter, so when whoever it was left it on one of the tables, I couldn't stop them."

Giulia set it on Sidney's desk. Smudged return address. She wasn't sure she'd have the guts to pick it up again. Sidney and Mingmei were staring at her, and she forced a smile.

"It doesn't matter. Frank told me we'd be getting a delivery today." *Liar. Confession this Saturday. Without fail.*

Mingmei poked Sidney's swimmer bobblehead. "Cute. You?"

Sidney grinned. "First place, 400 free relay, Big Ten championship."

"Wow. I'm impressed. I swim like a rock: straight down."

Sidney's face conveyed that she had just encountered an alien life form. "You can't swim, Mingmei? Really? That's terrible. Everyone should know how to swim. What if someone you love needed help? Here—" She reached beneath her desk and opened her messenger bag. "I teach kid and adult classes at the Y all summer, weeknights and Sundays." She handed her a brochure. "It's only thirty dollars for six weeks if you're a member. All the parents say I'm a real patient teacher."

Mingmei's blue-tinted eyelashes blinked at a rapid pace. "Um, thanks, Sidney. I'll check my schedule."

Another brochure appeared in Sidney's hand. "Ms. Falcone?"

"Been swimming since I was ten."

"Good."

Mingmei slid the brochure into her apron pocket. "Giulia, I forgot to tell you that someone was asking about you guys the other day."

"For business? Why didn't he come upstairs?"

"She. You weren't open yet. She wanted to have you guys check out a new personal assistant she was thinking of hiring. Wondered if I knew anything about you people."

"Ah, the upper class."

"You know it. She looked rich and dressed it, too: blonde, tall, fancy linen coat, fancy makeup, perfect hair, shoes that cost more than I make in a month."

"Good. Sounds like easy money for us."

"I never thought you'd be mercenary." Mingmei looked at Sidney. "A promotion can corrupt the best of us."

Sidney laughed.

Giulia said, "Oh, how I long to work with you again and give up eight hours a day with my polite, eager, funny officemate. Really." Giulia faked a glare at Mingmei. "By the way, shame on you for making this poor woman buy me coffee."

"Sidney, did it work? Was she nice to you?"

"I am always nice." Giulia pointed to the door. "You may leave now. I resent these slurs on my character."

"You know what they say about these ex-nuns, Sidney."

Sidney's mouth opened. "No. What? Tell me."

Giulia shook a finger at Mingmei. "I'll get you for this. Confusing the innocent. Think of purgatory."

"Not Catholic, doesn't apply, ha ha."

Giulia blew a raspberry at Mingmei, and she left. Then Giulia picked up the box, went into Frank's office without knocking, and closed the door behind her.

———

Giulia stared at the Barbie doll in the shoebox. "Why are her wrists handcuffed?" It also wore a brown, curly wig, exaggerated makeup, and a passable imitation of lingerie she'd seen in a *Cosmo* "Better Sex" article.

Frank lifted the doll's arms. "Why the slutty underwear?"

"Frank."

"There's no other word for it, Giulia. Nice girls don't wear bras with the nipples cut out and open-crotch panties. I didn't know you could get the legs to pose like that."

Never in this or any other lifetime did Giulia think she'd be standing next to her—male—boss discussing X-rated underwear.

The phone rang. A moment later, Sidney buzzed Frank's intercom.

"It's a Mr. Parker on one, Mr. Driscoll. He sounds kind of upset."

Frank looked at Giulia. "Let's hope it's just another pomegranate." He took a deep breath and straightened his tie before he picked up the receiver. "Frank here, Blake. What can I—"

Giulia watched his face take on that soothing look he'd used on Blake in the office three days earlier.

"In her mailbox? What was it dressed like? . . . I see. You too? . . . Oh. Of course . . . No, no, I'll come by and pick them up. Can Ms. van Alstyne bring hers to your condo today? . . . Yes, with the camera. I'll be there after seven . . . We'll discuss it then. Right."

He set the receiver into its cradle and fell into his chair. "He got a Ken doll in a bridegroom outfit, complete with two wedding rings. She got her own Barbie. No handcuffs. I didn't get exact details of the outfit, or lack thereof. The Perfect Fiancée apparently indulged in some shrillness." He dropped his head into his hands. "If this weren't so important, it'd be funny. Those two are utterly unprepared for this kind of love/hate intensity."

Giulia snapped her fingers. "Frank, the doll distracted us. Where's the note?" She turned over the lid. "Nothing in here. Can I pick her up?"

"Go ahead. I don't need more fingerprints. Did I tell you I sent the ones we got to a friend in D.C. to check?"

"Why not here?"

"Because Blake doesn't want police involvement yet, remember? My D.C. friend owes me a favor, so he's running the check on the QT."

The note lay beneath the doll.

"'Woe to you who are clever in your own sight. At every street you degrade your beauty, offering your body with increasing promiscuity to anyone who passes by.'" Giulia dropped the note like it singed her hand. "This is not in the Bible. Not like this. She's corrupting the text to suit her own hate."

Frank whistled. "I can just imagine what Pamela's said. No wonder she had hysterics . . . wait a minute." He searched his center drawer. "According to Blake, they found their dolls about half an hour apart. He gave me the time stamps from the cameras."

"Cameras. Rats. I forgot to tell you. Mingmei said a tall, rich-looking blonde stopped in there and asked about us."

"Us? You and me?"

"No. Sorry. About Driscoll Investigations. If only they used a security camera downstairs."

"When? What did she say? What did she look like?" Frank found a piece of paper and wrote several bullet points.

"Before we opened. According to Mingmei's description, she could only have been one of the exes. She was tall and blonde, and wore expensive clothes." Giulia stared at the Barbie. "She gave Mingmei a story about needing a background check on a personal assistant."

"Flimsy excuse. Did she think we wouldn't hear about it?" He wrote. "No, of course not. She let us know that she's on to us."

"Our plastic friend here told us that."

Frank jumped up. "You're right. What if she tried to jimmy the lock?" He threw open his door and strode to the main door.

"Mr. Driscoll? Is something wrong?" Sidney half-rose.

Giulia squatted beside Frank. "No, Sidney, nothing's wrong yet. Anything, Frank?"

Frank ran his fingers over the strike plate. "Can't see any scratches. Can't feel any, either. No wax residue, so she didn't try to make an impression of the keyhole." He stood, stumbling on his right leg.

Giulia put her hands on his arms. "Are you okay?"

"Yeah, it's nothing. Ever since they put pins and screws into my leg, I have trouble getting up from that position."

"Were you in an accident, Mr. Driscoll?" Sidney sank into her chair.

"Back when I was a cop." Frank rubbed his kneecap. "We were on a high-speed chase. Someone ignored the siren and plowed into our passenger side—and me—at an intersection."

"Ooh." Sidney cringed.

"Three months and two surgeries later, my choice was desk job or new career." He grinned at Sidney. "Now instead of a precinct that has ten men to every woman, I have a matched set of lovely servants."

Giulia and Sidney burst into speech at the same moment.

"Frank, you sexist pig!"

"Mr. Driscoll, how can you say that?"

Frank didn't answer right away, possibly because he was laughing too hard to catch a breath.

"You—you should see—your faces."

"Sidney, I vote we stage a walkout right now." Giulia stalked to her desk and took her purse out of the bottom drawer. "Ready? We'll see how he does without his 'lovely servants' for the rest of the day."

Frank spread-eagled himself across the door. "Insubordination. You'll regret such willful actions."

Sidney hovered by her chair, shifting from one foot to the other.

Giulia sat in her chair and crossed her legs. "You might be more imposing if you didn't try to threaten and laugh at the same time."

"All right—all right." Frank took a deep, shaky breath. "But you both looked like something out of a silent movie. Righteous indignation and the rights of women." He bowed to them. "I throw myself on the magnanimity of my invaluable—and equal in all human senses of the word—assistants."

"Should we draw upon our innate nobility and relent, Sidney?"

"Um, I guess, um, if you say so, Ms. Falcone."

"Very well. Frank, you are pardoned. Although a little groveling would have been preferable."

He straightened, giving his leg one last knead. "You would've had to help me up. I did want to retain my last shred of dignity."

Giulia returned her purse to the drawer. "Where's a video camera when you really need one?"

Frank stopped in the middle of the room. "Camera. Deliveries. We have to check something. Come in here, Giulia."

He dug his Pennsylvania atlas out of the bottom file drawer in his office and opened it to Cottonwood. "Blake lives on Fairfield. That's here. Pamela lives on Hunter's Court. That's six miles southwest, if you could travel in a straight line. If I believe Blake," he pulled a folded sticky note out of his pocket, "he found his box at 5:25, and Pamela's cook found hers at close to 6:00." He frowned. "If she drove, she could have used the Turnpike. These times are before the morning rush, which would be perfect for someone not used to a daily commute. That is, if we keep to our idea that one of the exes is making the deliveries."

"Who else would one of them trust? I can't picture Isabel taking her sister away from her wedding plans to deliver rotting pomegranates."

"Or Sandra calling her manicurist for help dressing the Barbie."

The image made Giulia chuckle. "They must have done it on their own. I'm sure the cars they possess are powerful enough to make it door to door in plenty of time." She looked at her box. "Wait. What about a delivery service?"

Frank's head snapped sideways at her. "Yes. No. A delivery service would keep records. She wouldn't risk it."

"But Mingmei was sure that a messenger delivered the Barbie doll." Giulia stopped herself. "Not thinking. She could've stolen—I mean surreptitiously borrowed—the clothes from one of the servants. Would someone of their social class stoop to theft?"

"Someone of their social class is slicing snakes and perverting childhood dolls." He made notes on the collage of Giulia's enlargements taped to the wall. "Did I tell you that making these copies of the case documents is a good idea? It's like a tactile flow chart."

"Thanks. I wanted to see everything together—spreadsheets, notes, Bible verses, everything. It helps me think."

"Damn, I'm good. Hiring you, I mean."

"Frank."

"Giulia, someday I'll hear you swear—and the six o'clock news will announce that Hell has frozen over."

THIRTEEN

GIULIA TRIED TO THINK of something neutral about the Barbie as the house lights blinked to signal the end of intermission for Friday night's performance. She'd taken the doll home to study it after Frank had compared it with the dolls Blake and Pamela received.

Okay, she shouldn't lie to herself. She'd taken it home to obsess over.

It festered. Not so much the blatant falsehood of the twisted Bible verse, but the idea that the stalker was trying to handcuff her by distracting her with false accusations. Because that's what she decided the handcuffs meant: *I'm smarter than you, neener, neener.*

Not if she had anything to say about it. At its heart this note-and-gift delivery was a childish game of wanting what you couldn't have. Giulia hadn't been a teacher for eight years for nothing; she could outwit this mentality. It was only Friday night. She had all weekend to work on it.

The Second Violin's black T-shirt looked even tighter tonight. He must've upped his workout. What if he wasn't gay? How would he react to her wearing lingerie like . . .

She nearly missed her cue.

Give it up. You could never wear that kind of wanton underwear. You're a repressed ex-nun. God didn't want you. Men won't want you. Too much baggage. Get used to it. And pay attention before you miss another cue.

———

The bus let her off at 11:10. People were still strolling arm in arm, enjoying the balmy June night. She could hear a late football game in the park—probably the guys from the dollar store against the mechanics from the corner gas station.

A little tea, some TV, and then bed. News of course, but an easy penance to endure to get to the late-night talk shows. Commercials blared at her when she turned on Channel 11. Back in the kitchen she stared at the Barbie until the kettle whistled. Plain green tea tonight. Nothing with caffeine.

She dunked the tea bag. Plain. Like her. Not like Blake's women. Not like the perfect plastic woman in front of her.

She'd never be good enough for someone like Blake. Ha. Who cared about a shallow pretty boy anyway? She'd never be good enough for someone like Frank. Decent, hard-working, honest, handsome. She wanted to be good enough for him, and a big part of her didn't care that he was her boss. But she was rejected goods. Like sniping little Sister Mary Hezekiah said the day she turned in her habits: God was better off without her.

She slammed down the tea, splashing the Barbie. She'd been repressing thoughts about that day for months. But you can only cap a boiling kettle for so long before the lid blows off.

Trapped in this apartment. Trapped in the work-home-cook-sleep rut. Day after day after day. Like today: another Friday night with the TV and a cold bed.

She had to get out. The galley kitchen walls looked like the tiny "cell" she'd had as a Canonical Novice, trapped like a cloistered Poor Clare for a year and a day. She hadn't known then she wasn't good enough. She hadn't known yet that the wedding ring she'd received at Final Vows would be a lie.

A quick snatch to transfer her keys from her purse to her jeans pocket and she was out the door and down the stairs. All the blocked garbage spewed into her head. The old nuns watching every move the Novices made. The backstabbing. The passive-aggressive power plays.

She couldn't run fast enough. Didn't matter. She couldn't get away. It was trapped inside her. It was part of her. Panting, she stopped in the park. Late—near midnight by now. No sounds of football. No happy girl on the arm of her man.

"I hate You!" There. She said it. No one to hear but Him. "Why didn't You tell me I wasn't good enough for You?"

She paced around the broken water fountain and up the path. "I wasted ten years on You, and You dumped me like a no-good boyfriend!" Tears dripped off her chin and her swollen nose. "You said You'd be closer than any lover and I believed You. You ruined my life!"

Thank God—ha ha, funny—no one was around to hear her. If she had to break down, at least she embarrassed no one but herself.

"Why did I ruin myself for everyone else?" *Stop dancing around it. Ask Him.* "Why did You dump me?"

A thin, strong hand clamped over her mouth and another grabbed her around the waist. "Shut up."

The hands dragged her off the path into the barberry bushes. The light from the old-fashioned path lamps barely reached here.

He said in her ear, "Stupid idea, walking alone at night."

His marijuana-and-garlic breath fogged around her and she gagged. Thought fragments slugged through her brain. *What did he ... Jesus, help ... No one around ...*

She jerked forward, but he yanked her back. "Think you're smart, don't you? Think you're better than other women."

He shoved her forward, and she fell to her hands and knees. Thorns from old branches gouged her palms. A shoe kicked her stomach. Her lungs emptied and she dropped onto her back

His hands grabbed her collar and ripped. Her breasts bounced and her bra's front hooks popped open.

Get him— She clawed his head but his hoodie blocked her nails.

"Bitch." He slapped her and she tasted blood.

Get him off— She dug her heels into the grass and bucked her hips.

"Begging for it, smart slut?"

He dug his hands into her breasts and pushed his tongue into her mouth. She gagged and bile choked her.

"Shit!" He released her breasts and spat on the grass by her head. Then he grabbed her hair. "I'm gonna hurt you now, bitch. Warriors show no mercy."

What? Get away! Get him off!

She spat at his face, and he punched the side of her head. Her ears rang and her eyes blurred. He dropped her head to the grass and yanked at her jeans. The zipper ratcheted apart and air brushed her legs.

Now! Get away!

But he planted a foot on her chest and pulled down his shorts. Then he dropped to the ground and pushed his knees into her armpits. She twisted away. He punched her temple. She gasped and he thrust his erect penis down her throat.

She bit.

He screamed and rolled off her, clutching himself.

She scrambled up, snatched her jeans, and ran.

"Bitch!" Distance muffled his high-pitched voice. It was lower a minute ago.

She heard a woman's giggle, high and on edge, and realized it was hers. Then she was crying and clutching her jeans over her bare breasts and unlocking the front door to her apartment building. She stumbled down the hall, one hand keeping her shirt closed. Her other hand shook so much when she tugged her keys out of her pocket that she dropped them.

"Come on, come on." Tears blurred her eyes, but she found the keyhole at last and fell into her foyer. On her knees, she slammed and locked the door and huddled on the carpet, sobbing.

"Oh God oh God oh God."

Eventually a burst of applause from the television distracted her. She stood and stumbled into the bathroom, ripped off the rest of her clothes, and stuffed them into the small trash can. Then she put her face into the sink and puked.

When nothing was left but dry heaves, she groped for the mouthwash and drowned her mouth in cinnamon. She gagged on that, but kept gargling until she emptied the bottle and her mouth blazed like a bonfire.

Shower. Get his touch off you.

You'll wake up the teacher next door.

Too bad.

She turned the spray on as hot as she could stand and scoured every inch of her skin twice over. She had to pull barberry thorns out of both hands, and the soap kept getting stained with blood.

When she faced the shower head to rinse her face, the spray stung her chest and she looked down. Red crescents from his fingernails circled her breasts. Several dribbled blood.

She sank against the far side of the tub and hunched over herself, sobbing louder than the noise of the spray hitting the shower curtain.

When the water grew too chilly to stay there, she shut it off and wrapped herself in her towel. Shuffling like an old woman, she inched her way to the couch. She pressed herself into the corner and stared at hours of mindless late-night sitcoms without really seeing them.

FOURTEEN

THE CONDUCTOR TAPPED HIS baton on his stand and waited through the applause. "Remember, people, no matinee tomorrow. I'm not a comedian, so I won't suggest you run through your music anyway."

Giulia stepped around her music stand to the First Cello's chair. "See you Monday, Frank." She dug into her wallet and counted out exact change for the bus ride home. She hadn't needed bandages for the thorn-pricks, and her hands weren't injured anywhere near enough to interfere with her flute-playing.

Frank scanned the theater seats as the Saturday night audience exited. "Yeah." His frown disappeared when he looked at her. "New shirt? Aren't you hot?"

Giulia glanced at her high-collar, long-sleeved henley. "Not really."

"Mmm." Frank tapped his cello case as the usher kicked the doorstop away and the swinging door closed. "Where is she?"

"Have a date?" She'd have to haul to make the 10:12 bus—the crowded one. Safety in numbers.

"With Yvonne and the new pizza joint on Main Street. The one with the unpronounceable name. It's supposed to have authentic Sicilian pizza—the thick kind."

"Have you asked an authentic Sicilian? What kind of sauce do they use?"

Good. Her light post-performance conversation sounded almost normal. She had all day tomorrow to get her act together for Monday morning.

"Dunno." Frank checked his cell phone. "No messages. Where is she?"

"Maybe she'll call tomorrow. 'Night." Giulia picked up her flute case.

"Giulia, wait." Frank put a hand on her shoulder, and she flinched hard enough to knock against a music stand. "Yvonne threatened to stand me up, but I didn't think she'd really do it. Would you commit a huge breach of professional etiquette and get pizza with me? I want to pick your brain."

Bad idea. She was still a walking freak-out. "I have to catch the bus."

"I'll drive you home. Please? I promise not to mention Barbies or the Bible. Besides, I'm hungry. Are you part Sicilian by any chance? Can you pass judgment on the pizza?"

He'll wheedle till I cave. I've got no reason not to go with him; he won't come on to me.

She hoped her smile looked genuine. "I'm all Sicilian. Twenty generations of women make me qualified to judge any pizza. Let's go."

"Yvonne is hot, you know? But that's about all she is. She doesn't read anything in the paper besides the lifestyles section, and she only watches chick flicks." Frank swallowed a quarter of his beer. "And she gossips."

Giulia sipped Chianti. "Then stop seeing her."

"It's not that easy."

The waitress set the pizza between them. Frank dug out slices with a miniature spatula and set them on their plates. Without smiling once, Giulia looked the pizza over with one eyebrow raised, measured the height of the crust with finger and thumb, and tasted the sauce. Then she bit through cheese, sausage, and green peppers and chewed. Slowly.

Aglio e Olio—quite an ethnic name choice for a new restaurant—certainly piled on the Old World charm. Empty Chianti bottles on red-and-white checked tablecloths held candles with artistic wax drippings. Waitresses dressed in "authentic" peasant costumes. Sinatra and Dean Martin crooned from ceiling speakers. And, of course, bunches of plastic grapes on dried grapevines hung from a trellised drop ceiling.

Why, of all places Frank wanted to try, did he pick a restaurant with "garlic" in its name? She knew she'd have to deal with garlic again sometime—she loved garlic, always bought it fresh and chopped it herself. But too soon, too soon.

Stop. Focus on not making Frank suspicious. Swallow this pizza and say something clever.

"It's a presumptuous little offering, but it has merit." She'd heard that on a wine-tasting show once.

Frank's worry lines faded, and he laughed. His first bite took half his slice. "This is great. Don't be such a pizza snob." He drank more beer and finished the slice. "See, Yvonne is like a tenth cousin twice removed. When I break up with her, a couple relatives won't speak to me anymore." He took another slice. "Maybe that won't be so bad."

Story of her life for the last year. "Frank, think of her rather than yourself. Call her tomorrow and then break it off in person. Not over the phone." More wine. "If I had a buck for every junior and senior who cried on my shoulder because their boyfriends texted their breakup . . ."

"Yes, Sister. You're the soul of fairness and decency, Sister."

"I'm not a nun anymore." She clipped the words and bit into more pizza. *Don't lose it.* She should have caught the bus. She wasn't fit company for anyone, let alone her boss. And she wasn't decent anymore. Her mouth hadn't formed a prayer since he'd stuffed his . . .

"Giulia."

Her eyes focused on her white-knuckled hand around her wine glass.

"Want to tell me what's been bugging you all night?"

"No."

"I could see it in the orchestra pit. You—"

"Frank, my personal life is my business."

"Of course it is."

"Then let's talk about something else. Where did you find Sidney?"

———

Frank parked two spaces from her building's front door.

"Thanks for the ride and the pizza, Frank. See you Monday."

"Giulia, how long have you lived in this neighborhood? Do they issue a can of mace with your house key?"

"It's not that bad. We all look out for each other. Besides, it's affordable."

"It's two derelict buildings away from becoming a slum. That punk on the corner's radiating attitude. Let me walk you to the door."

Was it Pot-Breath? She had to get out of the car. She had to put a good face on it. If it wasn't him, was that other guy near the doorway the right height? Could she get down the hall and lock her door before Frank drove away?

"Giulia."

Say something. Make a joke about defending yourself with your flute case. Turn this door handle and get out. Mary, Mother of Mercy, protect me.

"Giulia, what's the matter?"

Frank's hand came down hard on her shoulder, and she gasped and shied against the door.

"That's it." He shut off the car and pocketed the keys. Before Giulia could protest, he came around and yanked open the passenger door. "Out. Your chivalrous employer is seeing you to your abode."

She ghosted a smile up at him and put one foot on the curb. Hooray, her legs didn't give out. Frank stuck to her back as she opened her own door, but walked through each room while she locked them in.

His "Me Tarzan" act was funny and comforting in its way. But he should go home, now that she was safe inside.

Liar. Face it: what she really wanted to do was hide under the covers and not come out till Monday morning. She had to beat that fear into submission.

Frank settled into the corner of the couch near the window. "Nice couch. Come join me on it."

She squeezed into the opposite corner. If she thought of it like one of the girlfriend interviews, she could detach herself.

Frank leaned away, legs crossed, one arm across the back of the couch. "First let me tell you that I had another reason for taking you out to dinner and getting you to let me in here."

Her heart stuttered. Frank was the soul of decency. She thought. What if he really wanted—

"We need to talk about Pamela."

She nearly laughed. Work? That was his ulterior motive? Her legs unfolded, and she took a full breath. "You're reprehensible. I don't even get overtime pay."

"You got pizza. You said it was good pizza."

"You don't need to look so charming, Frank. What do we need to work on?" Piece of cake. She needn't have worried.

"Someone tried to rape Pamela last night."

Her heart stopped this time. It must have, because when it beat again a second later, a jolt of pain zapped her chest.

"At—at her house? Near the camera?"

"No such luck, if I can put it that way. She's running the Children with Cancer auction this year. First organizational meeting was last night at that French restaurant downtown. The one where you have to speak French or you could end up ordering steamed DVDs." He grimaced. "Bad joke."

"Yeah." She could relax. It wasn't related to last night in the park. It was just a weird coincidence.

104

"The women got gabbing and stayed late. Pamela's friends went to the parking garage, and Pamela realized she left her cell phone on the table. Then she got stupid and decided to take the garage stairs rather than the elevator."

"Is she all right?" *Please. Please.*

"Fortunately, yes. The guy grabbed her at the landing and ripped off her shirt, but her friends were still on that floor. She screamed and they came running and he took off."

"Thank God."

He scrubbed his face with his hands. "Blake called me at 6 a.m. I'm whipped. He thinks it's connected. I don't."

Good. Then neither was hers. "Why?"

"Too typical. Pretty girl alone in an empty downtown stairwell after dark? She might as well have had a target painted on her back."

Say something else. Act normal. "Did she see his face?"

"No. Too dark on the landing, she said. Blake gave me a summary of what she told the police. He was taller than her, and she's something like five-eight or -nine. All she remembered clearly was his breath. Like he'd eaten a garlic pizza and smoked a joint after."

The couch lurched. Frank receded like a movie special effect. His voice wobbled through the buzzing in her ears.

"Giulia? What's wrong?" His hand patted her cheeks. "It's okay, Giulia. She's fine. There's nothing to worry about. Blake and her family will keep her under lock and key now."

The room came back into focus. "That's not—" She cleared her throat. "That's not it."

His eyebrows scrunched together. "Tell me why you freaked out in the car."

"Last night." How to say it? "I was walking in the park last night."

"At night? Here?" His voice ratcheted up several notches. "Alone? Are you nuts? Do you have a target painted on you, too?"

"Stop, Frank." She heard the tremble. *Freaked out* didn't begin to cover her mental state. "I needed air."

"Giulia, you don't go out in this neighborhood alone at night. You—"

"Shut up, Frank. Just shut up. I know it was stupid." She couldn't tell him why she needed air. One hundred percent guaranteed he'd never understand. "I wasn't going to tell you—keep personal and business separate, you know. But we can't be sure anymore that the stalker is one of the exes."

"Since when? Where'd you get this idea? And what does this have to do with the punk on the corner?"

"Nothing."

"Then what do you mean about not one of the exes?"

"Because—" The words wedged in her throat.

He paced the length of the coffee table and back. "Giulia, it's after midnight, I had Blake screaming in my ear at 6 a.m., and I'm the walking dead. Do you have anything useful to say?"

A flicker of anger, enough to open her mouth. "I must apologize. I wasn't able to take notes last night. Next time I'll be sure to bring the Day-Timer. Listen: Pamela's attacker had a busy night. Straight from the garage downtown to the park on the corner here."

Frank stopped in front of the tomato plant. "What?" Sharp, not critical.

"Let me finish my report, Mr. Driscoll. I have a head for detail, remember? He dragged me in the bushes and called me a slut—you'll have to check to see if he used the same insult on Pamela. His breath smelled like pot and garlic. Now do you see? He kicked me and ripped off my shirt and grabbed my—" She dug her fingernails into her palms and barreled on before he could interrupt.

"I tried to get him off me but he straddled me and—" The rush of words choked her for a moment. "I bit—him. He rolled off and I got my clothes and ran back here and locked the door and that's what's been bothering me all night, okay? He stank like pot and garlic and he tried to rape Pamela and he tried to rape me." Her voice cracked and she hid her face against her knees, rocking and sobbing.

Frank's hands touched her shoulders and she jerked her body away, but there was no place to go.

"Giulia, I'm sorry. It'll be all right, I promise. If you're uncomfortable with just me here, I can call my mom. She's a born comforter. She won't mind if I wake her up—she loves to fuss over people."

She raised her head and actually laughed a small laugh. "Frank, I would never ask you to call your mother at this hour."

"Did he hurt you? Did the hospital take good care of you? Who'd they call from the station?"

"I didn't go anywhere till I had to go to tonight's show."

He jumped up again. "What?"

"I needed to get myself together."

"Have you been living in a cave?" He pulled her off the couch. "You should've gone straight to the ER. They need to get semen samples, look for hair, test you for STDs. Did you scratch him?

They'll swab under your fingernails for skin samples. DNA testing, Giulia. What the hell were you thinking?"

She yanked her hands out of his. "Get out."

His face changed to a Greek tragedy mask: wide eyes, open mouth. Then: "What?"

She stalked to the door and shot back the bolt. "Get out of my apartment, Frank. It's after working hours. You can't order me around." Her hand shook when she popped the lock on the handle. "If you think you should be able to give orders day and night, you can have my two-week notice Monday morning."

What was she saying? She needed her job. She needed Frank. As someone to admire if nothing else. *Say no, Frank. Please say no. You're a decent man and I'm falling for you—there, I admitted it— and I need decency right now.*

He scrambled to the door and stopped her hand before it turned the handle. "What are you talking about? This scum committed two crimes in one night. You have to report it. You have to get treatment. What if he got you pregnant?"

The righteous anger vanished. "He didn't, didn't get that far."

"There was no penetration?"

"He put it in my, in my mouth." Her other hand clamped over her lips.

"Oh, Giulia." Frank pulled her into his chest and held her. "We have to get you looked at. Make sure you'll be okay. Come on. You know you have to do this. Where's the clothes you had on yesterday?"

"In the bathroom trash."

"All right, I'm going to get them. You get your purse and I'll drive you to the ER. I'll call my ex-partner and he'll meet us there. You'll like him. I'll stay right there with you, too."

She'd have to do this. It did make sense, really.

She'd have to describe it all.

And? She'd thought of nothing else for the past twenty-four hours.

He doesn't want you to quit. Focus on that. He was holding her. Just comfort, but strong and safe and oh God she wanted to kiss him, touch lips that weren't foul and spewing hate.

Frank spoke before she could raise her head and humiliate herself by acting on that thought.

"Come on, *a mhuirnín.*"

"Huh?"

"Nothing. Sorry. Come on. Let's get this done."

FIFTEEN

CAPTAIN HOGARTH WAS AS sweet as Frank promised. Giulia sat on the cot in the treatment room, legs folded as close to her chest as possible, as he keyed in her answers to his questions. He was way too tall for that flimsy plastic chair. Frank leaned against the wall next to him. At any moment the nurse would return with the rape kit and tell Giulia to take off her clothes.

She inhaled a lungful of sweetish hospital disinfectant. Gack.

Hogarth unbuttoned the top button of his shirt and loosened his plain navy-blue tie. "Did you see his face at all, Ms. Falcone?"

He had a good voice, too. A little gruff, but fuzzy. Like his pale brown beard.

"No. The path lamps don't give off much light, and he pulled me into the bushes. When he, when he stood over me, shadows from his hoodie pretty much covered his face."

"Tell me everything he said."

Detach yourself. Report it like those girlfriend interviews. "He called me a slut. He said, he asked me if I thought I was smart."

Frank stuck his head forward. "Why smart? What did he say next?"

"I don't know . . ."

"Use that memory thingy you told me about. The one you used to remember the interviews. Come on, Giulia, you can do it."

She closed her eyes. "He said . . . Do I think I'm better than other women?" She opened her eyes before the sounds and odors from last night drowned her.

Hogarth tapped into the laptop on the crowded table. "Anything else?"

"He punched me in the head. It made my ears ring."

Frank muttered something she couldn't understand. More Irish, she supposed.

Giulia frowned. "I didn't think about it at the time, but he did something really weird. When I was on the grass, he put one foot on my chest like . . . how do I describe it? Like a general in one of those old Roman Empire movies." She chewed her bottom lip. "He said, 'Warriors show no mercy.'"

Frank stared at her, brows furrowed. "That was a weird thing to say. 'Slut' and all that—" he waved a hand—"typical rapist-speak. Why would he talk about you being smart? Why better?"

"I told you. Because it's connected to—"

"Shush, Giulia." Frank looked down at his former partner. "Confidentiality. You know."

"I knew it would come up. I'll talk to you later about that." Hogarth smiled at Giulia. "If only Frank had given us a chance to warn you what he's really like, Ms. Falcone. Sure we can't talk you into working for us? You'd be in much better company."

What a puppy dog. She couldn't have hoped for a better interrogator.

"I have a few more questions, Ms. Falcone. They're a little awkward, so if you'd like Frank to leave, I can kick him into the waiting room."

Last chance . . . No. What would be the point? He'll need to know the perp's MO. She nearly smiled. Since when did she turn into a whiz at jargon?

"That's okay. He said he'd stay with me, so he might as well listen to the gory details."

Frank pushed away from the wall and sat on the bed next to her, but she moved away. "No, Frank. I need a lot of space for this."

He slid to the edge of the bed and hung his legs over the footboard.

Hogarth tapped more keys, and another page filled the screen. "Ms. Falcone, was there penetration?"

There. He said it. That hadn't been so bad. "No."

"Was there exchange of body fluids?"

Oh.

"Ms. Falcone?"

Still gentle. Giulia wondered if he talked to small children a lot. "He stuck his tongue in my mouth. The taste made me gag and he got mad. I spit in his face and he grabbed my hair and told me he was going to, going to hurt me."

"Ms. Falcone, could you speak up just a bit? I learned on a manual typewriter, and I always bang the keys."

Frank said, "You spit at him? Good for you."

"Frank, either shut up or get out." Hogarth's voice froze Frank in position. Then his next words returned to the soothing gravel. "What happened next?"

"He punched me in the side of my head and stood on me. I got woozy for a second. The next thing I saw—"

"A little louder, please."

She cleared her throat. "Then his knees straddled my chest and he . . . put his . . . penis . . . in my mouth." All those years of teaching Sex Ed weren't helping her with this at all.

Frank remained motionless.

Several keystrokes. "Did he ejaculate?"

Almost done. "No. I bit him—it."

The keystrokes stopped, then restarted. "And then?"

"He fell off me and I grabbed my clothes and ran home."

"Did he chase you?"

"No. He yelled at me. It sounded like falsetto."

Frank burst into strangled laughter as the nurse opened the door.

"The doctor is ready to examine you, miss. If these gentlemen would step into the hall?" Her Amazonian body filled the doorway. Hogarth hit two keys and closed the laptop. The nurse moved aside and Frank followed Hogarth through the door.

The nurse waited in front of Giulia until she looked up at her. Her fuchsia lipstick and matching eyeshadow framed the kindest face Giulia had ever seen.

"It's okay, honey. We'll be real gentle. Here." She reached up and pulled the green curtain all the way around the bed. "Get undressed behind there and make sure the gown opens in the front."

Giulia managed to get the puke-green paper gown on without looking at her gouged breasts. On the other side of her cocoon she heard tiny clinks and rustles. The rape kit. She twitched back the curtain, the rings rattling. An array of swabs, slides, boxes, and plastic bags covered the movable bedside table.

The doctor's head only reached to the bottom filigree ball of the nurse's dangling earrings. Giulia stared at his back as he opened his own laptop and set it where Hogarth's had been. His short, sharp movements contrasted with the nurse's gentle ones. If he thought no one could tell he used styling gel, she wasn't about to disillusion him.

"All right, Ms.—" The doctor glanced at the laptop. "Ms. Falcone. I understand you were attacked last night. It's unfortunate you didn't come right to us. We could have gathered more evidence." He shone one of those little lights in her eyes and up her nose. His delicate hands matched his small body and meticulous black beard. "This injury is more than a day old."

Giulia had almost forgotten the karate chop. "I took a self-defense class the other day, and my partner didn't stop his demonstration in time."

"Ah." He touched the bridge of her nose and pressed her sinuses. "Does that hurt? No? The bruising should dissipate and the tissue return to normal in two days." He typed for a moment. "Please recline on the bed. Nurse, position the lamp for a pelvic examination."

"No." Giulia scooted against the head of the bed. "That isn't necessary. He didn't get that far."

"This will proceed more quickly if you follow standard procedure."

"I said no."

His precise voice acquired a clipped edge. "Then please sit on the edge of the bed and hold out your hands."

The nurse handed him a series of cotton swabs and opened several plastic bags. He swiped them beneath Giulia's fingers and dropped them in the bags. The nurse labeled and closed them. When the doctor turned his back to them to type, she mouthed *tight-ass* at Giulia, and Giulia hid a smile.

114

The doctor spoke over his shoulder. "Please recline on the bed."

Giulia looked at the nurse. She nodded.

The doctor untied her gown's thin plastic belt—did they make these things from recycled trash bags?—and opened her gown.

"Oh, that pig did a number on you." The nurse patted Giulia's hand as the doctor pushed the scabbed crescents on her breasts. "Did you kick his sweetbreads before you got away?"

Giulia kept her eyes on the nurse. Another minute of the doctor's precise, cold hands on her, and she'd forget manners and slap him so he'd remember it.

"He stuck his—penis—in my mouth. I bit it."

The nurse crowed. "You are my kind of woman!"

The doctor frowned at the nurse. "I shall return in a moment."

When the door swung closed behind him, the nurse helped Giulia sit up and she closed the useless gown.

"He's a robot, but he knows his stuff. I try to team up with him when women come in here because we're such opposites."

Giulia held both her hands. "It works. Thank you." She glanced at the door. "Why did he leave?"

"To tell your cop friends to call a police photographer."

"What? What for?"

"To take pictures of your injuries. Gotta have 'em for when they catch the pig."

Giulia buried her head on her knees.

"Don't you worry, I'll be in here the whole time. You want your friends in here, too?"

Her head jerked up. "No!"

"I didn't think so. A woman's gotta have some privacy." She squeezed Giulia's hands. "I'll keep them out."

The doctor returned with two syringes, a color-capped vial, and more packaging. "The police photographer will be here shortly, Ms. Falcone. Did I understand you to say that you inflicted a bite on the attacker's penis?"

"Um, yes."

"I must assume you drew blood and thus put yourself at risk for various STDs and HIV. I have a combination Hepatitis A and B vaccine here. The complete Hep B requires two more vaccines from your primary physician within the next six months." He frowned at Giulia. "The STD tests require a cervical swab. Nurse."

"Real quick, over in a minute." The nurse rolled a lamp to the foot of the bed and switched it on.

Giulia gripped the sides of the bed and opened her legs. A cold speculum touched her, then disappeared.

"Done, honey."

Giulia clamped her legs together and sat up. The nurse wrapped the tourniquet around Giulia's upper left arm and drew blood. Then she injected the vaccine into her right arm.

The doctor closed the laptop. "Ms. Falcone, you are free to leave after the photographer finishes. Your primary physician's office will notify you of the test results." He held out his hand, and Giulia shook it. "You should be proud of your resourcefulness. Goodbye."

A new policeman came in as the doctor left, carrying a digital camera, a ruler, and Captain Hogarth's laptop. He looked all of eighteen years old.

Giulia leaned her arms on the bed to hold herself upright. It was clinical. Nothing more. She wanted Pot-Breath caught and thrown in jail. Therefore she had to let this kid take pictures of her torn breasts. Oh, God.

" 'Evening, ma'am. This shouldn't take more than a few minutes." He opened a different form on the laptop.

Noise from the hall crept in as the top of Frank's head appeared around the door.

"We'll let you know when you can come in, gentlemen." The nurse's hand hit the door closed.

The photographer pointed to the wall next to the bed. "All right, ma'am, if you'll stand there and take the gown down to your waist, we'll get the first set."

Giulia faced forward, left, and right. She didn't think. She looked above his crew cut to the pain-indicator chart on the opposite wall and counted its smiley and frowny faces. She repeated all three positions a second time, holding the ruler beneath each breast.

"To get the correct scale of the injuries, ma'am." He snapped one more photo and took the ruler. "All done. I'll fill in the rest of this form outside so you can get dressed. 'Night, ma'am."

Giulia pulled up the gown and sank onto the bed.

"Betcha can't wait to get home."

She smiled at the nurse. "You know it. Half of me wants to hang from the ceiling and scream, and the other half is so tired I could almost sleep here."

The nurse handed Giulia her underwear. "It's three o'clock in the morning. I sure wish I was in my own bed."

When her bra and underpants were on, Giulia felt secure. Illogical, really. They were just a thin layer of cotton between her and anyone touching her. Despite logic, these might just become her favorite jeans and shirt. A security blanket for the paranoid adult.

"Thank you for staying here with me."

"I've got three girls, honey. I just think of how I'd want some-one holding them up if—the good Lord forbid—they landed in here." She looked Giulia up and down. "You've got circles behind those fading shiners, but you look just fine otherwise." She enveloped Giulia in a hug. "You ready to face the cops out there?"

"One's a cop, the other one's my boss. He's a PI."

The nurse patted her and stepped back. "He'll get the pig for you, then. You're gonna help him, right?"

"Yes."

"You go, girl." She opened the door, and Giulia turned left into the hall and the nearly empty waiting room.

Frank jumped up from a battered chair in the corner. "Hey, there. All done?"

"Yes. Can I bum a ride home?"

Frank fell into step beside her. "We have to give your ripped clothes to Jimmy before we go."

"So we can check them for hair or saliva," Hogarth said from her other elbow.

Giulia shuddered as the automatic doors slid apart and they stepped into the night breeze. "Captain Hogarth, can you hit me in the head at just the right spot to induce temporary amnesia?"

"So you can forget about agreeing to work for Frank? I have a better idea. First thing Monday come to the station and ask for me. I know I can find you a job working for us decent, honorable, ready-to-serve police officers."

"Jimmy, you are not taking Giulia into that cesspool of dirty jokes and hard-ass thugs. She's different."

Giulia snorted. "Is that a compliment?"

"Of course it is. Here's the car." Frank opened the trunk and handed Hogarth the grocery bag filled with Giulia's torn shirt, underwear, and grass-stained jeans.

"We'll need to keep these for a while, Ms. Falcone."

"Giulia. And I never want to see them again, so don't worry." She shook his hand and didn't wince when his large hand squeezed the healing thorn pricks. "Thank you."

"Glad to help. We'll let Frank know if we get a hit on anything." He unlocked his unmarked sedan. "That job offer still stands."

"Go away, Jimmy. Thanks for coming down." Frank opened the door for Giulia and walked around to the driver's side of his Camry. "I'll call you Tuesday or Wednesday."

Giulia leaned back and closed her eyes. Frank was a careful driver. Some might call him boring. Her life could use a long stretch of boredom. Or, better yet, a permanent lifestyle change to cozy and domestic. House in the suburbs. No, the country. Close to State Route 66 but far enough away to be considered the sticks. A couple of dogs, a big vegetable garden, a good man. Like the good man next to her. As if he'd ever look at her as anything other than an employee.

And an ex-nun. She could tell by the way he acted around her sometimes. As though he could see her only in habit when she really wanted him to see how hard she tried to be a regular woman. That maybe she'd absorbed a lesson or two from *Cosmo* and raised her allurement quotient.

Except now. Two fading black eyes, a nose still not back to normal, and gouged breasts. Not only did she look like five miles of bad road from the neck up, but under her dowdy clothes the rest of her looked like, well, like a sexual-assault victim.

And didn't that sound all detached and professional.

Frank kept quiet until they stopped in front of her apartment building.

"Giulia, why didn't you tell us about the marks on your breasts?" His voice held a little of Captain Hogarth's fuzziness.

"Because I didn't think you needed to know." Temporary amnesia looked better every minute.

"Of course we needed to know. It's evidence. You aren't thinking."

She opened her eyes and turned her "disruptive student" glare on him. "On the contrary, Frank. I've been thinking about nothing else since it happened. I was hoping to keep a shred of privacy and not have my employer see photographs of my naked breasts covered with gouges from a disgusting, evil pervert's attempt to use me as a sex toy."

"It's not sex, Giulia, it's power. Rape is always about power."

Before she screamed loud enough to shatter the safety glass, Giulia pulled at the door handle. "Thank you for the ride. Thank you for making me get this taken care of. I'll see you Monday."

"Giulia—"

"Do you understand that I can't talk about this any more tonight?"

"If you don't talk it'll keep building till you go off like a shook-up pop can."

An edgy giggle escaped her. Before she disintegrated into hysterics, she opened the door. "Tell Captain Hogarth that he's a big, fuzzy teddy bear, and I love him to death. Good night."

SIXTEEN

"Giulia, my office, please. Now."

Giulia and Sidney looked up from Sidney's monitor. Frank marched past them without pausing. Giulia glanced at Sidney and followed him.

When she closed the door, he was tapping his desk and muttering, "Hurry up" to the monitor.

"Am I in trouble?"

"Huh? No, of course not. Finally—" to the screen. He banged in his password. "She killed the lovebirds."

"The lovebirds . . . you mean the ones she dyed pink and blue? How?"

"Opened Blake's deck door, probably with a credit card. Idiot doesn't have a deadbolt on it. I never thought of putting a camera on the back door. Broke their necks and left this." He took a pink phone-message note from his inner pocket. "'Love is as strong as death, its jealousy—'"

"Unyielding as the grave."

"Giulia, what the hell is it with her and this Bible poem? I dragged Blake to the station and forced him to report the breaking and entering, but she didn't take anything, so it's a minor incident for them."

"Why did she use a message slip?"

"She didn't. The cops kept the original as evidence. I scribbled the verse on this while we waited. She wrote it inside a blank card in that floofy wedding-invitation writing. The photo on the front was two little kids in wedding dress-up." He ran his hands through his hair till it stood up. "God, I'm tired. He called me at six a.m. again. Did you sleep in yesterday?"

"Till eleven. I had to get up for Mass anyway."

"If ever you had a reason to skip—never mind. I have this discussion on a regular basis with my mother. I know how it ends."

Giulia would've loved to sleep the whole day. That meant not thinking. Or remembering.

Frank's stomach growled. "Do we have anything to eat around here? What time is it?"

"Close to one. I'll send Sidney across the street for subs."

"Did you two eat? No?" He dug out his wallet and handed her two twenties. "Get what you want and get me a foot-long turkey club, extra bacon. And a can of that stuff they named the New York MLS team for—Red Bull."

As she went out, he called after her, "Tell Sidney she's on her own this afternoon—you and I have work to do in here."

———

Frank taped maps next to Giulia's enlargement collage and they covered it with notes and questions.

"I still think there's a possibility the two attacks were coincidence. No, wait." He held up a pickle slice before Giulia could interrupt. "How do we know he's not just a plain old pervert who didn't try and fail—or succeed—with one or more women in between Pamela and you? It's possible."

"What about the 'smart' comment?"

"Inadequate or angry man taking it out on easy targets." He set the pickle next to five others on his sub wrapper. "Which reminds me. You're not walking out alone at night anymore, right?"

"I'm not walking anywhere. Bus to work, bus home. In for the night." Giulia mashed her sub wrapper into a ball and tossed it at the trash can.

"You don't need to turn into a hermit. Just take basic precautions." He tossed his wrapper and rejected pickles in the trash after hers. "Back to which ex is after Blake, and why she's mixing the Bible with slutty dolls and dead birds."

"I have more on my theory of why she uses the Song of Songs."

Frank slugged the last of the Red Bull. "Try me."

"Because it's the perfect love song, and she's telling Blake he's her perfect mate. For example, Groesbeck's sister is having the perfect filthy-rich wedding. Groesbeck could be telling Blake that he belongs in her perfect storybook world."

"You said Moreton was too snooty to live, right? What if she thinks Pamela is too low for Blake . . . no, that won't work. The van Alstynes are practically the top of the money and social pyramids here." He drew a hot-pink X with a highlighter across the piece of paper headed *Moreton*.

Giulia stuck a finger on Osborn's name. "Solomon was one of the richest and smartest kings. Blake's business career is taking off. Osborn's the only one with a real job and a business head."

"So she could see it as a business transaction—marriage to the king? No, I got it—a hostile takeover." He laughed.

"Cute."

"Gotta find some lighter moments in between dead birds and rotten fruit." He drew fluorescent question marks on Osborn's and Groesbeck's sheets. "Bischoff?"

"I'm not sure. Nothing she said stuck out, not like the rude ones or the happy-happy ones."

"Question mark, then." The highlighter squeaked on the paper. "Falke?"

"She's supposedly an interior designer. That might count as a job under the 'business transaction' reason to stalk. Did I tell you her nail polish matched her upholstery?"

"You're kidding."

Giulia shook her head. "She also threatened to tell me about their sex life."

His eyes popped. "What?"

"She wouldn't have. She just wanted to humiliate me." Giulia tapped the pencil on Falke's sheet. "She acted calm and poised, but I get the feeling I missed something underneath, like the poise was a cheap paint job."

Frank waited, and finally Giulia shrugged it off.

"Chalk it up to nerves. She was my first interview. Here, look at one thing she said: 'He maintained public and private control, and he liked submissive women.' I can't picture her strangling birds and dressing up dolls to get Blake to marry her. She's going to marry someone who wants to be dominated."

"Agreed." Another X. "Matching nail polish. Picture that anal-retentive sex."

"Frank—"

"Sorry. I'll behave." He capped the highlighter. "I don't want to rule any of them out altogether, but this makes Groesbeck and Osborn our best bets, with Bischoff an iffy third."

Giulia leaned on the windowsill. "We should find out what religion they are. I'd be willing to rule out anyone not Christian or Jewish."

"Right, the Bible."

"She'd have to know it well enough to twist the passages from the Prophets. Paging through a *Strong's Concordance* wouldn't be enough."

"I'll take your word for it."

Sidney knocked and poked her head around the door. "Mr. Driscoll, I'm pretty much stuck without Ms. Falcone, so would it be all right if I left early to get my car out of the shop? They said it'd be done by four."

Frank checked his watch. "It's four-twenty already? Sure, go ahead. Do you need a ride?"

"My boyfriend's picking me up. See you tomorrow."

The outer door closed a minute later.

"Giulia, can you lock up? I'm meeting Yvonne at five for a drink." Frank dropped the highlighter in his center drawer. "I'm going to break it off face to face."

"You can tell me how right I am tomorrow morning."

"Only if she doesn't toss a sloe gin fizz in my face."

———

The breeze died just before Giulia finished cleaning the floors. She tossed the disposable mop pad into the bathroom trash and stuck her head out the window. She wanted iced coffee.

Why not? Her day finished an hour ago. The next bus came at 6:20. Plenty of time to lock up and splurge on an extra-large. She knew she worked late to avoid staring at the apartment walls. And she knew that the 6:20 bus would get her home well before dark. It wasn't fear. Of course not. Just common sense.

She pulled in her head at two sharp raps on the outer door. Blake Parker flung it open before she had taken a single step.

"Where's Frank?"

SEVENTEEN

"Mr. Parker, what happened? Can I do anything?"

He dropped a black leather gym bag by Sidney's desk and pushed her aside. "Frank!" He stopped in Frank's empty office. "Where is he?"

How she wanted to slap this man. "Mr. Driscoll's out. I am also working on your case, Mr. Parker."

"Sugar, I need a professional with experience. Dammit, why isn't he here when I need him?"

Didn't they teach common courtesy in business school? "Mr. Parker, if you'll sit down, we'll assess the situation."

Blake flung up his hands. "Fine. I doubt you can do anything, but what the hell."

If ever someone needed a ruler across the knuckles . . .

He rolled Sidney's chair next to Giulia's desk. "That bag was locked in my car all day. Whoever she is, she knows my keypad combination."

"To your car?"

He rolled his eyes and shoved back in the chair. "Of course, my car. You don't open a Lexus with a key."

"I see." *Count to ten. Keep counting.*

"I play in the Businessman's FC—football club. That's soccer, not American football. Tonight when I hit the gym to change for our game, I found this in the side pocket."

He pulled out a square jewelry-type box and thrust it at Giulia. Inside, a gold-painted padlock gleamed on a wad of silver tissue paper. It reeked, but not with "Passion."

"Was there a note? Oh, I see." She pried it out of the lid. "'I arose to open for my lover, and my hands dripped with myrrh, my fingers with flowing myrrh, on the handles of the lock.'" She inhaled a combination of sweetness and spice. "So that's what myrrh smells like."

"Who cares?" He slammed a hand on her desk. "I'm paying good money to this company and I want results. When is Frank going to pin down the right one? I've had it with this psycho bitch and her obsessions. Thank God Pamela knows what's expected of my future wife."

Someday Giulia would be sending Pamela a sympathy card. "Mr. Parker, I'll give this to Mr. Driscoll first thing tomorrow. How early may he call you at home?"

"At home?" Blake stood and paced the room. "I can't go home. She got into my condo once already. She got into my car. What if she's waiting there for me?" He leaned over Giulia's desk into her face. "Frank has to find me a safe place. All my exes know the only type of hotel I patronize. I need someplace that none of them would think of. I have to show up to work tomorrow like everything's perfect—I'm chairing a big cost-cutting meeting. I need sleep and peace of mind. Frank promised me, and he damn well better deliver."

What should she do? Suggesting he undergo spinal insertion surgery would be a start. But he wouldn't appreciate that, and anyway who was she to judge him? She was hiding in her apartment every night.

"Sugar, are you going to help me or do I have to find another PI in a real town? Pittsburgh, for instance?"

For a spineless pin-up he could sure fake the testosterone. The case might be hers to lose if she didn't make the right decision.

"Please wait here while I make a phone call."

"Good. Call Frank. Get some instructions. You got a bathroom in here?"

"Through that door. I'll be right back." *Jerk. Bully. Jellyfish.*

She closed Frank's door and dialed his cell. Half a ring, and "You've reached Driscoll Investigations. Please leave a message and we'll get right back to you."

Of course. He turned it off for Yvonne.

She tried paging him. Another message. Now what? She had an irate client threatening to pull the business.

Ninety-nine percent sure it's an empty threat.

What she really had was a scared spitless client in the next room afraid to go home . . . and a PI-in-training in this room afraid to walk from the bus stop to her apartment building alone.

. . . It could work. He could crash on her couch. She'd get safety in numbers. He'd get the comfort of using a nobody who couldn't embarrass him socially or professionally.

And maybe a crick in his neck from the arm of the couch. Small price to pay?

What about her reputation?

Same deal: he couldn't embarrass her. She had no social circle. Frank would file it under "general client assistance" and add the time to Blake's bill.

It could work.

She dialed Frank's cell again. "Frank, she left Blake another package. He doesn't want to go home because of the break-in, so I'm taking him to my place for the night. Keep your mind out of the gutter—he'll be on the couch. See you in the morning."

Giulia opened the door. Blake still paced the room like a caged lion. One of those pampered, raised-in-captivity lions they use in outdated circuses.

"Mr. Parker, I think I have a solution."

EIGHTEEN

"Spare towels are in the bathroom if you'd like to shower. I'll make up the couch for you."

Blake's top-of-the-line business suit didn't belong in Giulia's lower-middle-class apartment. Neither did Blake, and his pained expression showed it.

Giulia sniffed. Nope, nothing smelled bad in here. All in his imagination.

"May I put your bag in the closet?" *A "thank you" would be nice, Mr. Perfect.*

His nose smoothed out, and he looked down at her. She watched his business training kick in and the gears crank a mechanical smile in place.

"Thank you."

Before he closed the bathroom door, Giulia caught his sneer at the tiny proportions of everything. His probably had one of those whirlpool tubs, a marble sink, and a heated towel rack. He'd be roughing it big time tonight.

She flipped on the lights in the living room and her bedroom. At least her spare sheets were newer than the ones on her bed. Unfortunate that they had a roses-and-baby's-breath pattern. Not quite the first choice of a star executive.

Three books lay open on the coffee table. Better straighten those. Should she offer to make coffee? Would that look like a come-on? Lord knows that was the last impression she wanted to convey. How far did hostess duties constrain her? She certainly didn't want another half-hour of pretending interest in his job prospects and Pamela's virtues. And serving him . . . she loved to cook, but not when common courtesy would be misinterpreted as the superior male's entitlement.

By the time she stripped the extra pillow from her bed and stuffed it into the flowered pillowcase, he'd turned off the shower. She bent over the couch cushion to make a hospital corner, and the bathroom door opened.

"Sugar, I need the shorts and T-shirt from my gym bag, unless you don't mind my sleeping in the buff."

The man had an ego the size of Texas. "Your bag is in the hall closet, Mr. Parker. Right next to—" She stood and turned around and her brain seized up like an overworked engine.

Blake stood at the opposite end of the couch, one hand loosely clasping the ends of a towel around his hips.

The towel didn't meet in front.

His tousled blond hair gave a boyish look to his square face. His chest hair curled around droplets of water that kept dripping off and rolling down his six-pack abs, down behind his hand, down into the curlier blond hairs above—

She snapped her eyes back up to his face. His soft grin had a cocky edge. *Bet you want this, sugar*, it said. *You'll never have any-*

Every syllable carried with painful clarity. She never realized the walls were so thin.

"She doesn't have cable. Where did Frank find this chick?" Another thump and his voice muttering. Then the television clicking on.

Giulia flung off the sheet and restacked several books on top of the bookshelf with a series of bangs. A laugh-track volume increased.

Maybe celibacy wasn't that bad. Giulia and her plants. Like Miss Silver and her knitting.

That future was supposed to change when she jumped the wall. What was she doing wrong? She had a real job. She had friends . . . no. She had no one. She was alone, scared, and confused.

A smart, modern *Cosmo* woman would've ripped Blake's towel off and wrestled his willing, wet body onto the area rug. So long, virginity; hello . . . what? Promiscuity? Guilt? Unemployment? The latter without doubt, once she compromised the professionalism of Driscoll Investigations.

Would sex get the specter of the rapist out of her head? Would Blake have pushed her onto the couch and tried to use her mouth like Pot-Breath did?

She had to get a grip. She was safe in her own bed, and a tower of masculinity lay on the other side of her locked door. A tower of willing masculinity.

So take him. Be the aggressor, not the victim. Choose what kind of sex you want.

And she'd deserve the slut label. She reached for her Bible. The Holy Card bookmark from her mother's funeral caught her eye, and she opened to Second Peter. "They are blots and blemishes, reveling in their dissipation, carousing with you. They have eyes full of adultery, insatiable for sin."

"I get the point." She slammed the book shut and threw it onto her nightstand. The clock radio bounced.

"Sugar, you want to keep it down in there? Thanks."

She flung off the covers and stalked to the bookshelf, tugging her T-shirt down when the breeze hit skin that should've been covered. Sherlock Holmes? No. She already had an arrogant male invading her space. Saint John of the Cross? No, she wasn't in the middle of a Dark Night. Not yet. Italian fairy tales. Perfect. A million miles removed from real life.

The breeze puffed in, warmer than before. She kept the sheet off, propped her pillow, and rested the book on her knees.

Two sitcoms later, the television switched off. Amid much grunting and squeaking springs, the arrogant, sexy, annoying, lust-inducing Blake Parker settled in for the night.

Did he dream of the women he's slept with? The women who refused him? What would sex with such a perfect physique be like? He'd kiss her with those full lips and put her hand on his firm butt cheek. She'd give it a tentative squeeze. He'd slide his hand under her T-shirt and knead her breasts—and then he'd make a snide remark about the scabs.

He was a narcissistic, superficial, drop-dead-handsome sexpot. If she gave up her virginity to him, he'd take it as his due and toss her in the trash like a fast-food wrapper.

Ten minutes later, rhythmic snoring floated through the wall.

Turn out the light, Giulia. You don't want to sleep with the client.

NINETEEN

"A PADLOCK?" FRANK SET the box on the windowsill the next morning and rubbed the back of his neck. "That stinks to high heaven. You're certain it's myrrh?"

Giulia held out the note. "It has to be. The padlock is symbolic of this verse, so therefore the scent is myrrh."

"Isn't that one of the gifts the Three Kings brought to Jesus at Christmas? I wouldn't want to smell this mixed with cow dung."

"Frank, how often does your mother pray for your irreverent soul?"

"Every night, she tells me. I'm keeping her happy. She loves a project, and I'm her perpetual straying lamb." He kneaded his left shoulder.

"Did you hurt yourself?"

"Migraine. Woke up with it. That myrrh is killing me."

"Do you need me to, um, rub your shoulder or anything?"

"Ms. Falcone, where are your professional boundaries?" He attempted a chuckle. "And don't you dare take that seriously. I took serious drugs as soon as I got up. It'll go away in half an hour, I hope." He closed the blinds and turned away from his glowing monitor. "Now tell me what happened last night."

"He came in here around six looking for you. When he had no other options, he talked to me." She put the lid on the box and set it on the floor outside Frank's doorway. "By the way, please don't ever call me 'Sugar.'"

"Sugar? You're kidding."

"I am not."

"Did you dump coffee on his lap?"

"Of course not. Professional boundaries, remember?"

"Touché. And I'm sorry I turned off my cell. Yvonne analyzed our failed relationship and potential life-mate types for two solid hours."

"Serves you right. Did you sever the relationship like a gentleman?"

"I did indeed. I told her about all the 'correct way to break up' advice you gave me."

"You didn't."

"She said you ought to host the late-night call-in show on WLTJ." He dropped his forehead on his desk and yanked at his hair. "Can you get me an espresso? Or my gun. I'll give you the key to my apartment." He pushed the heels of his hands against his temples.

"Don't even say that as a joke. Be right back."

He was asleep on his desk when she brought the espresso.

———

At 11:30, Frank's door opened.

"Sorry about that, ladies." His face had lines from the papers on his desk, and his ginger hair stuck flat to one side of his head.

Giulia hit *Save.* "Better?"

"Almost normal."

Sidney handed him a printout. "Mr. Driscoll, have you tried feverfew? Lots of people don't think of holistic remedies, and they're so much better for you than synthesized drugs."

"Thanks, Sidney. I'll look at it later."

Giulia plucked the empty coffee cup from her trash can and waved it at Frank. "Do you want me to get you another espresso? I drank that one."

"Never let good caffeine go to waste?"

"That's my motto."

"I need food more than caffeine now. Who's up for an early lunch?"

"I brown-bagged," Giulia said, "but I'll get something for you."

Sidney planted herself in front of Frank. "Mr. Driscoll, you should eat healthy foods, natural ones, after a migraine. Like organic salad with tofu and vinaigrette. No MSG or preservatives. And nothing with carbonation. Spring water is best; it'll flush the toxins out of your body."

Frank's eyes closed. "Sidney, if you try to feed me tofu, you'll get two weeks' notice."

She shot Giulia a panicked glance, then backed toward her own desk. "I'm sorry, Mr. Driscoll, I didn't mean to overstep my boundaries. I won't mention anything like this again. I—"

He held up a hand. "That was supposed to be a joke. All right. I'll eat a salad if there's a burger attached to it." He pulled out his wallet and looked at Sidney. "Do you mind going?"

"I planned to get takeout today anyway. I'll be right back."

Giulia gave Sidney time to get outside. "Stop teasing that poor girl. She's new to the working world." She pulled out her client chair and shoved it toward Frank. "Sit before you fall."

"Haven't had a migraine this bad in a while. I must've eaten one of my triggers." He sat. "We didn't finish the story of last night."

Frank closed his eyes and rubbed his left shoulder with a light touch, so she could indulge her urge to simply look at him. The censored version of last night arranged itself in her mind, excluding Blake's nudity and her (suppressed) lust.

A good four or five minutes passed while Giulia attempted to relax her mind the way Frank was trying to relax his tight shoulder muscles. When the silence had stretched to the point of awkwardness, she said, "When you didn't answer the phone, I got inspired. He and I were both worried about what might be waiting for us when we got home." She tapped two keys with her index fingers; PC doodling as cover. "I did think he was a bit of a weenie to be asking me for protection, but I suppose he was really asking the firm, not me, myself."

Frank opened his eyes and gave her a penetrating look. "Giulia, maybe you should crash with someone for a while."

"With who? Quinn? Mingmei? Evelyn of the disastrous date nephews? No. If I give in to this, I'll end up pushing all my worldly goods in a shopping cart and sleeping under bridges."

He raised an eyebrow. "Isn't that a little extreme?"

"I took it to the worst possible conclusion. Therefore, I'm not giving in. To continue. I suggested my couch."

"Blake agreed right away?"

"You know better than that." She banged the keys harder. "He started to laugh and didn't manage to disguise it as a cough."

"Oh. Yeah. He'd think, well, you know."

She most definitely did know. "I called upon my years of explaining English grammar to thick-headed teenagers. Mr. Parker realized that, lowly as I am, he could use me."

Frank sat up. "He could what?"

"*Tsk.* Not in that way. As if."

He leaned away. "*As if?*"

She snorted. "Sidney's a bad influence."

Sidney stopped with one hand on the door handle and the other filled with bags. "Ms. Falcone? Did I do something wrong?"

Giulia stepped around Frank and took two bottles of water from under Sidney's arm. "You polluted my conversation with your slang."

Sidney's brown eyes rounded into root beer barrels. "Um. I'm sorry, I didn't mean to say anything bad, really, I can stop talking—"

Frank and Giulia laughed.

"You wouldn't be you," Frank said.

"I was kidding," Giulia said. "I used one of your expressions, and Frank called me on it."

"And you told me to be nice to poor Sidney." Frank opened his salad container and grimaced. "What's this white stuff?"

"Feta cheese. It's all natural, made from goat's milk, very healthy. I spritzed plain vinegar on top. Vinegar is good for cleansing the system, too. There's cheddar on the burger but no bacon. Nitrates are a leading cause of migraines in men under fifty." She split the pile of napkins between them. "I looked it up."

"I—thanks."

Sidney rooted in her skirt pocket. "Here's your change."

Giulia carried the water into his office. Frank followed, salad in one hand and cheeseburger in the other.

"Bring in your lunch and close the door." While she unwrapped salami on homemade pumpernickel and swallowed a bite, he stabbed lettuce, feta, and cucumber on a plastic fork and said, "Anything else I need to know about last night?"

"Nothing important. He bought dinner, my lack of cable caused him to miss a soccer game, and since he didn't call this morning, I gather he found no one lurking in his closet when he went home to change."

Frank chewed his first bite of cheeseburger, and his eyes rolled back in his head. "God, that's grand." With a contented sigh, he swallowed and drank half the water. "Okay, sounds like you did good. I won't tell him that Man U lost to Wigan, biggest upset in Premier League history."

"Should I understand any of that?"

"Just soccer talk," he said through a mouthful of salad. "And I'll tell Mom to add you to her devotions. Inviting an engaged man to sleep in your apartment, unchaperoned. I'm shocked."

"Francis Xavier Driscoll, you know better than to think anything happened."

The burger thumped into its plastic box. "How did you know my middle name?"

"A good Irish Catholic boy named Francis can only have one possible middle name." She crossed her arms. "What's mine?"

"How should I—oh. Wait. You're a good Italian Catholic girl. Mary. No—Maria."

"Bingo."

"You can take the kid out of the Catholic, but you can't take the Catholic out of the kid." He waved her out. "Go finish your lunch in the sunshine, or at least someplace that doesn't have a biblical scent diffuser. And log all the hours Blake foisted himself on you as billable time."

As soon as Giulia crossed Frank's threshold, Sidney waved her over.

"Come here, Ms. Falcone, come here and listen to this."

Sidney double-clicked an MP3 e-mail attachment. A man and woman sang a bouncy song in painfully cheerful voices. A guitar and piano accompanied them.

"Hats and gloves,

Snug and wooly.

Socks and scarves

Keep you cozy.

When winter bites,

Laugh and play,

Keeping warm

The alpaca way!

Meier Farms, two miles west of Cottonwood on Route 19, all-natural alpaca yarn and odor-free fertilizer. 555-WOOL. Meier Farms—it's Spin-tastic!"

Sidney closed the file. "What do you think, Ms. Falcone? I wrote the lyrics, my sister wrote the music, and that's my mom and dad singing."

Giulia hunted through her mental thesaurus for a compliment. "It's catchy."

Sidney clapped. "Oh, good. It's the first time we're advertising on radio and TV. It's the same jingle for both, but for TV we have a short movie of my mom spinning the wool in the backyard with the prettiest alpacas roaming behind her. One of them came and looked over her shoulder while she was spinning, and Dad got it on film. My boyfriend says it puts the cute factor through the roof."

The phone rang. Sidney put the call through to Frank in a textbook-professional voice.

Giulia set the remains of her lunch on her own desk. "The farm supports your whole family?"

"Once we got out of debt. Alpacas are wicked expensive. Thirty-two thousand dollars for two proven females—meaning they successfully gave birth once—and twelve thousand for two non-gelded males."

"Good heavens."

"That's why I needed the swimming scholarship. When I applied to colleges, Jingle and Belle were only on their third pregnancy each."

Giulia coughed. "Jingle and Belle?"

"Sure. Mom's the original Christmas elf. The males are Comet and Blitzen, and the six babies are the other reindeer names."

Giulia tilted her head and scrutinized Sidney. "And you're not a Christmas elf?"

Sidney gave her a *duh* look. "Of course I am. Nothing beats Christmas. But Mom out-elfs us all. That's the real reason I haven't moved out yet. The whole month of December is one long Christmas orgy. It's so great. Did you know that goat-milk eggnog tastes just like the cow kind?"

Goat milk. And Giulia would bet— "From your own goats?"

The big eyes got bigger. "Where else? Ms. Falcone, once you've tasted chilled goat's milk that you milked yourself the night before, you'll never touch pasteurized, hormone-filled, store-bought cow milk again."

Sidney pulled a small photo album out of her tote bag. "This is my whole family on the cover. My twin sisters are the oldest, then my brother, then me. Dad's blurry because he set the timer too short and didn't make his spot behind Mom in time."

"What's in the small laundry bags by your sisters' feet?"

"Alpaca poop."

Giulia plopped into Sidney's side chair. "What?"

"It makes the best fertilizer. It doesn't stink, and it comes out shaped like raisins. Not wrinkly, more like chocolate-covered raisins."

"Gross."

"Well, if you like that candy, maybe, but as fertilizer it can't be beat. You can use it on indoor plants, and your house won't smell like the toilet overflowed."

The weak basil. "Does it work on herbs?"

"Anything. Do you have a garden?"

"Herbs and tomatoes in pots."

"Tomatoes love our fertilizer. I'll bring you a sample bag tomorrow. It's not expensive at all, either."

Frank appeared in his doorway.

"Am I losing my mind, or did I hear someone singing about alpaca poop?"

TWENTY

The photographs surrounded the Driscoll Investigations lettering on the frosted window Wednesday morning. The hall light behind Giulia's head reflected off them in different spots, obscuring a face here, an arm there.

Blake Parker stood naked in one, the bath towel at his feet. She lay on her bed in another, her knees propping a book. Except the book that should be there wasn't. Instead, Blake's head was buried between her legs.

Her on her knees, eyes closed, her open mouth filled with Blake's very erect penis. She'd knelt on the bed and yawned. She remembered, because just then Blake had laughed out loud with the laugh track on the TV. But in the picture, she knelt on the floor.

Her bent over the bookshelf in her T-shirt, looking for a book. Only in this photo Blake stood behind her and even she would swear they'd spent an X-rated night together.

Clunk. Her travel mug slipped to the hall floor.

"Giulia? You up there? I saw you get off the bus." The street door slammed and Frank's head appeared at the top of the stairs. "I got an idea about us doing surveillance in shifts, and I want you to work out a schedule—"

He stumbled on her coffee mug, his eyes following hers to the door display.

He stepped backward, looked at her, looked at them, stepped forward. The bookshelf photo, on top of the *D* in DRISCOLL, sat exactly at his eye level.

His head jerked left, right, up, down.

"Frank, I don't know—"

He snatched the bookshelf photo and tore it in half. He ripped down the one where she should have had a book on her knees. Then he stopped, inhaled, and exhaled. With care, he pulled the remaining photos off the door, bending onto their backs the pieces of tape holding them.

Giulia reached out to help. Frank jerked his head *no*. She picked up her mug. A few drops had spilled. She hadn't noticed the aroma of French-vanilla hazelnut filling the narrow hall until just now. Her fingers fumbled the key out of her purse, but she managed to unlock the door.

Frank shoved the door open ahead of her and strode into his office. Giulia leaped and caught the doorknob before the door crashed into the wall.

"Can you come in here, please?" Frank's words snapped like karate students breaking boards.

He should be angry at the faked photos, not her. Maybe that was it—they were too nasty to keep, but they were evidence of the stalker's willingness to pervert the truth.

She'd have to analyze them. With Frank. And discuss how cleverly their stalker made it look like she and Blake spent an . . . athletic night together.

He held the pieces of the torn photo in his hands. "Tape."

She ran to her desk and back with the tape dispenser in her hand.

"Set it down. I'll put them together." When that one was repaired, he dealt the photos onto his desk like a game of solitaire. "A full-frontal shot of our client naked and wet. Did he take a shower?" Icicles edged his voice.

"Yes, when we got in."

"My partner on her knees to our client." He glanced sideways at her; his freckles made too sharp a contrast to his skin. "Did they teach you those prayers in the convent?"

Giulia shied but stood her ground. "Frank, you can't possibly think these are actual pictures." An irrelevant thought captured her attention: she was glad she'd worn her dowdiest gray skirt and shapeless slate-blue blouse today.

"Blake on the couch, looking—I see a pattern here—looking very happy. As though he'd just finished doing something pleasurable."

Giulia pinched her lips between her teeth. When she could control her voice, she said, "He watched sitcoms because I don't get cable."

"I especially like this one. My partner's double bed seems to be plenty big enough for one adult to inspect the other for . . . what? You'll have to tell me."

Icy fingers crawled down her back.

"And what book were you looking for so diligently? I'm glad Blake was able to help you." He lined up the last one at the edge of his desk. "This might be my favorite. Not every PI can hold up her hips at just the right angle to accommodate the client's cock."

She sat in his client chair before her legs gave out.

"Did you need to get a closer look?" He offered her the last one.

"They're faked." Her voice wobbled.

"Your tomato plant is doing quite well. I can almost smell that broken stem on the far side."

"I told you yesterday that nothing happened. We went to dinner, he slept on the couch, he drove me to work in the morning."

"He took a shower, too."

"Yes. So?"

"You omitted that detail in your report." He brought that photo closer to his eyes. "You really should buy larger bath towels. How can our clients get ready for you to accommodate them if they have to use substandard bathroom supplies?"

"Frank!"

"It seems you omitted several details in your report yesterday. When were you planning to tell me about this new service you're bringing to the firm?"

"Of course I didn't tell you about the shower. Everyone takes showers. It wasn't important."

"What do you consider important?" He picked up the bookshelf photo. "Which book you needed?" The bed photo. "How adept he was at oral sex?" He slammed it down. "How many times you came for him?"

"Stop it!" Giulia swept the photos off the desk and they scattered over the floor. "Yes, he came out of the shower like that. He gave me that arrogant grin and said it was my choice whether he slept naked or not. I told him that we were professionals and that we expected the same of him, and to put on his clothes. I locked myself in my bedroom, he watched TV, and we both went to sleep."

Frank's teeth ground together, and he breathed in a too-steady rhythm.

Giulia searched the floor for the Blake-on-the-couch photo and the Blake-by-the-bookshelf photo. "Look." She set them side by side on the desk. "Look at Blake's smile. It's identical in both photos. Head a little thrown back, the same number of teeth showing. Even his hair has the same curl on the side of his fore-head. Whoever took them just flopped the photo to trick us."

"You're going to stand there and tell me that Blake Parker stood naked in front of you and you refused him? What runs through your veins? No woman's ever said no to Blake." He grimaced. "In-cluding two of my girlfriends."

"Yes, I refused him. Look at these." She dived and came up with both bed photos. "I had a book on my knees here. I remember, because it was hot and I didn't want the sheet." What she wanted to show him wasn't clear in the 4 x 6 print. "Do you have a magni-fying glass?"

"I'm not Sherlock Holmes."

"Yes, you do—in the fingerprint kit." She squatted before the filing cabinets and opened a bottom drawer. Her still-shaking fin-gers needed two tries before she dislodged the jeweler's loupe from its form-fitting plastic slot.

He had to believe her. He had to see that they were fakes. Clever and detailed, but all lies. She respected him. She was try-ing desperately not to fall in love with him, but she couldn't think about that right now. She'd stumble over every word she wanted to say to him.

She moved the loupe up and down her thighs in the bed photo. It had to be there. A line, a blurry patch, something the eraser program missed. Nothing. She switched to the kneeling photo. There must be a stray fold of bedsheet. Under her toes, or between her knees— "There. Look."

Frank bent over the loupe. "What am I supposed to see?"

"Behind my right knee. That's not my area rug, it's a piece of my sheet."

"It's blue. The rug is blue."

"It's a different texture. It's wrinkled. Don't you see?"

He flicked away the loupe and the photo. "You're digging yourself a deeper hole."

"I did not do anything wrong!" Giulia bit her lips to squelch the shrillness in her voice.

Frank leaned back in his chair, crossing his legs. "You lied so well yesterday that I can't wait to hear what you're about to say."

"I didn't lie to you yesterday." *Don't cry. Absolutely don't cry. Reason with him. You're both adults.* "Frank, you know me better than this. You know I would never compromise the company. I would never take advantage of your trust."

"My oldest brother once told me never to trust a nun, because they were out of touch with reality."

"I'm not a nun anymore."

"And you're certainly making up for lost time."

Try another way. Explain it photo by photo. Forget that they're nothing more than porn. You have to convince him.

"Where's the towel one? Here." Giulia pointed to the left side of the photo. "You were just in my apartment. Look at . . . aha. Look at the angle of the couch against the bookshelf on the far wall. When Blake pulled his studmuffin act, she must have crouched outside the window with the tomato shelf. That's why you can see the tomato plant and why the TV doesn't block him."

"You're going to tell me how she—and I do agree that our stalker is responsible for this entertainment—how she took these through closed curtains. You closed them when it got dark, of course, so no one could see in. Because you're a . . . lady."

If he'd slapped her across the face it couldn't have stung more. "No, um, I was making up the couch. It was hot. I didn't think about the curtains till I felt a breeze when he came right up close to me."

"I see."

"And this one." She deliberately stared at herself lying on the bed. "I got a book from the shelf because him being on the other side of the wall distracted me."

Frank emitted a sound somewhere between a laugh and a groan.

"The last time I saw a naked male was when my little brother was a baby and I gave him baths. Blake offered himself to me, all naked and wet. He's, he's . . . " Her tongue chose that moment to bond to the roof of her mouth.

"A walking magazine cover." Frank's jaw clenched.

"The image of him stuck in my mind and mixed up with the guy in the park. I needed to think about something else." She dropped the bed photo and picked up the bookshelf one. "Compare him in this one to the one from the living room. He has the same expression on his face. His image is reversed."

Frank raised his eyebrows.

"Look at it."

"I got quite an eyeful in the hall, thank you."

"Don't tell me you're jealous." *Shut up! Stupid broad. Mouth like a scolapasta.*

His mouth curled into a sneer, slowly, like he wanted her to catch each muscle twisting into contempt. "You seem to have forgotten the boundaries of polite society. I must admire how quickly you learned to do whatever it takes to please the client. A lie here, an offer of service there. Should I have wished that you offered to please me first?"

He turned his face away a moment and inhaled sharp and deep. When he turned back, he'd adopted an aloof smile. "For example, I'm interested in hearing you try to explain how that's not Blake Parker's blonde and chiseled head shoved into your—" He cleared his throat. "Give it your best shot."

Ten minutes ago, she would've sworn he trusted her implicitly. "I got a book and went back to bed. The curtains were closed, but the window was open and they blew in on the breeze. I spread the book on my knees. That's why my legs are up and why she could make it look like, like . . ." In her mind, another image superimposed itself on the photo. "She made me look like the Barbie she sent me."

TWENTY-ONE

FRANK TOOK THE PHOTO from Giulia's hand.

"Isn't that nice of our stalker. Now I know what to get you for Christmas. Franciscans wear black, don't they? I'm sure I'll be able to figure out the right sizes from the photos. They're so clear."

The crotchless underwear and cut-out bra appeared in Giulia's mind. The hot, airless office closed in on her the way her apartment walls had last Friday.

"Frank." Her voice cracked. "I thought you trusted me."

"I did."

"How can you not believe me?"

"I believe what's in front of my eyes. I believe that you lied to me about Monday night and you're lying now to cover yourself." His hand brushed the impossible oral-sex photos. "Cover yourself. I'm such a comedian."

"I never touched him!" Her hand covered her mouth. If she took it away, would she scream at him?

"Of course not. You had nothing to do with Blake's erection that you're so attentive to." He snatched that photo and pushed it into her face. "How fast you learned to prefer sucking to biting."

She slapped him. Surprise filled his eyes. She hadn't realized how empty they'd been.

"Oh, Frank, I'm sorry." She rubbed her stinging hand. "I lost my temper."

"Was it as easy as losing your virginity?" He steepled his fingers in a classic Sherlock Holmes pose. "That is, if you still had it to lose. One does hear stories about the goings-on in convents these days." He smiled through his tented palms. "I wonder about the real reason you left."

A ball of fire and ice filled Giulia's stomach and boiled into her throat. She willed steadiness into her voice. "I swear on the Cross of Christ I am innocent of everything these photos imply."

"Don't blaspheme the Cross, Ms. Falcone. I might not be a good Catholic, but I do remember that Dante punishes blasphemers by eternity in a desert accompanied by a continual rain of fire. You might want to study up on that."

He gathered all six photographs and slipped them into his jacket pocket. "Before all this excitement, I remember I had an idea about surveillance. Please make up a schedule that has you and I watching Blake's condo and Pamela's house in alternate shifts from four a.m. to six a.m."

"All right." She walked to her desk on rubber legs.

"I think we'll start running this as a business, not a chat room. Please knock on my door only for situations that can't be handled by my staff. If our current client drops in, Sidney will interface with him. She's new, but she seems to know the appropriate employee-client boundaries." He closed the door between them.

Giulia sat without moving in front of her monitor. She was going to lose this job. The photos were practically seamless. She could see the errors—but that was because she knew where to look. How could Frank believe she'd knelt on the floor in front of Blake or invited him into her bed? She thought she understood Frank, a little. Apparently someone should also sell her the deed to the Brooklyn Bridge.

She would've smiled if her muscles remembered how.

Would Frank use the photos as an object lesson for Sidney? What look would fill Sidney's eyes after Frank showed them to her?

The door opened and a waft of kiwi shampoo scent preceded Sidney's boisterous alto. "Fight on, on, on, on, on, fight on, on Penn State!" She tossed a "Green Tea-Green Planet" satchel on her desk. "Good morning, Ms. Falcone. Wow, it's dim in here. And hot. How come you didn't open the windows? Never mind, I'll do it."

The yank and rattle of the venetian blinds woke Giulia. She booted her computer and sipped her tepid coffee. She didn't want it. Or the carrot muffin in her bag.

Sidney looked like a Creamsicle in a bright orange shirt and white pants. "You look tired, Ms. Falcone. Bad night? Warm milk with nutmeg works for me. Puts me out like a light in ten minutes."

A thump and unintelligible words from Frank's office.

"Mr. Driscoll's early. Did you guys get a break in the stalker case? Hey." She grinned. "I'm learning the lingo."

Giulia unfroze her numb lips. "No, no breaks. We're going to start early-morning surveillance."

"Ugh, better you than me. I'm so not a morning person." She uncapped a bottle of green tea and drank. "Have you tried the whole-wheat bagels downstairs? I'm so glad they offer healthy stuff. Oh, here." She unzipped a side pocket and handed Giulia a double-bagged bunch of what looked like chocolate-covered coffee beans.

"Um, thank you. These look delicious. Does your mother make the chocolate with milk from your goats?"

Sidney giggled. "This isn't chocolate, Ms. Falcone. It's our fertilizer. You can't eat it." Her phone buzzed and she hit the speaker button. "Yes, Mr. Driscoll?"

"Good morning, Sidney. Would you please tell Ms. Falcone I expect the surveillance schedules by noon? Thanks."

She turned off the speaker function. "You heard that, right, Ms. Falcone?"

Giulia nodded. Frank's voice sounded the same as always. Of course it would when talking to Sidney. She was a sweet, innocent puppy. Giulia'd been innocent once. Still was, technically. Technically. Like that mattered anymore.

Sidney set her bag on the floor beneath her desk and booted her computer. "Surveillance sounds so *CSI*. I know I have lots of work and stuff to learn, but can I help somehow?" She glopped all-fruit spread on the bagel and took a large bite. "Will you need anything done late at night? Like, I don't know, digital photos to upload?"

Giulia clenched her teeth. *Wrong example to use this morning, Sidney.* "I don't know. I'll ask Mr. Driscoll."

Frank might promote Sidney after he fired her. Sidney had zero experience, but neither had she when Frank hired her. Sidney's enthusiasm should make up for it, with plenty left over.

When Giulia labeled tabs in the surveillance spreadsheet, the flaw jumped out. It didn't take anywhere near long enough to cross the room and knock on Frank's door.

"Come in."

She closed the door. He didn't look up. Today he hadn't chosen to imitate any of the classic detectives. His khakis and rugby-striped shirt made him more boyish and attractive than ever.

"Frank, surveillance won't work at both houses."

He continued typing. "Did your extensive field experience tell you this?"

Because she'd sat through innumerable sermons from her Superiors with a neutral countenance, she didn't react to his rudeness. A little imp on her shoulder suggested she write them thank-you notes.

"Pamela's street is too exclusive. Your car or a rental would be spotted before an hour passed. The same if you or I dressed in all black and walked up and down the street or loitered or hid behind a hedge."

Frank's hands hovered over the keys, then came down hard on the desk. "Damn. You're right. Blake's condo is one neighborhood over from the exclusive area he'd like to live in. Actual poor people can be seen there. Just passing through, of course." He started to grin.

It switched off. "All right. Revise the schedule. I will take into account any suggestions you have for Pamela's surveillance." He clicked the mouse. "Please close the door behind you."

She stared through her screen, not really listening to Sidney's chatter. Maybe a rosary on her knees would clear her mind, even though she wasn't guilty of anything but lustful thoughts. Over an unworthy object.

The schedule for Blake's condo took her all of twenty minutes. One column for time, one for day, one for location. Assuming it didn't rain, she could hide behind the porch swing or the woodpile. Even if it did rain, she supposed. The light rail stopped a quarter-mile from his street. She could incorporate it into her exercise routine. Frank could sit in his car every other morning.

Her ideas ran out at Pamela's worksheet.

"Sidney, how would you stake out a house in one of those super-rich neighborhoods? The kind where the lawns could double as putting greens and the nanny is paid more than both of us combined. Early morning, four to six a.m."

"That sounds like the house my boyfriend lived in. Two boyfriends ago, I mean. My current sweetie works for a landscaping company while he gets his MSW. He's so sexy when he picks me up, all sweaty and smelling like fresh grass. I'm going to miss that when he graduates and sets up in private practice." She kept going when Giulia didn't smile. "Um, well, you couldn't just hang out on the corner or across the street, because the servants would be up by five to start laundry and breakfast—no joke. They'd open the curtains and see you and call the cops, and the cops would rush right over."

"That's what I thought."

"Oh! I know! You could dress up like a landscaper and write down stuff on a clipboard—make it look like you're comparing colors of flowers, eyeballing the topiary, stuff like that. The people next door to my old boyfriend had a huge one right in the middle of their lawn. Two swans touching beaks, or bills, or whatever. So they formed a heart, you know? Ew."

"I'd still be a stranger lurking at an odd hour."

"That's okay, because you'd be a hired-help stranger. It probably wouldn't work more than once or twice, because the regular landscapers come around a couple times a week and they all know each other."

Giulia searched used-clothing stores on the Web and typed their information and Sidney's idea below the schedule.

The mail arrived at eleven. Sidney gave Giulia brochures for spy equipment and a flyer soliciting donations for the Children with Cancer auction. She looked over her shoulder and leaned into Giulia's ear. "Did you and Mr. Driscoll have a fight or something? It kind of feels like an ice-skating rink in here today and I don't have skates. I'm not being rude or anything by asking, am I? I don't want to butt in where I don't belong. It's just that you two are always so cute, making jokes and teaming up to brainstorm ideas and stuff, but this morning it's like, well, you know. Do you?"

Ice. Appropriate. The atmosphere after what they'd said to each other could freeze three circles of Hell. Poor Sidney, getting sideswiped by this train wreck.

"Just a disagreement, Sidney. It'll pass." What was one more lie? "I'll be sure to give you credit for the landscaper-disguise idea."

"Wow, thanks, you're really going to use it? That's so cool."

Giulia set the spreadsheet on Frank's desk.

"A phony landscaping company? Good work, Ms. Falcone."

"It wasn't my idea. Sidney came up with it."

"Then I'm glad to see that one of my employees has justified my choice in hiring her."

Giulia bit the inside of her cheek. *Don't say anything. Keep a neutral front. He'll get over this when you prove the photos are faked. Or he'll fire you and it won't matter.*

The phone rang and a moment later Sidney yelled, "Mr. Parker on one!"

Giulia and Frank smiled, and for an instant the rapport returned. Then the ice formed again as he glanced at her, then the door.

"Sidney," Giulia said after she closed it, "always use the intercom."

"But his door was open."

Giulia smiled at the genuine puzzlement on her face. "This is an office. What if a client walked in? Professionals modulate their voices. If you remember always to make the professional choice, it'll become habit."

Frank stepped out of his office and over to Sidney's desk. "Ms. Falcone and I are meeting Mr. Parker. Go ahead and take lunch; the machine can get the calls for an hour."

TWENTY-TWO

FRANK HELD THE DOOR of Tutti Mangia for Giulia in silence. She wondered when he would speak to her. Not a word from him during the twenty-minute car ride. Any small-talk ideas withered on her lips before she opened them.

This restaurant catered to sophisticated diners. No dripping candles in straw-wrapped wine jugs. No imitation peasant costumes. Italian opera played at a discreet volume through invisible speakers. Stainless flatware that almost looked silver graced linen tablecloths.

Giulia wanted to snatch a menu. It was 99 percent guaranteed they served greens and beans as an appetizer at $4.95 a bowl. A small bowl. She could make an entire pot of greens and beans for three dollars. The thought would've made her smile any other day. She would've explained the joke to Frank, and he would've laughed at the pretentiousness of passing peasant food off as gourmet. On any other day.

A hostess led them to a corner booth already occupied by their client.

"Blake."

"Frank. Ms. Falcone." He waited for the waitress to open her pad. "Merlot for Mr. Driscoll and myself. Water for Ms. Falcone."

When she left, the cold smile returned to Frank's mouth. "I didn't realize you knew my assistant's drinking preferences."

"She stuck to water Monday night, so I figured it was a good bet."

Giulia kept silent. Whatever she said would make it worse. Especially since she wanted to grab Blake by his silk tie and demand he tell Frank the truth.

"Are you ready to order?" The waitress set their drinks in front of them. Crystal goblets, even for the water.

"Rigatoni Fra Diavolo for me. Frank?"

"Linguine primavera."

Giulia wondered if anything would stay in her chaotic stomach. "A small antipasto, please." Their manners were slipping; she should've ordered first.

The waitress brought a bowl of steaming marinara sauce and breadsticks in a silver-plated basket. Giulia took one and began picking the crust to pieces. Anything to keep herself occupied.

"Do you have any progress to report?" Blake dipped a breadstick in the dish of sauce and took a bite.

"Yes. In addition to the cameras, we'll be watching your condo and Pamela's house every morning from four to six. All the house deliveries were made between those times. We think it's our best chance to get a decent look at her."

Giulia noticed he still referred to them as a team. Keeping up a good front for the client.

"Yeah, well, you missed a delivery this morning." Blake opened a briefcase on the seat next to him. From a 6 x 9 plain brown envelope, he handed Frank a pile of photographs.

Giulia let out a tiny gasp. "Oh."

Frank glared at her.

Blake laughed. "Nothing to get jealous over, Frankie. Right, sugar?"

If Frank's laugh was forced, Giulia couldn't tell. He grinned at Blake. "Our friend taped a set to my office door sometime last night or this morning. Quite a wake-up call."

"She put them under my windshield wiper."

"Care to explain them?"

Giulia shredded more bread.

"What's to explain? My ex decided to try amateur photography and digital manipulation."

"She must have had some interesting images to work with."

Their food arrived. Frank slid the pictures together and dropped them in his lap.

Giulia swallowed bile at the mixed odors of sauce, hot peppers, and salad dressing. Her stomach cramped and burned, but she picked up her fork and played with the julienned salami.

Blake gestured for the photos and spread them on the table. "I didn't realize your curtains were open, sugar. My ex sure got an eyeful of what she's missing."

Frank speared shrimp and macaroni into his mouth. Blake stabbed a hot pepper and swallowed it whole. Giulia hid the salami beneath the lettuce.

"Come clean, Blake." Frank slugged his wine. "You're not telling me this one of you in all your glory is faked."

Blake laughed and poked his own abs. "Of course not. I work hard at these muscles. The important muscle down there, well, that just comes naturally."

Frank brayed. There was no other word for it. "Always the stud, Golden Boy. But I have to object at seducing my assistant."

"Your sweet little assistant offered me a place to crash. What was I supposed to think?"

Frank spread the photos along the center of the table. "So this one of you happened when, exactly?"

"Right out of the shower, just like it looks. I asked sugar here if she wanted me to bother with clothes. Struck you speechless, didn't I?" He chucked Giulia under the chin.

Frank nudged the one of her kneeling before Blake. "Not for long, obviously."

Giulia swallowed, trying to reverse an attack of cotton mouth. "Mr. Parker." She coughed. "Mr. Parker, Mr. Driscoll is under a misconception—"

Blake laughed. "Misconception? Good one, sugar. When I take a girl sack-wrestling, she knows she better prevent a misconception."

Giulia hooked her fingers under the edge of her antipasto dish, ready to chuck it in his face.

No. If you make a scene, Frank will misquote Shakespeare and say you're protesting too much.

Frank caught her eyes. He looked down at the dish and up again, and she could swear he was thinking, *You turn shrewish when you're rejected.*

Could this get any worse? In the movies, that question was the signal for the bad stuff to happen. Even though she honestly could not imagine this farce getting any worse. No, not farce. Theater of the absurd.

Frank tapped his index finger on the same photo. "What about it, Blake?"

"As much as I'd like to tell you all the details, Frankie, it didn't happen."

The waitress arrived with Blake's second glass of wine.

"I'm good, thanks," Frank covered his glass with his hand. After she left, he shook his fork at Blake. "You're not going to tell me that a boner like that sprang up on its own."

Blake slapped Frank on the back. "I have a good imagination, Frankie-boy."

"Uh-uh. You're shoveling it pretty deep."

Blake set down his fork. "Listen, Frank. I've had some hot women come to my bed. Your little girl here, well," he let his eyes roam from Giulia's hair to her waist, and back to her breasts, "she's not up to my standards. Sorry, sugar. I know you wanted me, but it wasn't going to happen."

Giulia's facial temperature soared past the heat index of the Fra Diavolo peppers. From the corner of her eye, she watched the sneer return to Frank's mouth. He'd never believe she hadn't slept with Blake now. Blake's locker-room act would convince his own mother.

"By the way, sugar, did your last bed partner give you that double shiner? You don't look like the kind of girl who likes it rough. Guess you never can tell, can you, Frank?"

Dear Jesus God in Heaven. She had to get away. But what would they say about her if she hid in the ladies' room? Did it matter? She had no career to ruin now. *No. Cowards ran.* She survived ten years in the convent and a sexual assault. She could survive Blake's slander.

Frank pushed the photo of Blake's head between Giulia's legs toward Blake. "You're telling me that flagpole wasn't from this oral exercise? It looks pretty hot to me."

"Well, if you ask Cammy or Mags, they could tell you some stories." Blake winked at Giulia. "But I'm telling you, Frank, the photos aren't real. Here's how it was: your girl didn't have cable; I got bored. I decided to reminisce about some of my best lays and apply a little elbow grease. Of course, knowing sugar here was only a thin wall away helped." He turned that grin on Giulia again. "Did you hear anything? I wondered if you were peeking."

Giulia couldn't keep her eyes on his wide baby blues. Her gaze dropped to the soggy salad in front of her. *Jesus, Mary, and Joseph, save me from this hell.*

"Blake, you're full of it." Frank tucked the photos in his pocket. "You've never stopped yourself when there was a willing female within shouting distance. Save that story for Pamela when she catches you with a stacked file clerk."

Blake guffawed. "I'll be the soul of discretion and a credit to the van Alstyne name and fortune. I've changed."

"You have?" a cultured, feminine voice said.

Everyone looked up. A beautiful blonde stood at the end of the table, a brown envelope dangling from one manicured hand.

Blake half-rose. "Pamela?"

TWENTY-THREE

She's everything I'm not.

Giulia stared without embarrassment because the men sat in a tableau of open-mouthed surprise.

Pamela van Alstyne's shining hair curled just at the tips: a blonde Julia Roberts. Her linen skirt skimmed her narrow hips; her sage-green silk shell draped with just the right amount of cling. Her makeup accented her flawless complexion. A touch of brown mascara brought out the highlights in her hazel eyes.

Blake really was marrying the perfect woman. Next to her, Giulia was both of the Ugly Stepsisters combined. Mousy, unimportant, and frustrated. No wonder Blake thought she'd be easy.

"Pammy, sweetheart, what are you doing here?" Blake pushed his dishes toward the wall. "Sit down and have lunch with us."

"Thank you, no, Blake."

Even her voice was perfect. Low without being sultry, flat vowels probably trained out through elocution lessons.

"Do I have the pleasure of meeting Mr. Driscoll?"

"Of course, forgive me, my manners must be out to lunch." Only Blake laughed feebly at his own joke. "Frank Driscoll, Giulia Falcone, allow me to introduce my fiancée, Pamela van Alstyne."

Frank stood in the cramped space and shook her hand. "My pleasure."

When Giulia held out her hand, Pamela's dropped to her side.

"I've seen so much of you already, Ms. Falcone. I feel as though we've no need of a formal handshake."

Giulia kept her eyes away from the envelope in Pamela's hand. She had to say something, or Pamela would think she remained silent out of guilt. Well, what else could she think?

Frank sat. "I didn't know you and Giulia had met, Ms. van Alstyne."

"Not in person, no." Pamela opened the envelope. "But someone was kind enough to give me some photographs of Ms. Falcone. I do wish I could thank the photographer for the informative morning I spent with these."

The room wavered, and Giulia's ears buzzed. She dug her short fingernails into her palms, and the slight pain brought her back. She might wish the Second Coming would happen right now, that very moment, and save her from this humiliation, but she'd salvage what dignity she could and not slump into her antipasto.

"Thank you," Pamela said to the waitress hovering at her elbow, "I won't be staying to eat."

The waitress glanced at the men and Giulia.

"Thank. You," Pamela said again through her rose-tinted lips. The waitress tore her eyes from the photos in Pamela's hands and scurried to the next booth.

Blake tried to take the photos from her.

"Blake, dear, it's very rude of you to grab."

Frank said, "Ms. van Alstyne, I—"

"Excuse me, Mr. Driscoll. I haven't finished. If you'll allow me?"

Frank inclined his head. A waiter carrying a loaded tray looked over Pamela's shoulder and stumbled, nearly upsetting three bowls of pasta fagioli.

Giulia's body no longer threatened to faint. That would be a release she didn't deserve. She'd spewed her rage and hate at God last Friday—only five days ago? When she renounced Him, He'd obviously bowed to her whim. Look what happened in the park as she spat out her last curse.

Pamela set the photos on the table. "Blake, darling, I can see you passed a delightful evening—Monday, wasn't it?"

"Pammy, I can explain—"

"Ms. van Alstyne, let me assure you—"

"Gentlemen." Pamela's voice, softer than theirs, still silenced them. "I think the explanation is obvious." She clasped her now-empty hands in front of her. "This common whore spread her filthy legs for my fiancée and he mounted her like a bull in heat. Have I omitted anything?" She gazed at all three of them. "Oh, yes. Blake, dear, I wondered about that odd smell on your face when you kissed me Tuesday afternoon. How foolish of me not to recognize the musk from another woman's cunt." She finally looked at Giulia. "That is the word, isn't it, Ms. Falcone? I looked it up to make sure someone like you would understand me."

Giulia dropped her eyes to the ravaged breadstick. If she concentrated on counting the crumbs, maybe she could trick her ears into not hearing another word.

"Blake, Mr. Driscoll, Ms. Falcone, thank you for a most enlightening experience. And may I compliment you on your hiring acumen, Mr. Driscoll. You certainly found an enthusiastic employee.

Blake," she gave him a tight smile. "I believe this belongs to you." She removed the one-carat diamond from her left hand.

"Pamela, please listen." Sweat beaded Blake's forehead as she let the ring fall to the table. It bounced and landed against Blake's knife with a high-pitched ring.

"I really must run. I have an auction meeting in ten minutes." She transferred the smile to Giulia. "Should I advise you to get tested for HIV and sexually transmitted diseases, Ms. Falcone? Or is it Blake who needs to worry? Perhaps you should share your sexual histories over dessert. Enjoy your lunch."

TWENTY-FOUR

"Damn." Blake shoved the ring into his briefcase. "Frank, I have to get her back. Find out who's doing this. Spend any money. Do whatever you have to." He threw two twenties on the table and ran out.

The waitress returned. "May I get you some dessert?" Her eyes never left Giulia.

"We're fine, thanks," Frank said. "Come on, Giulia."

Giulia's legs moved when she told them to, but her numb fingers tried three times before they caught hold of her purse.

The busboy stared at her. A waiter caught her eye and licked his lips.

Hot sunshine on a smelly city sidewalk was delightful. Why couldn't she get warm? She shivered all the way from the restaurant to Frank's parking space. The car was stifling, but she kept the window up.

Frank rolled his down. "Aren't you hot?"

"No." She wrapped her arms around herself like a straitjacket.

Twenty more minutes of silence. When Frank parked in his usual spot behind the building, Giulia pried one arm away from her body and reached for the door handle.

"Giulia."

She waited, not looking at him.

"Tell me . . ."

"Tell you what, Frank? That I should never have offered Blake a safe place to spend the night? I'm not stupid. I figured that out already." She kept speaking to the dashboard. "I understand that working with me is offensive now, but stopping this stalker is more important than our personal likes and dislikes, correct?"

"Yes."

"Then I'll put every effort into identifying her. You can treat this time as my notice. As soon as she's caught—"

"I'll terminate your employment. Is that what you want?"

No. I want you to say you know everything Blake said about me was a lie. I want you to trash professional boundaries and hold me and say you'll make Blake apologize.

"I thought you were—" Frank's voice stopped. A moment later, he said, "You used to be a nun, Giulia. Holy. Untouchable. When I bought coffee from you and you started talking to me, I thought you were sweet and clever and I was kind of ashamed for being attracted to you. When you said you'd work for me, I thought maybe there was a slim-to-none chance that you might not only look at me as your boss."

This is hell. Trapped in an airless, ninety-degree car listening to the man I admire and want tell me why I now repulse him.

"Instead, you screwed Blake and lied to me about it." Frank didn't raise his voice, but she flinched.

"No." He wasn't going to believe that if she could help it. "Listen to me, Frank. I. Did. Not. Sleep. With. Him. I don't care what those photos make it look like. They're lies."

He banged the back of his head against the headrest. "Damn. Damn. Who do I believe, Giulia? You? The tangible digital evidence in my coat pocket? Blake?"

"I've never told you a lie, Frank."

"Everyone lies, Giulia. I lie to my brothers about how successful I am. Nature-girl Sidney might be a closet Twinkie addict. You lied about Blake standing naked in your living room. You're no different."

"Don't you dare equate—"

"Don't you tell me what I can or can't do, Ms. Falcone. Don't try to assume the all-holy nun mantle when it suits your convenience."

"I never do that. I want you to listen—"

"I want you to be who I thought you were. What kind of a— never mind. When the stalker is stopped, you'll no longer be my employee. Correct?"

"Yes." She opened the door before her stoic front crumbled. She preceded him inside and went straight to her desk.

Sidney came out of the bathroom. "Hey, Ms. Falcone. How was lunch?"

Frank's door slammed. Giulia typed like the keys were cheap meat that needed pounding. Sidney tiptoed to her own desk and read the document on her screen.

———

"Sidney, if I had the money, I'd give you a raise," Frank said Thursday morning. "Two dog-walkers and one jogger passed me this morning, and none of them gave me a second glance."

He moved to Giulia's desk. Today he dressed like any off-duty detective. Khaki pants, blue shirt open at the collar, linen-weave blazer. "Anything to report?"

"No. I switched from behind his porch swing to his bushes when the sun started to rise, then jogged the block for the last half-hour. Four people drove to work—probably—between five and six. Nothing else."

"Fine. Here are my notes."

"The spreadsheet will be updated before noon."

"What's your plan for tomorrow morning? We can't use the landscaper disguise two days in a row."

"Eager college student."

His forehead crinkled. "What?"

"Before sunrise, I'll jog down the street or across the intersection where I can still see. As soon as it gets light enough, I'll bring out a sketch pad and draw. If anyone asks, I'm analyzing styles for my MFA in architecture."

———

"Envelope for you, Ms. Falcone." Sidney turned it left and right in her hand. "I can't make out the return address."

Giulia took it like it held a live scorpion.

Sidney knocked on Frank's door and opened it. "Mail, Mr. Driscoll."

"Anything important?" He didn't look up from his screen.

"Phone bill, junk, résumé-looking envelope, and an envelope for Ms. Falcone."

"What? Ms. Falcone, bring it in here. Thanks, Sidney, that's all."

Giulia dragged her feet across the room. Zombies must function like this. Her only clear thought was how much she did not want to open this plain, square envelope.

Frank made the *gimme* gesture with his hand. "Let me see it. Smudged return address, of course. Use my letter opener."

Giulia slit the flap and pulled out one of those cards that play music when opened. Her fingers touched the battery-powered computer chip in the back.

"What does it say? Show me." Frank came around to stand next to her.

Her face. On a camel's body. It made no sense. She'd expected a new X-rated photograph.

"A camel?" Frank looked from Giulia to the card and back. "Is this biblical?"

"I suppose."

"Open it."

She started to breathe a quick prayer. Useless. She'd renounced God.

"Open it, Ms. Falcone."

Cackling laughter. She closed it. Opened it again. Sort of like the Wicked Witch of the West mixed with Woody Woodpecker. She read the cartoonish text: "'Although you use an abundance of soap, the stain of your guilt is still before me. Consider what you have done. You are a swift she-camel running here and there, sniffing the wind in her craving— in her heat who can restrain her?'"

Giulia flung the card to the floor. "You bitch!"

Frank caught her arm as she ground her heel into the computer chip. "Stop! I need to see it."

She kicked it into the far corner and it popped open. The laughter slurred into a drunk-sounding Woody Woodpecker.

"What for? So you can point out how each word applies to me? Let me save you the trouble." She stalked to the corner and clawed the card up from the floor. "This is probably Jeremiah or Ezekiel. Let's see. Nothing can make me clean again. That's clear. She's acquired a sense of humor, too. That's a pretty mangy camel she put my head on. I especially like the lively translation she used for the quote. The RSV and King James are so stodgy when it comes to sex."

"Giulia, calm down."

"We're back to Giulia now? Of course. Women like me don't need the dignity of last names. Everyone in Tutti Mangia knows that now. Did you see how the busboy stared at me? Maybe he was wondering if his tips would cover a quick blow job."

"Giulia, stop it."

"Are you afraid I won't give you a full day's work after yesterday? Or that I might try to sabotage this investigation out of spite? After all, I'm a liar, right? I'm the filthy whore who spread her legs to keep the client happy. No, wait." She held up the card and pointed to it like the teacher she'd been. "I'm a she-camel in heat—nobody can restrain my lust."

"Giulia Falcone, shut up!"

She let the card fall to the desk. The slow-motion laughter petered out at last.

God, she was tired. Too many nights of sleeping in snatches between rape nightmares, photograph nightmares, homeless nightmares. If the landlord evicted her when she lost this job, would she sleep better under the Delaware Street Bridge? Was the convent really worse than all this?

She tucked her trembling hands into her skirt pockets. "Do you want me to leave now, Frank?"

"Yes."

Oh. Well. That's that. "I'll clean out my desk."

"What? No." He stood toe to toe with her until she looked up. "I want you to go home and get some sleep. You look like death warmed over. Just set your alarm so you make it to Pamela's house on time tomorrow morning."

This sounded like the old Frank, before those photographs appeared on the door. His face showed concern—but the minimal kind. The boss making sure his employee was able to do her job. Well, it was more than she expected.

"Thanks."

She shuffled to her desk and shut down her computer.

Sidney wasn't even pretending to work.

TWENTY-FIVE

Friday afternoon, Giulia poked her head around Frank's door.

"Frank, let me see the clue collage. Something's bugging me."

"Come in." He waved to the wall on Giulia's left.

She read and made notes and compared interview quotes and background information until Sidney buzzed Frank's phone. "I'm leaving, Mr. Driscoll. Break a leg tonight and have a nice weekend."

Frank typed a moment longer, then closed the document. "She only says goodbye to me? Don't you count?"

"She's afraid of me."

"Of you? Why on earth—oh. Yesterday."

"Duh, Frank. If you'd explain what the blowup was about maybe she'd try to understand."

"Ms. Fal— Giulia—"

"But since you still believe the photos and not me, there's no point, is there? After I leave, she'll have a great story for the next admin. All about the crazy ex-nun who slept with the client and wrecked her career."

———

The conductor closed his music as the applause dwindled.

"Good show, everyone. Nice job on the Minuet tonight. Sounded like cats yowling. Keep it up."

Giulia broke down her flute and clipped her score together. Just after ten o'clock. In five hours, her alarm would ring.

"Excuse me, First Flute."

Giulia looked up into broad pecs under a tight black T-shirt. Up higher, into the smiling face of the Second Violin.

"This is the right moment to give you this." A chocolate rose appeared in his hand.

"I—it is?"

"To be honest, I meant to give it to you last Saturday, but I lost my nerve."

Giulia's brain short-circuited.

He held out the rose. "I'm glad I didn't, though, because you look like you really need it tonight."

To her left, Frank slammed home the locks on his cello case.

Giulia took the rose.

"Do you have any plans tonight?"

His physique was even more impressive up close. She caught a whiff of the same shampoo she used. A frisson of intimacy ran through her. She willed her brain to connect with her mouth. "I have to be at work at four a.m."

"Ouch. Can I talk you into one drink?"

This was the Second Violin asking her out. Forget five hours of sleep. She'd manage on three. "Fair warning: at midnight I turn into a pumpkin."

He grinned. "Then I'll see you to your door at eleven fifty-nine."

Giulia smiled. *Hey—I can still smile.*

Frank heaved his cello case into his left arm and brushed past Giulia. "Good night, Ms. Falcone."

After Frank disappeared through the exit, the Second Violin said, "The Cello's your boss, isn't he?"

"Yes."

"Jealous?"

"Not likely."

"Gay, huh?"

Laughter nearly choked her. There was no way to explain the whole soap opera. No way at all.

He offered her his arm. "Ready to go?"

———

"I've never been to an Internet bar before, Scott." Giulia sipped her vodka cranberry and watched pockets of people banging away at keyboards.

"Not a gamer?" Scott pulled at his ale.

"Don't even own a computer."

"You're kidding."

Giulia smiled again. She hadn't been this relaxed in days. "I'm the exception that proves the rule. I only use a computer at work."

"Ms. First Flute, I foresee a series of long evenings at my place during which I seduce you into the universe of MMORPGs."

"Of what?" She liked his use of the word *seduce*. Maybe it'd erase the bad connotations from her mind.

"Massively multiplayer online role-playing games."

"Like Dungeons and Dragons?"

"Shh. Don't let the gamers hear you say that. You'll forever be branded as out of touch. D&D is ancient history. I'm talking about Combat Realm."

A woman in the back squealed and hugged the man next to her.

"She probably just won a battle or completed a quest. Maybe defeated a supernatural monster." He nodded toward a table with six laptops arranged like place settings at Thanksgiving. "Now I can confess that I had an ulterior motive for bringing you here. The Raging Death Clan challenged Flight of Terror to a battle tonight. That's why this place is so crowded. My roommate's in Raging Death." He looked over Giulia's head. "There he is. Hey, Kyle, over here."

A pale man with a shaved head marched over to them, talking into the air: ". . . just waiting for Nightclaw. She had to fill in for the kid working the drive-through tonight. See you in five." He touched his ear, and Giulia saw the matte-black cell phone earpiece.

"Scott, dude, come to cheer me on? Who's the babe?"

Scott smacked the back of Kyle's head. "Watch your mouth, clod. Giulia, I'm ashamed to say this is my roommate, Kyle. Kyle, this is Giulia Falcone, flautist."

"What-ist? Just a second." He tapped his earpiece and turned his back to them. "No, dude, I don't see him yet. Battle's scheduled for quarter to eleven . . . He'll be here. Right." He faced them again. "Sorry. Those your chicken fingers? I'm starved."

Scott slid the basket of chicken and fries toward him. "Where's Lugal?"

"In the alley, sucking a cig and getting into character." He stuffed half of a long piece of chicken, dripping with ketchup, in his mouth. "Hold that thought." He swallowed and tapped his ear again. "Yeah? Cool. I'm there." He shook Giulia's hand. "Nice to meet you. Gotta get ready."

Giulia just then saw the messenger bag on his shoulder. As he walked away, he drew out a green-and gold cape, flourished it over his shaved head, and tied it at his throat. Several people whistled and applauded.

Scott hung his head. "Sorry about Clod-boy, there, Giulia. He spends more time online than in the real world."

Giulia said around a mouthful of her cheesesteak hoagie, "Does he have a regular job?"

"IT tech for all the local hospitals, now that they merged. So 99 percent of the time, the only warm bodies he interacts with are fellow geeks."

Giulia smiled again. "I speak a little geek, Scott. The species just needs proper handling, anti-static suits, and a good conversational dictionary." When he laughed, she got a glow in her cheeks that wasn't embarrassment. "So give me a crash course in Raging Death."

"Easy. They're all ogres, so they have major attitude."

She stifled laughter. "That helps them in battle?"

"Sure, for when they fight zombies and—ah. Here comes Urnu the Snake."

Giulia looked on the floor. *Wait. He means an ogre. A person playing ogre.* "Which one is he? Or she?"

"That tall, skinny guy in the black T-shirt and jeans. Looks like nobody, right? Wait'll you see his eyes during the battle. He's the ultimate warrior."

Three young men left their barstools, and in hushed voices began chanting, "Ur-nu. Ur-nu. Ur-nu." Several gamers left their screens to add their voices to the homage.

Mob psychology. More than that—religious fervor. "Quite a reaction. The others on his team do what he says?"

"You bet. He's a master strategist. Hrunting—that's Kyle—controls lightning, casts spells, and is awesome with a two-headed axe." Scott pointed to an older woman with a 1970s 'fro. "That's Nightclaw. She's a hunter. Ishtaria's a mercenary—she's the bleached blonde next to Hrunting. The Indian guy is Wulfaxe, the other warrior. He's nowhere near Urnu's level, though."

They looked like a cross-section of average people to Giulia. She'd assumed they'd all be pale, pimply, and stoop-shouldered. *Never believe stereotypes.*

Urnu the Snake sat at the head of the monitor-covered table and folded his hands like a priest at Consecration. He looked familiar. Maybe if she heard his voice . . .

Melted ice in her drink had watered it down, but she sipped anyway. "And who are you in all this?"

"Tonight I'm just me, rooting for Hrunting. When I'm in the game, I'm his apprentice. Anything to get into Raging Death."

A true bodybuilder took the seat at the opposite end of the table from the snake guy.

Urnu raised his eyes and Giulia blinked at the power and pull in his expression. *That's why they follow him.*

Scott leaned into Giulia's ear. "Lugal's toast after the battle."

"Who?"

"Lugal the Spear. The walking muscle that just sat down. He should've been first at the table to cast protective spells."

"Maybe he had to work late."

"When Urnu schedules a battle, his Clan is there. No exceptions. Hrunting called in sick to be here."

Lugal the bodybuilder . . . no, Lugal the Spear attached his headset. Everyone raised a fist. Lugal raised both, revealing a silver and green spear tattooed on his left forearm. He spoke for a good two minutes, gesturing to each player in turn, saving Urnu for last. Then he stood. The others followed and slammed their fists on the table. "Death rages on!"

The clock over the bar read 10:44.

TWENTY-SIX

"HERE COMES THE CLIMACTIC battle." Scott pulled Giulia closer to Hrunting's monitor.

A hundred voices like fingernails on a chalkboard screeched out of the earpieces. All the players except Urnu and Lugal flinched. Ishtaria yanked off her headset, but put it back on a moment later. Leopard-vulture-spider creatures swarmed over the remaining opponents, dissolving one in venom, disemboweling another, slicing a third into strips just like giant cats used to do on Saturday-morning cartoons.

On-screen Urnu gestured, and all the creatures gathered behind him. With measured steps, he walked to the center of the battlefield where only the opposing leader remained. Urnu smiled. Giulia looked over the top of the monitor. Real-life Urnu had the same smile. He tapped several keys, and ogre-Urnu released a deafening shout. The others pounced on the vanquished leader, shredding and stamping. Urnu snapped his fingers. They fell away as Urnu reached a massive hand into the gore and came out with a tattered heart.

The gamers and the crowd began chanting in hushed voices. "Ur-nu. Ur-nu. Ur-nu." Giulia, almost caught up in the moment herself, opened her mouth to join the chant.

Urnu swallowed the enemy's heart.

The bar erupted in cheers. Giulia gagged. On screen, the Raging Death Clan crowded around Urnu as text and numbers appeared and disappeared over them and the victims. Their alter-egos tapped keys, never losing focus.

"Wasn't that awesome, Giulia?" Scott squeezed her against his side. "The strategy, the cunning, the bloodlust."

Giulia kept silent rather than ruin Scott's mood with her true opinion. Scott finished his second ale and set the bottle on a table. "I'm almost powerful enough to petition Urnu for full membership. Kyle couldn't give me details of his initiation, but he said the price was worth it."

Snake-handling, maybe? How biblical. Giulia could picture Urnu as a Great Awakening preacher, a dozen harmless corn snakes twined around him, mesmerizing his followers with those eyes. And skinny, cute Kyle taking one of those snakes, trembling because he wouldn't know whether it was poisonous or not.

The gamers, laptops closed, mingled with their fans. Hrunting high-fived Scott and followed two redheads to the bar.

Scott leaned into Giulia's ear. "Want to meet Urnu?"

"I don't really—"

He turned on the pout. "Come on, Giulia, he's almost as mysterious in person. Then I'll take you home—it's almost pumpkin time."

She could resist the pout, but why? He'd made her forget the last few days. Meeting this role-player was easy repayment. "Sure. Introduce me to the lead ogre."

As they weaved through the groupies, Ishtaria stopped in front of Urnu. He bared his teeth and snarled his fingers in her long blonde hair. She touched her tongue to her upper lip, and Urnu jerked her forward. His eyes took in the fans around them. Then with one hand in her hair and the other kneading her buttocks, he thrust his tongue in her mouth. She clamped her lips onto his and ground her hips into his pelvis.

Giulia looked away, looked back. In rhythm with Urnu's hand, Scott kneaded her waist.

Good Lord, I hope that woman is wearing underwear. Did I just think that? The hand on her own waist made longer strokes. *Don't move that hand any farther up or down, Scott.* Her eyes locked on the victory tableau. *Lady, please stop rubbing yourself on his leg.*

"Scott, dude! Did you see? Weren't we awesome?" Kyle/Hrunting and his redheads returned, beers in hands.

Lugal the Spear pushed past Giulia as the blonde turned toward the bar. In half a dozen slow steps, Lugal stood before his leader like a penitent, his Schwarzeneggerian muscles drooping before Urnu's wiry height. Giulia couldn't hear their conversation over Kyle and Scott's jabber, but she had the distinct impression that if the two men were alone, Lugal would be on his knees.

Urnu touched Lugal's chest, right above his heart. A tattoo of a snake extended to strike ran from his wrist to his elbow. Lugal touched his forehead to the snake.

That proves it. The game is their religion. Well, I promised to play nice for Scott's new preacher. She touched Scott's elbow to get his attention, sure that Lugal would leave after his obeisance.

Instead, Urnu replayed the last scene. He twisted his fingers into Lugal's hair, grabbed his muscled buttocks, and crushed their lips together. Lugal clutched Urnu's rump and pulled him closer.

Not in public—good Heavens.

Scott breathed, "I'd like to get a woman to dry-hump me like that."

Giulia stiffened.

"Oh, not you, Giulia. I mean, not yet. I mean, this is just a first date and all. I'm a gentleman, really. Ask Kyle." He yanked Kyle's arm. "Right, Kyle?"

"Huh? Yeah. Sure. Scott's a throwback to the fifties. Prince Charming and all that." Kyle put an arm around the waists of his bookends. "I'm his foil. He tries to keep me honest, and I regale him with my conquests. You're safe with him."

Urnu and Lugal finally separated, and Scott took his place in the receiving line. "Urnu the Snake, you are awesome!" Scott high-fived him.

Urnu bared his teeth in his alter-ego's smile. "I accept your homage, apprentice." His greenish-gold eyes scrutinized Giulia. "Is this your consort?"

Scott smiled at Giulia. "I'm working on it. Urnu the Snake, this is Giulia."

Urnu's twisted smile expanded. "Indeed." He held out his hand.

Politeness compelled her to take it. His grip was dry, and his hand trembled the slightest bit. Residual excitement, she supposed. Up close, she could see the metallic scales on the snake tattoo. Green and gold. The Clan took its colors from Urnu's eyes. *Strange* didn't begin to describe the groupies, the gamers—heck, the entire bar.

"I look forward to our next meeting, Giulia." He released her hand, inclined his head to Scott, and walked to the bar. Ishtaria and Lugal opened a space for him between them.

"You've made a conquest, Giulia." Scott stared after Urnu with just a hint of Lugal's lust in his eyes.

Giulia flushed, then got a touch of the crawlies. "I don't think so."

"I don't want the lord of the manor to exercise his right to take you from me anyway. You're okay with dating a future ogre, right?"

"Let no one say I'm species-intolerant."

"Ma'am, you've won my scaly heart. Shall we go?" As they passed the bar, Scott slugged Kyle's shoulder. "Don't drive home, Wizard."

"Got cab fare stashed with the bartender." He kissed the right-hand redhead. "Don't expect me before morning, dude."

Giulia would've liked to kiss Frank like that. Well, maybe not at first. There was zero chance of it happening anyway. That window had closed and locked when those photos appeared on the office door.

They crossed the parking lot, and Scott held the passenger door of his dark green Pathfinder for her.

Get a clue, Falcone. A hot, eligible man is driving you home.

She was going to take the plunge. He was willing and she was tired of being a throwback to Victorian times. Maybe she didn't know how to dry-hump, but she could kiss. What had the February *Cosmo* said about red-hot kisses?

Scott braked hard and Giulia's seat belt caught her.

"Oh, dear. I think I've been a colossal boor." Giulia gave him an apologetic smile. "Please tell me we haven't been driving long."

Scott reached for her hand. "A few blocks. I tried to talk to you, but when you didn't answer I figured I'd wait till you came back to earth."

"You take me out and I ignore you. That's got to be on the top ten list of reasons people don't get a second date."

"Giulia, the only way I wouldn't ask you out again is if I dropped dead before tomorrow's show."

"Oh." She squeezed his hand in return. "You're in good health? No terminal conditions? No tendency to fall off roofs or jump in front of moving trains?"

"Damn. We're here." He escorted her to the door. "Barring fire, flood, or earthquake, I'll see you at the Marquee tomorrow."

"I'll be there."

"Kyle's wrong, you know. I'm no Prince Charming."

She knew a twinge of disappointment for the buried desire of every little girl to really, truly meet Prince Charming. "I didn't expect you to be."

"Prince Charming always seems to be too much of a wuss to show his feelings for the rescued princess. Myself, on the other hand—"

He cupped his hand on the back of her head and kissed her. She embraced him, and he trailed his other hand up and down her back. She shivered. A good shiver. Tomorrow night she'd pull that clingy red sweater out of the back of her closet. Never too late to become a consort.

TWENTY-SEVEN

GIULIA BLEW THROUGH HOUSECLEANING and grocery shopping Saturday morning. After lunch, she threw on capris and her black-and-white DMHO T-shirt and took the bus to Common Grounds.

Deep female singing voices hit her as soon as she opened the door.

She'd forgotten Evelyn's open-mike Saturdays. Whoever these three were, at least they could carry a tune, unlike that Beach Boys tribute band on Memorial Day.

Giulia knocked on the counter and said to the back of Mingmei's apron, "Hey, Mingmei. Can I get a medium iced chai?"

Mingmei started and turned around, raising her voice over the music. "Hey, Giulia. You working overtime?"

"Not really. Don't you get off shift soon?"

"Three o'clock. Ten minutes." Mingmei leaned forward, her striped hair brushing Giulia's ear. "Something wrong?"

Giulia shook her head. "Need your advice."

"Okay. No worries. Evelyn's niece is working second shift today. She's always on time."

Sure enough, five minutes later Mingmei's replacement walked in, waved at Giulia, and headed straight for the counter. Three women toting shopping bags followed her, debating in lawyerlike fashion about strawberry versus blueberry smoothies.

"Whew." Mingmei slid into the chair opposite Giulia and drank sixteen ounces of water without taking a breath. "Okay, I'm all yours. What'cha need?"

"Makeup advice. I have a date tomorrow." She patted her homemade messenger bag.

"Yes!" Mingmei high-fived her. "It's about time. Do I know him? What's he look like? Where are you going?"

"One at a time. Come upstairs to the office with me, and I'll tell you on the way."

As they climbed the stairs side by side, Giulia said, "His name's Scott and he plays violin in the theater with me."

"Is he the one with the great pecs? You mentioned him the day after that cast party."

"That's the one. He gave me a chocolate rose after last night's show."

Mingmei clapped her hands. "It's only a short step to real flowers. Is he nice? How's he kiss? He has kissed you, hasn't he?"

An overnight delivery envelope hung on the doorknob in a plastic bag, addressed to Frank from someone in D.C. She slid it over her wrist and turned her key in the lock.

"Yeah, he has. I think he kisses, um, well, great." Her ears tingled. "I don't have a lot of experience to compare him with, though."

"Girl, you are such an amateur." Mingmei hugged her. "But I am so proud of you."

"I have a ten-year drought to overcome." Thank God for Mingmei. Who else would put up with her klutzy attempts at girl stuff?

"Just a sec." She opened Frank's office door and hung the delivery on his chair.

"What can I do to make him want you?"

"Mingmei . . ." She closed Frank's door, shaking her head.

"Come on, Giulia, you've got that look in your eyes." She glanced around. "Small office. Which desk is yours?"

"By the window. The one behind you is Sidney's." She set her messenger bag next to the phone.

Mingmei rolled Giulia's chair into the center of the room and sat in it. "The fashion genie is out of her bottle. I hereby grant you three wishes."

Giulia took a deep breath. She could—no, she would do this. Scott was going to ask her out again, and she was not going to look like a repressed, makeupless frump.

"Genie, please bring out your makeup wand. Scott should want to kiss this face." She pulled out a quilted makeup bag.

"Let's see your ammunition." Mingmei dumped its contents on the desk. "Base matches your skin tone, good blusher, two lipsticks; let's see here." She opened the first tube. "A little orange for you." She opened the second. "Metallic crimson. I like it."

"It's not too forward?"

"Forward?" She giggled. "Giulia, sometimes you talk like my grandmother. What colors of eyeshadow do you have?"

"Three shades of blue that are supposed to blend together, but I never figured out how."

Mingmei held the two-inch rectangle by Giulia's face. "Maybe . . . I'd prefer a gray to blend with the darkest blue."

"I have that." She sorted through the pile of samples sent to her as promotional gimmicks.

"Yes." Mingmei set them side by side on the desk. "These are the right ones. Okay. Eyeliner? Mascara?"

"Brown? Black? That's all I have."

"Not brown. Black. You want drama." She lined up everything on the desk. "All right, Cinderella. Prepare for transformation."

After Mingmei left, Giulia went into Frank's office to study the clue collage. Out of habit, she started to rip the overnighted envelope open, but stopped. She wasn't the admin anymore. Face it—she wasn't really an employee anymore. Plus, she would not open anyone else's mail. No exceptions. End of discussion.

Sipping the chai, she pulled out a pen and some blank printer paper and brainstormed at Frank's desk.

"Camille. You can make it to Blake's and Pamela's mailboxes and still be on time for work. Are you the Bible type? Would you strangle birds?" Giulia sketched two rows of attached boxes and filled in the exes' names. "Sandra. You'd dye birds pink and blue. You might kill them, if it didn't ruin your nails. Margaret." She stirred the last of her drink with the straw. "I still get no feeling either way. Why are you such a mystery? Is your real self too hidden? Or are you simply a nice person who happens to be rich enough to attract Blake?

"Isabel. I saw a classic guardian angel painting in your hallway. You could be the Bible-quoter. Your cheerful face could easily hide a hellfire Protestant upbringing." The chai faded into slurps of spiced air and she tossed the cup into the trash. "Elaine, being snooty doesn't preclude being psycho. You could kill birds.

Would you dye them? That's what maids are for, right? You'd have a helper."

Giulia's slouch vanished. "Good heavens. What if she's not working alone? That changes the whole dynamic. They're all the type to have personal assistants. And if she's using an assistant for all this, how far does she trust her?"

She pushed back her chair and paced the stuffy room. "It's too dangerous. This stalker is one step from the edge. Would an assistant risk being named as an accessory just to keep a lucrative job?"

Giulia wouldn't, but the lure of money . . . And if this hypothetical assistant had also been dumped by a lover . . . She'd be exactly the kind of person the stalker could talk into playing this game. In another set of boxes, she scribbled reasons each of the exes might use a partner in her "Blake or Bust" program.

She checked the time and had to unstick her watch from her wrist.

"Oh, no—did I sweat off the makeup?" She ran to the bathroom mirror. "Whew. Still looks the same. Kind of *Cosmo* girl-ish."

Below her sketched charts, she wrote a note for Frank: *What if she has an accomplice? Unlikely, but we should consider it. See boxes above.*

She put the pages on his chair beneath the overnighted envelope and locked up.

"Something wrong?"

She jerked upright and spun around. "Frank." Amazing how fast her heart rate could ramp up.

He was frowning, but that was his habitual expression when he looked at her now. "Why are you here?"

"I was brainstorming and needed the spreadsheet collage."

"Shouldn't you be out looking for your next job?"

"Shouldn't you be pleased that I'm devoting extra time to finishing this case?"

"I managed without you for quite a while, Ms. Falcone. No one is indispensable."

All her frustrated desire to kiss him burned to a crisp. "What's your real problem, Mr. Driscoll? Worried I'll bring undesirable companions into the office?" She pried open the circular clip on her key ring with one hand. Damn the man. If he was so pigheaded that he couldn't let go of one wrong idea—

"What brilliant insights came to you in there?"

"Nothing brilliant. Just an idea we hadn't thought of before." *Stupid key. Now of all times it decides to jam.*

"Excuse me. You might not have thought of it. Give me credit for seeing a few more possibilities than you would. I am a professional." He crossed his arms and smirked at her struggles with the key ring. "By the way, I see you're painting your outside to match your new, improved inside."

Her fingernail ripped. *Bite me, Frank. No, don't say that. But don't be a doormat for him to smear his assumptions on, either.* "What are you doing here on a Saturday afternoon, Frank? Sherlock Holmes needed only a bit of cigarette ash and half a footprint to catch criminals. You should be sitting in your easy chair, eyes closed, with Yvonne massaging your feet to relieve stress and increase blood flow to the brain." There. The key came free.

"Not everyone requires foreplay to do their job."

"Damn you, Frank Driscoll." She seized his hand and thrust the key into it.

He closed his hand around hers. "I'm sorry. That was uncalled for."

"I agree. So is just about everything you've said to me since our friend learned to play with photo-manipulation software."

He opened his hand and hers fell away. "You're not going to beat that dead horse again, are you?"

"Here's a bulletin for you: you know those tabloids that show photos of space aliens landing World War Two biplanes on the moon? Build on those fakes, and we may be able to have a civil discussion again."

He pocketed the key. "Sidney e-mailed me. She's uncomfortable when you're in the office. What do you think should be done about that?"

Just like that, it all became too much. All Giulia wanted was never again to see this building or this office or this man she once admired. "You win, Frank. I quit. Tell Sidney she can do what she likes with the stuff in my desk."

Giulia pushed past him, but he put out a hand to stop her. "What? What else do you need to say that you haven't said with nauseating precision already?"

"You took me too literally. I didn't mean—"

"Yes, you did. You didn't have the guts to fire me, so you tried to push me into quitting." She wrenched her shoulder away. "Why am I still talking to you?"

She reached the stairs, and her sandals slapped and echoed in the stairwell. She had to get out before she said something worse. Why wouldn't the blasted street door open?

"Giulia, this has gotten out of hand." Frank's voice, right behind her.

She turned and faced him. "It got out of hand four days ago."

"Perhaps we should revisit the problem. I told you how I think—thought of you. I want—"

"The problem, Mr. Driscoll, is you. Not my perceived behavior, not Sidney's first harsh experience in dealing with co-workers, not your tomcatting client or his unhinged ex. Remind me to send a sympathy card to your future wife. Unless she's Mother Teresa, she's going to need a degree in psychology to make the marriage work."

He flinched like she'd slapped him again. "I'll mail you your last paycheck. Don't feel you have to make polite conversation in the orchestra pit tonight, Ms. Falcone."

"Already figured that, thanks." She held out her hand, ingrained politeness overriding her anger. "Goodbye."

He shook it. Firm. Businesslike. Distant. "Goodbye."

TWENTY-EIGHT

"Stupid bus schedule. Stupid cheap shirt. Stupid, stupid, stupid me. Ow!" Giulia sucked the blood from her fingertip and jammed the needle into the shoulder of her new long-sleeved black shirt. "Serves me right for buying clothes at the dollar store."

She knotted the thread and bit off the excess. Even though she only had seven minutes to make the bus, she retouched her lipstick, wiped away a few flakes of mascara from under her eyes, and dabbed on a bit more concealer. "There. Almost as glamorous as this afternoon."

6:29. She snatched her flute case and sheet music, and of course the key slipped out of the lock and of course she fumbled it on the second try. *What's wrong with this lock?* It turned sticky, then smooth, then sticky again. *Must be the humidity.*

6:31. The building's front door slammed into her heel, she ran half a block, and plopped onto a sideways bus seat.

Now what was she going to do? She could've dealt with Frank's attitude at least for another week, but no, she had to let her mouth run like a sewer. It didn't matter that Frank was a pig-headed, gutter-mouthed jerk. She wanted him to look at her the way he used to. She certainly didn't think of herself as sacrosanct, but if Frank did, that would explain his occasional fits of shyness. His odd moments of gentleness, too, in the middle of banter or accounting or spreadsheet creation.

Scott didn't know about her past, so he'd never look at her that way. That could be an advantage. A blank page to draw herself on however she wished. Giulia Falcone, twenty-first century woman ready to embrace life. Sounded like a talk-show hostess speech. Bring on the makeover consultant, the shrink, and the volunteer male escorts.

Focus on the checking account balance. If nothing else, she could temp. She hated temping: always a new set of people to get used to. Sometimes people just looked right through her, because temps weren't officially co-workers.

She weighed invisibility against the past week of working with Frank. No contest.

In the distant past—last month—invisibility had been one of her goals. She'd lost sight of it in the temporary happiness of Frank promoting her to partner, learning how to piece together clues, falling for Frank, teaching Sidney.

She was going to miss Sidney. No more Penn State fight song at 8:30 in the morning. No more lectures on the benefits of tofu and green tea. Her throat closed and her eyes blurred. How had her life disintegrated so completely in a mere four days?

"Wanna bite, lady?"

Giulia blotted her eyes on her sleeve. The mechanic from the garage on the corner sat opposite her, winking in an exaggerated manner and holding out a brownie. The diamond studs in his ears glinted beneath his long blond hair. He smiled, and a matching diamond on his left incisor glistened with saliva. "You look like you could use a hit of happy. No charge or nothing. You always say hi and stuff when I see you. Makes me feel human."

"Thanks, no. Have to work tonight."

"Cool. Nobody wants to have weed-breath talkin' to the boss." He bit off half the brownie, chewed slowly, and swallowed. A lazy smile spread over his face. "Anytime you need to feel good, you come by. After the place closes, you know."

"Thanks. You be careful. Stay out of trouble."

He slid the rest of the brownie into his mouth. "I got no troubles."

The bus pulled up at the theater, and Giulia hustled through the stage door.

"Giulia! There you are." Scott took her music and walked beside her to the orchestra pit. "Guess what? Urnu PM'd me tonight!" They weaved among the music stands, Scott jabbering about Urnu and Hrunting and Raging Death.

"Breathe, Scott. I'm glad you're so happy about this." She positioned her music and unlatched her flute case.

Scott took her hands off the lid. "Set up later. Listen. Urnu says he wants to expand Raging Death in a new way: a Siren-Wizard pair. That's where you come in."

"Me?"

"Absolutely. Urnu's initiation is tough, but the rewards are worth it."

"Scott, I don't know the first thing about RPGs. And I don't own a computer, remember?"

"Not a problem. I know this guy who rooms with the Wizard of Raging Death. He's good-looking and almost a gentleman, and he'd just love to show you all about quests and battles." Scott turned on a thirty-klieg-light grin. "What do you say?"

She didn't care. She needed a job. She needed . . . She needed a vacation from her current life. Why not a fantasy alter ego? "You make it sound like fun."

"It is. It will be. You and me, sharing a chair in front of my PC late into the night, a bottle of wine, developing character skills." Scott nudged her chin up. "Hey, you look awesome tonight. Is that beautiful face for me?"

Giulia attempted a coy smile. "Maybe."

"Well, then." He treated her to a lingering version of last night's kisses.

When they parted, Giulia took a deep breath and said, "I'll give your idea serious consideration, apprentice, um . . ."

"Wizard. Maybe I should print you out a character chart."

"Sure, but you've distracted me long enough. It's seven o'clock, and I'm not set up yet." She leaned to her right to see the violin section. "And neither are you, Second Violin. Git."

"Bully. Talk to you at intermission."

Giulia smiled and lifted the lid of her flute case. He was a kid at heart, kind of like Sidney. A month or two of Scott might be just what she needed right now.

A plain-white piece of paper folded into sixths lay on top of her flute's head joint. Her smile stretched even wider. Scott stuck a note in when she wasn't looking. What a sweetheart.

Your day has come, the time for you to be punished. Now then, listen, you wanton creature. All your friends have betrayed you; they have become your enemies. There is no one to help you. Disaster will come upon you, and you will not know how to conjure it away. Your enemies will look at you and laugh at your destruction.

I have to tell Frank. She turned it over and saw a line of minuscule type across the bottom: *Fallen are you, never to rise again.*

Oh, shit.

She never swore. She needed to regain control. The stalker wasn't threatening her, she was taunting her with the past. The photos and the job—how would the stalker know about the job? She had to be assuming. Maybe she'd been in the restaurant on Wednesday. Sure, she'd be following Blake to see everyone's reactions to her photos. But Pamela broke off the engagement. That should've made the stalker happy, so why this new note?

Giulia refolded the paper and slid it in her pants pocket. With mechanical precision, she opened her music, put her flute together, and warmed up.

What if Pamela got a note, too? No, not like this. Pamela wasn't being painted as a seductress. The stalker seemed to be jealous of her, Giulia, the one Blake slept with.

But she hadn't slept with Blake. If the stalker was the photographer, she'd know this.

Good heavens. The stalker did have an accomplice.

Giulia balanced her flute on the closed case and headed toward Frank, who'd finished tuning and was talking to the drummer. She waited behind him a moment, then touched his arm. "Excuse me."

Frank turned his head, frowned, and turned back to the drummer.

Giulia touched his arm again. "It'll only take a moment."

Frank's mouth smiled at her, but the rest of his face radiated irritation. "I'm afraid I don't have a moment."

She stared at his back for a beat, then returned to her stand and ran up and down scales on her flute. C, E, A-flat, D, B-flat, one after the other, fast and loud.

Insufferable jerk. Arrogant, know-it-all, pig-headed moron. He wasn't her boss anymore. She had zero obligation to share her insight with him, let alone this latest note. She wouldn't put it past him to repeat the worst bits out loud with that sneer on his face. And what would anyone in earshot think?

Fine. He had the experience. Let his superior skills reach the same conclusion. Now that Giulia wasn't working for Driscoll Investigations, Blake's stalker wasn't her problem anymore.

———

Scott pounced on Giulia as soon as she exited the ladies' room during intermission. "So what do you say to tomorrow after the matinee? We can grab a pizza. I'll move my laptop to the coffee table, and we'll snuggle on the couch as we learn."

Giulia fingered the note in her pocket. What if Scott was the accomplice? No one else came near her flute case. No. No, not possible. Scott was too straightforward, too little-boy-ish.

Frank had to be told. She could deal with him being rude if it gave them the telling clue. No one had approached Pamela's house between four and six that morning, but the ex in her messenger disguise could've delivered something later.

"Kyle's working two shifts tomorrow to make up for Friday, so we'll have the place to ourselves."

If she'd received "death by Prophets," Blake had most likely received something, too. He might have given it to Frank by now. In a perfect world, the camera trap had finally caught her face when she sneaked into Blake's yard.

"Are you still working at four in the morning? I get out at six. That'd give us at least two hours on weeknights before you had to get home."

Unfortunate that she hadn't memorized the Song of Solomon. What verses could top the last set? Something about the ex's breasts, most likely. Solomon liked cleavage.

Scott's breath warmed her ear. "Earth to Giulia."

"Mm?"

"Have you heard anything I said?"

She replayed the noises his voice had made while she considered the note's ramifications. "Battle training?"

The lights blinked off and on. A pause. Off and on.

"Rats. Intermission's over." They walked back amidst audience and orchestra members. "Here's the gist. You. Me. Pizza. Tomorrow after the matinee."

"I might have to . . ." No. Not anymore. No more job. "I'd love to."

Scott stopped her at the conductor's stand. "We will make a kick-ass team." He leaned down and kissed her.

The sound of a throat being cleared broke them apart. The conductor raised an eyebrow and gave pointed looks toward their respective seats.

Giulia sidled to her stand and warmed her flute. When she looked up, Frank's frown assumed biblical proportions.

———

"Call is one-thirty tomorrow, people. Kindly forego the Pirates game and be on time." The conductor stared at the clarinet and piano players. "And no texting until intermission."

Giulia pulled a cleaning cloth through the flute body and shook it out. Frank loosened his bow and tucked his music into the case's inner pouch. Giulia waited until he'd fastened all four latches and walked up to him.

"If you have a minute, Frank, there's something—"

"Excuse me, Ms. Falcone, but I'm in a hurry." He picked up the case. "An employee quit, and I have to cover her duties as well as my own."

"Frank, stop being so pig-headed. I got a new—"

"Enjoy your date tomorrow. Remember to smile for any hidden photographers. At least your face is camera-ready this time." He turned his back on her and walked away as fast as the unwieldy instrument allowed.

Giulia slammed her flute case. Her music slipped through the back of her folding chair and scattered.

Damn the man. Because of him, she'd cursed more this past week than in her entire life. If she hadn't violated her service contract with God, she'd badger the angelic host to send down . . . Yes. To send Frank a particularly cranky messenger angel who'd whack him upside the head. And when he couldn't do anything but hold an ice pack on the bump, the angel would give him the true explanation of everything that happened since the night she let Blake crash on her couch.

"Ms. Falcone?"

Giulia looked up at the first row of seats. "Sidney?"

"We could hear your flute. You play really well."

"Thanks." Why on earth had Sidney come here? With the landscaper/social worker boyfriend too.

"I, um, well, do you have to be anywhere right now?"

No rest for the wicked. Sidney and boyfriend must need advice. "No. Did you want to go for coffee?"

Sidney's always-cheerful face got its "health lecture" expression. "Green tea, Ms. Falcone."

Giulia weighed something invisible with both hands. "Chai?"

Sidney smiled. "Deal."

TWENTY-NINE

"Olivier has the highest GPA in his class, Ms. Falcone. He's not just a hunk." Sidney leaned her head on her boyfriend's shoulder, easy to do as even sitting next to each other he was a foot taller than her. "But you have to admit he is a hunk, isn't he?"

"I admit it freely." Giulia brushed a few verbena leaves off the table from the lush plant hanging overhead. "And I'm interested to see that you do wear something besides earth tones, Sidney." Giulia smiled at Sidney's instant blush. "You look good in hot pink and black. Did you ever think of getting a permanent? The waves you put in it frame your face just right."

"A permanent?" Sidney shuddered. "Abrasive chemicals soaking into my hair for hours? Oh, no. And you should talk, Ms. Falcone. Who did your makeup? Do you have a date or something later?"

Giulia didn't quite stop a grin. "Tomorrow. Mingmei showed me how to do a little more with makeup today. I just hope I remember what she did."

"You look really good. Um . . . your date's not with Mr. Driscoll, is it?"

Giulia's smile shut off. "No." A quick sip of chai had trouble getting past the rock in her throat. *Frank and me. Not likely. Not ever.*

She sipped more chai, and it went down easier. The Garden of Delights made the best chai in Cottonwood, and even at eleven p.m. the café was three-quarters full. Possibly related to their white-chocolate crème de menthe cake, which sold out almost every weekend.

A verbena leaf fell on Olivier's short, rippled black hair. Another on his green silk shirtsleeve.

"At least it stayed out of my mocha and strawberry pie this time." Olivier's voice was like a good mocha: smooth and deep.

Sidney brushed them off. "His only imperfection is his accent."

"I'm sorry?" Giulia looked at Olivier, who affected a martyr's expression.

Sidney said, "He was born in Jamaica, but he talks just like you and me."

"Ms. Falcone, my parents emigrated when I was six months old. My brothers were all born in Cottonwood. I ask you: how else should we talk?"

Sidney gave him her theatrical sigh. "I know, I know, sweetie, but I still wish you sounded mysterious and exotic."

"Sidney, you know I love you, but I refuse to say things like 'Hey, mon, do you feel da riddems?'"

Giulia laughed. "Olivier, please call me Giulia. Did I say how glad I am you haven't asked me to produce a guitar and sing 'Dominique?'"

"That's right, Sidney told me you used to be a nun. We are therefore kindred spirits in our war against stereotypes."

Sidney's brow wrinkled. "Ms. Falcone, were you annoyed that first day when I asked you about *The Sound of Music*?"

Olivier groaned. "Sidney, you didn't."

"I, well, the convent is mysterious and exotic, just like Jamaica, you know? I never met a real live nun before. I've only seen them in movies and stuff. I was curious."

"Don't worry about it, Sidney. Everybody is curious. I'll show you a picture of myself in habit sometime so you can laugh."

"I'd never laugh at you, Ms. Falcone." Sidney dropped her dessert spoon with a clatter. "I think you're sweet and funny and sad." She bit her lips. "I didn't mean to say that."

Giulia stirred her tea. She should've thought about poor Sidney, caught in the middle of this mess.

"Tell me the truth, Ms. Falcone, all that caffeine doesn't keep you awake at night?" Sidney stared into her soy-milk decaf white chai and spoke much faster than normal.

"Sidney, I could've ordered espresso and I'd still be asleep five minutes after I got home." Giulia smiled at her and watched her shoulders un-hunch. "And I did want to ask you if you're feeling okay."

"Sure I am. Why?"

"You're eating ice cream."

"Oh, no, Ms. Falcone. I'd never eat processed ice cream. This is frozen tofu with berry puree and sweetened with—"

"Honey. Sidney, you're an example to us all. I am mortified, and shall finish my whole-milk chai with a contrite spirit."

A shadow flitted across Sidney's clear, open face. "Ms. Falcone, I don't always understand your sense of humor."

"It's just self-deprecating sarcasm."

"That's another thing I don't understand about you, Ms. Falcone. You're so thoughtful and good. Why do you hide behind sarcasm? I asked Olivier about it, and he told me—"

"Sidney, you said you wanted to keep that between ourselves." Olivier set down his forkful of strawberry pie. "Ms. Falcone—sorry. Giulia, Sidney's worried about your office situation and because I'll be receiving my Master's in Social Work in December, she thinks I have all the answers."

"You do, sweetie. You were such a help to my last boyfriend when his new girlfriend dumped him and he wouldn't come out of his room and nearly lost his job."

Olivier kissed the top of Sidney's head. "Your confidence is quite the ego-boost."

Giulia smiled. Only Sidney could convince her new boyfriend to help her old one out of a jam. She was the perfect companion for a psychologist: Giulia could picture Olivier coming home to her after a long day of navigating other people's complexes and obsessions and relaxing in her presence like in a favorite chair.

"Sidney, I appreciate that you're only trying to help."

"Ms. Falcone—"

"Please stop calling me Ms. Falcone. It makes me feel like a fossil. My name is Giulia."

Sidney sipped her tea like she was buying time. Still holding the cup, she said, "You're my supervisor."

"Not anymore."

Sidney gulped too much tea and coughed. "He didn't—just a sec—" she snatched her napkin and hacked into it. Olivier rubbed her back and she took several deep breaths. "Mr. Driscoll fired you?"

"No. I quit this afternoon."

"This afternoon? It's Saturday. Why were you at work on Saturday? You already had to get up at four to watch one of the houses, too." She held up one hand. "Wait a minute. All that's not important right now. Why did you quit?" Sidney leaned across the tiny, round bistro table and lowered her voice. "Was it anything to do with Thursday's mail?"

Giulia's mouth quirked. "In part." She caught Olivier's eye, and he found an immediate need to stir his mocha. So he knew. Her chai soured in her mouth and she pushed the remains to one side.

"Ms.—Giulia—why did you say those terrible things about yourself? I didn't mean to listen, but you left the door open and you were kind of yelling. You used to be a nun. There's no way you'd be, well, selling yourself like you described."

Olivier put a hand on Sidney's arm. "Too loud, Sidney."

"Yeah, the people two tables over may not be able to hear you." Giulia pushed back her high bistro chair. "Olivier, please allow me to thank you for speaking to me like I was still a decent human being."

"Ms. Falcone—Giulia—"

"It's all right. I never expected Sidney would share our daily soap opera. I apologize for making you uncomfortable. Good night."

Sidney caught Giulia's sleeve as Giulia slid to the floor. "Ms. Falcone, wait. I know I shouldn't have said anything to Olivier, but Mr. Driscoll shouldn't have yelled at you like he did."

"It's a long story." She shook off Sidney's hand.

Olivier's mellow voice penetrated the blood pounding in her ears. "Ms. Falcone, please sit down with us again. We've given you the wrong impression."

Giulia stopped but kept her eyes on the polyurethaned wood floor. She wanted out. She wanted away from people.

"Ms. Falcone, I don't believe you've ever done a bad thing in your life." Sidney jogged Olivier's arm. "Tell her what you told me."

"Ms. Falcone, from Sidney's description it appears that you're the victim of hate mail. That's a crime in Pennsylvania. Because it now seems to have adversely affected your livelihood, you might want to look into taking legal action."

"Do you know who sent it, Ms. Falcone? Do you know why Mr. Driscoll is so off the wall about it?"

Giulia looked up for a moment to meet their eyes. "We don't know specifically. We're—Frank—is narrowing it down from a pool of five." She switched her gaze to the floor again. "I appreciate your suggestion, Olivier, but when Frank finds out which one's doing it, I don't want to listen to a courtroom recital of all the disgusting things she's written about me. That's the trouble with innuendo. Like those supermarket tabloids, they're scandalous and exciting and once the idea is planted it's so easy to believe it—because it's in print."

Sidney's voice squeaked. "Mr. Driscoll believes the hate mail? Is he on crack?"

Giulia laughed. After a moment, Sidney laughed too. When tears started rolling down their cheeks, Olivier reached a long arm to the next table and snagged several napkins. Giulia and Sidney wiped their faces and honked into them.

"Here, Ms. Falcone. Have some tofu. This kind is my number-one comfort food." Sidney slid her melting dessert to the edge of the table near Giulia. "You can use my spoon; I never get sick." When Giulia hesitated, she said, "And don't even think you're not good enough to share our table or anything so, so, asinine as that."

214

The part of Giulia that had been freezing solid since Wednesday began to thaw around the edges.

"Sidney, you're a perpetual ray of sunshine." Giulia scooted back into her chair. "But I really don't like tofu."

Sidney shook her head. "Ms. Falcone, if you only knew the health benefits—"

Olivier waved a forkful of glazed strawberries and flaky crust beneath Sidney's nose. "Giulia obviously knows the true bliss of butter, processed sugar, and refined flour."

"Olivier, I was wrong. You have two imperfections."

This time Olivier laughed. "Some people get married and sleep in separate bedrooms. When we get married, we'll have to build a house with separate kitchens."

"No, sweetie, once you see how much better you feel when you go 100 percent natural, you'll—" She paused. "What did you say?"

"We'll talk about it later. Right now we're here for Giulia." He gave Giulia a *Change the subject?* look.

Giulia tapped the back of Sidney's hand. "Hey. Listen. Frank's going to need your help on Monday with this stalker case. Do you have a pen and some paper? There are a lot of details."

Sidney stared. "Me? Ms.—Giulia. I'll remember, I promise. Giulia, can't you take it back? Saying you quit, I mean."

"Uh, no. We both said irrevocable things. And besides, it'll be easier for you now. You told him I made you uncomfortable."

"What? No, I didn't. I told him that it was hard to work with you two all tense and snarky. After I said it, I realized I was way out of line and I apologized six or seven times. He said I didn't do anything wrong, and he'd take care of the situation."

"He did indeed."

Olivier finished his pie and brought his mocha to the counter for a refill.

Sidney grasped both Giulia's hands. "What changed? I was sure you and Mr. Driscoll were practically a couple. Besides, you made the office fun. I liked coming in and sitting behind a desk, and I never thought that'd happen. Whatever you said can't be that final. Please come back on Monday."

Giulia shook her head. "It wouldn't be fun anymore. You're better off with Frank and me in two different zip codes."

Olivier returned with a flyer for yoga classes and a pen with *The Garden of Delights* in an ivy-leaf design. "Here you go. For the notes."

Sidney tipped her glass bowl and drank melted tofu-berry slush. "I can't do what you and Mr. Driscoll do. I barely know the filing system."

Giulia waved that away. "I didn't even know that when I started. You'll do fine."

Sidney frowned, although her facial muscles appeared out of practice. "I'll take notes if you give me your phone number. I'm going to need lots of help."

"That's not a good idea. It could cause friction between you and Frank. Now, here's an outline of Blake Parker and the stalker suspects."

———

Giulia leaned into the passenger window of Olivier's Jeep an hour later. "Thanks for the ride, Olivier. Now, Sidney, when Frank asks you to be his new assistant Monday, what's your response?"

"If you think so—"

Giulia slapped the windowsill. "Confidence! Any time an employer asks you to take on new responsibilities, your only response should be, 'I'll be happy to. When would you like me to start?'"

Sidney rested her forehead on Olivier's shoulder. "All right."

"That's the spirit. You'll be raring to take this on when Monday hits."

Sidney put her hands over Giulia's. "Mr. Driscoll will realize what a jerk he was for not believing you. You'll see. He'll call you in a few days and apologize and everything will be back to normal."

"You're sweet. Good luck. Olivier, I'm very glad to have met you."

"Likewise, Giulia." He leaned across Sidney. "I think perhaps Sidney's intuition is correct, and you'll be working together again very soon."

Giulia smiled. " 'Night."

She was inside her building before they turned the corner. Just because she didn't see anyone lurking didn't mean she should tempt fate.

Theirs was going to be an interesting wedding—just the kind those "food stations" were made for. Half would serve only all-natural, soy-based appetizers, and half would no doubt serve carnivorous creations. Two cakes, as well? One with carob and spelt flour and the other a vision in sugar and butter.

Mail. She forgot to check her mailbox this afternoon. Going into work and fighting with Frank threw off her Saturday schedule. Tucking her flute under her arm, she flipped her key ring around to the tiny silver mailbox key.

College alumni letter—that meant a request for money. Office-supplies sale brochure, postcard asking for animal shelter volunteers. The return address on the last envelope stopped her right under the dusty ceiling light. *Office of the Superior General.*

```
Dear Ms. Falcone,
    October 3rd will mark the 125th year of the
founding of the Sisters of Saint Francis of
Greater Pittsburgh. In the spirit of Community,
we are asking all former Sisters to join us for
our three-day celebration of the life of Saint
Francis and the anniversary of the SSFGP.
    All Sisters of the Community will return to
the Motherhouse for this momentous occasion. Un-
fortunately, this means that there will be no
rooms available for former Community members. On
the back of this letter you will find a list of
hotels within a ten-mile radius of the Mother-
house. When you make reservations, mention the
code "Franciscan" and you will receive a ten
percent discount on a single room for Friday and
Saturday nights.
    In addition, please contact the Motherhouse
by August 1st with your acceptance, so we will
have accurate numbers for the celebratory ban-
quet. The price for this banquet is $25.00 for
former Sisters, and $30.00 each for spouses and
children, if any. Make checks payable to the
Bursar General.
    On behalf of Sister Mary Fabian, Superior
General, we hope to see all of our former Sis-
ters on this joyful occasion.
    In the Spirit of Saint Francis,
    Sister Mary Beatrice, Bursar General
```

The light flickered. A police siren swelled and blared and faded. "I always knew that woman had brass balls." *Lord, what a vulgar expression.* Her father used to say that after a weekend shift at the power plant. *Dad, no shift supervisor ever came close to Sister Mary Fabian.*

Her lock turned like normal. Must've been the humidity. She turned on the kitchen light and set everything on the table, marveling at the fact that some people enjoyed opening the mail.

I know the response I'd like to send. Dear Hypocritical Tightwad: I'll be happy to spend money I don't have renting a car and buying gas to drive to Pittsburgh if you'll be available to do me one favor. I'll climb on your antique mahogany rolltop desk and you can kiss my butt.

Giulia started to laugh, but she must've been more tired than she thought. Her throat closed and a couple of tears formed in her burning eyes.

"To hell with you, lady." She crumpled the letter into a ball and shoved it into the coffee grounds at the top of the trash can. "And you, too." She popped her flute case and wadded the stalker's note into a tighter ball.

Wait. She couldn't do that. She had to figure out exactly what the stalker was talking about.

Giulia un-mashed the note and dragged it over the edge of the table to iron out some of the wrinkles.

The clock read 12:20. Her brain was fried. She'd only reread it over and over and over. Probably get pieces of the reunion letter mixed up with it, too.

Forget it. Bed.

THIRTY

Giulia groped for the alarm's *off* button. 3:30. "Awake, O sleeper, arise from the dead. It's your turn for Pamela's street," she muttered into her pillow.

No. Wait. She quit yesterday. Surveillance was Frank's problem now.

———

Early Mass a stressful memory, frying pan scrubbed, plate and utensils drying in the dish rack, Giulia studied the want ads over her second cup of coffee. Two bucks for the Sunday paper would be thievery except for the expanded classifieds.

Lifeguard. If she had to, but she wanted to work past Labor Day. Waitress. No. Not after the disaster at her last waitressing job. Bookstore clerk. Painless, and heavy lifting would be no problem.

All the hotel chains needed housekeepers. That was code for "maid," but so what? She could work an institutional buffer. Might pull her above the other applicants. Those years polishing the chapel floor might finally pay off.

Doughnut baker. There. Start early, end early, just her and the ovens. A little hot now through August, but she could punch in at four a.m. every day no problem. Piece of cake after ten years of two a.m. Vigils and five a.m. Mass. She circled the ad with a magic marker. It said to call between six and seven a.m. Sweetness and Lite must want to hear only from true early risers. Worked for her. Tomorrow at 6:01 she'd dial that number.

She pulled out her interview suit and the ironing board. Early Mass gave her the whole day free. The wrong attitude toward the Sacrament, but . . . really, why was she still attending Mass?

Easy. Guilt. Ask a harder one. Okay. Why was she still attending Mass?

Force of habit. No pun intended. Ask a harder one.

Oh, just admit it.

She was still attending Mass because she wanted to believe He didn't really boot her to the curb.

That's why. So shut up, iron your suit, and get out your résumé disk. The library opens at eight tomorrow; you can update it and be back here on the phone by nine, calling other ads.

She was still avoiding the note, and she knew it. She could study it out in the courtyard if she didn't want to be trapped inside with it. Fear of the stalker was going to consume her life if she didn't take control of it now, today.

Giulia wrung the dishcloth tighter and tighter.

"Fine." She threw the twisted cloth in the sink and lifted the toaster off the still-wrinkled stalker note. It didn't bite her. Did she have a wacko dream about the letter last night? Yes . . . And the convent . . . Sister Mary Beatrice's desk had chased her through the Motherhouse halls. The rolltop snapped at her and spewed out Barbie dolls and pomegranates and reams of letters.

Time to shake it off. She'd escaped the nunnery, she had enough money to make rent this month, and Scott wanted her bod. That was antidote for quite a few obsessive stalker letters. Now to analyze this one and get on with her life.

She carried it to the living-room window and laid it out on the floor in the sunshine. She would not get her Bible. That'd be just another excuse. It didn't matter what Prophet the stalker took the quote from. What mattered is what it meant.

"Your day has come, the time for you to be punished." *I've already been punished. No job. Reputation in shreds.* "All your friends have betrayed you; they have become your enemies." *In Frank's case at least.* "There is no one to help you." *I suppose that's true. I'll have to find a job on my own. Common Grounds doesn't need another barista.* "Your enemies will look at you and laugh at your destruction." *Could that mean the ex is still spying on me? Why? I'm no threat to her getting Blake back. Any woman who wants him is welcome. If the ex wants to gloat over me as I ice doughnuts at six a.m. . . . Nah. No one's that obsessed. Ms. Bible-Twister will leave me—and Pamela—alone now that Blake's free.*

"Fallen are you, never to rise again." *Does that woman think I'll never get another job? Is she waiting for me to throw myself off the nearest overpass?*

"Forget it, broad. I'm not going to lie down and die to make you happy." Giulia tore the note into a pile of ragged little squares. She didn't need to keep it—Frank didn't care, and she was no longer working on the case. He'd figure out which blonde had a Blake-and-Bible fetish. It wasn't her problem anymore.

THIRTY-ONE

"Scott, do you know a good locksmith?" Giulia sat on the First Violin's chair while Scott unwound a broken E string.

"At least the stupid thing didn't break during the show. A locksmith? Why?" He took a new string out of its square envelope.

"My front door is acting up and my landlord moves in slow motion." He didn't need to know the other reason.

"Excuse me."

Giulia looked up past a purple case, way up to the First Violin's multiple blue-and-blonde braids. "Sorry, Lois. Talk to you at intermission, Scott."

Scott grunted in her direction as he plucked the new string and turned the tuning peg.

If she'd been hitting on all cylinders yesterday, she would've thought to check the lock last night when her key stuck. But what about the possibility that someone had accessed her flute case while she talked to Scott? That meant someone in the orchestra might be the stalker's flunky. A scary thought, that the hands of a fellow musician strangled lovebirds in anger. Did the ex pay her assistant so little salary that he or she needed the twenty bucks per performance to make the rent? Possible. Blast, that widened the field. Or maybe narrowed it, since she—no, no, no. It narrowed the field for Frank, since he no longer employed her. Driscoll Investigations, aka Frank Driscoll, would soon realize he had access to all these people Friday nights, Saturday nights, and Sunday matinees. He could study the Clarinet's hands, the Bass's hands, the Piccolo's hands. Sidney could research them for her first assignment.

The conductor walked past her, talking on his cell phone. She put her flute together in record time and warmed up. To her right, Frank ran scales and adjusted tuning pegs. On the other side of the half-circle of musicians, Scott played the opening measures of "Till There Was You" and gave the E-string microtuner one more tweak.

———

"Ready for an evening of pizza, beer, and the finer points of ogredom?" Scott plucked Giulia's flute head joint from her hands and blew a piercing note through it.

"Ouch! Give me that." She snatched it and pushed her cleaning cloth through it again. "Philistine. Keep your spit to yourself."

"How would you like me to apologize?" He kissed the back of her neck.

She giggled. "Stop that."

"Okay. For now." He sat on the Second Flute's chair. "So what do you say?"

"Have you ever had homemade pizza?"

"Uh, no. Why?"

She nudged the small cooler under her chair. "I didn't think so. In this magic box are the ingredients for traditional Sicilian pizza. After tonight you'll be spoiled for anything else."

"You're going to cook for me? Awesome. No woman's cooked for me since mom."

She rolled her eyes and finished stowing her flute. "I am not your mother."

"You bet you're not." He picked up the cooler. "Ready?"

"There's one minor difficulty. I'm applying for a new job at six a.m. tomorrow, so I have to get home early."

Scott looked over at Frank and lowered his voice. "I thought you had a job."

Giulia didn't lower hers. "Time for a change."

Frank slapped his music folder onto his chair.

Scott's eyes seesawed from Giulia to Frank and back to Giulia. "What happened?"

She was not going to dredge any of it up. Her imaginary X-rated past was in the kitchen trash with that last shredded note. Giulia Falcone was going to create her own future. "Nothing happened. Some jobs just aren't a good fit."

His hand came down on hers as she closed her case. "You're a lousy liar, Giulia. Did he try something? Is that why you want your lock changed?" He squeezed her hand. "If he did anything to you, I'll make sure he never touches you again."

Giulia shook her head. "Nothing like that happened. It's just a personalities thing." *Liar. Big, fat, hairy liar.* Good thing none of her former students could hear her. Some example she was setting now.

Well, she wasn't a repressed, obedient high-school teacher anymore. She was a modern woman who was going home with Scott to explore RPGs and the muscles under his tight shirts.

Scott said, "I've got a printer. We'll fix your résumé while we eat."

"I knew I liked you for a reason."

"I have several reasons." He wagged his eyebrows. "And I'll be showing some of them to you very shortly."

Frank walked past them without a glance at her. The Percussion and Clarinet, each talking on cell phones, snaked in opposite directions between chairs and stands. The Saxophone and Tuba emptied their spit valves and went out the stage-right door. Except for the ushers banging chair seats into their upright positions, she and Scott were alone.

"And as though I'm not tempting enough, Urnu wants you, too. In a few weeks the groupies will applaud us and lick their lips as my hand kneads your back. And the lower parts, maybe."

Giulia pasted on a polite smile. Learning intimacy behind closed doors was one thing. Public groping . . . no. Modern Giulia still had standards. "You're such a tease."

"Consort, I always deliver." He traced her ear with one finger. "I thought of names for our characters. Tammuz—that's me—and you can be Veiled Siduri. Cool, huh? I'll show you where I got them from later."

"The Gilgamesh epic."

He blinked. "How'd you know?"

"I used to teach high-school English."

"I'm looking forward to learning all about you, my Siren." He slung his violin over his shoulder and squeezed her with his free arm. "Kyle clued me in on Urnu's initiation process. I'll tell you about it later. Ready?"

"Just have to hit the bathroom. Be right back."

Locked into a toilet stall, Giulia tucked the cheap T-shirt into the zipper pocket of her purse. The red sweater came out wrinkled, but it was the tiniest bit too small, and the creases disappeared when she smoothed her hands down her front and sides.

Two bra straps were the first things she saw in the mirror.

"Bad." She tugged the neckline, but her straps were too wide to conceal. Instead, she slid them over her shoulders so they rested on the tops of her biceps. *That's what they mean by décolletage, Veiled Siduri. Veiled. Sheesh. Wonder what he'll say if he ever finds out where I spent the past ten years? Hopefully he'll laugh at the irony.* She reapplied lipstick and concealer. Everything else was holding up.

Should she unbutton one more button? Why did she buy a sweater that buttoned top to bottom? It screamed *temptation.*

Shut up, dowdy self. Unbutton it. Whoa. Cleavage. She rebuttoned it. Not dowdy now, just modest. Why did she want to be modest in a sweater that revealed every single curve she had? Scott was waiting. *Go on, unbutton it. Just one more. There.*

Before her former-nun self could claw her back to spinsterhood, Giulia opened the door.

———

"Scott, do you have a large knife or a cleaver? I have to slice the mozzarella." Giulia touched the grocery-store dough ball in its bowl on the counter. Almost room temp.

"Isn't it pre-shredded?" Scott handed her a chef's knife after rummaging through a crowded, noisy drawer.

"I weep for your palate. Come here and be educated, Prince Charming." She slit the cheese's plastic wrapping and carved it into narrow slices.

He leaned one elbow on the counter. "A Prince Charming has a bevy of kitchen wenches for these tasks."

"And I've read about how Prince Charmings like to exert their charm on said wenches."

"Not while they're holding ten-inch knives."

"Which is why we're so skilled with them." She set the knife in the sink. "The dough should be ready. Watch how true pizza is made."

Giulia let the dough hang by its own weight, turning it ninety degrees twice, until it fit the oblong pan. "Sauce, please."

"Yes, ma'am. The spoon, too?"

"Yes. You take three or four tablespoons of sauce and spread them over the dough. Not too much, or the finished product will be a soggy mess. Now lay the cheese over it. Leave space between each slice because cheese spreads as it melts."

"See what a quick study I am, kitchen wench?"

"No lip, or I'll take a wooden spoon to you." She ripped open the sliced pepperoni package. "Now lay these in rows. Just touching, not too many. Good. In about twenty minutes we'll have supper." She sealed the bag. "Do you have any plastic wrap for the extra cheese?"

"I'll get it. You wash your hands."

Giulia turned off the water and reached for the towel when Scott's arms appeared around her waist. "Prince Charmings give favorite kitchen wenches extra attention."

"I, I thought your time was spent learning to rule wisely and sit regally on a noble steed." Her breathing picked up speed.

"And looking manly in those puffy shorts."

Giulia laughed. Too breathy.

"Did I tell you how much I approve of this sweater?" Scott's hands traveled up her ribs to the curve of her breasts.

"I thought it, um, might be, um, too revealing."

"Not at all." He kissed her neck. "You've unbuttoned just the right number of buttons." He kissed her collarbone, and his hand snaked over her shoulder and into her cleavage.

Giulia let out a tiny gasp. Scott's hand slid farther.

What if he felt the scabs? She wasn't ready. Yes, she was. *Cosmo* said to go for it.

She twisted around and kissed him.

Scott paused a moment, his hand bent at an awkward angle. Then he tugged it out from between them and returned the kiss. His tongue touched her lips, pushed between them, brushed her shrinking tongue.

Pot-Breath did that—in the park. Giulia almost gagged at the memory, but then tasted peppermint. This wasn't any rapist. It was Scott. Her muscles unlocked and she opened her mouth.

Scott's hand dropped to her butt and kneaded. Giulia pressed closer. Then his fingers slipped between her legs and touched . . . Giulia stopped breathing.

It didn't feel anything like in the park. It made her tingle. What should she do? If she opened her legs she'd signal "yes" to sex. She wasn't ready. She was an idiot. But his touch felt good . . . He'd think she was easy . . . but wasn't she? This was only their second date . . . His fingers moved against the seam of her jeans and her legs wobbled.

Her own voice, eight years younger, came back to her. *I, Sister Mary Regina Coelis, do hereby vow to Almighty God and to you,*

Sister Mary Fabian, Superior General, His representative on earth, perpetual poverty, chastity, and obedience . . .

A high-pitched *Meep! Meep! Meep!* made them both jump.

"Damn. Stupid printer." Scott's voice came huskier than usual. "Sorry, Giulia. Be right back."

Giulia braced herself against the cutting board. What was she doing? Who was she trying to become? A she-camel, sniffing the wind in her lust?

She should leave. But what could she tell Scott? That she couldn't drag herself kicking and screaming into the twenty-first century? That Jesus was busting a gut laughing at her? That she finally might've driven away the Holy Spirit?

She ran water on a scouring pad and scrubbed the cheese dregs off the cutting board.

From the living room came the unmistakable sound of a printer top snapping open and paper *zzzzipp*-ing through rollers. "Giulia, the printer ate two résumés. Give me a second to reset it."

Thank you, printer. You're a true deus ex machina.

THIRTY-TWO

"Giulia, you were right. All pizza should taste like this." Scott leaned against the back of the couch and finished his third slice. His laptop sat in the middle of his coffee table, his pizza and beer on one side of it and hers on the other.

"Thank you. The cook always likes it when the Prince appreciates her food." She sipped beer and started her second slice.

"No, fellow ogre, you're my consort, not my subject." He took her free hand and nibbled her fingertips.

She shivered—a good sensation—and smiled at him. "So tell me about becoming a Siren."

"You're going to love it. Here, let me log in and I'll show you what my new character looks like. I can help you design yours today." He looked at her chest and nodded. "I recommend red body armor. It's your color."

Her cheeks grew hot.

The printer repair had taken longer than expected, and the pizza was cut and on plates when he'd finished. Hunger and cold beer became their priority. She still hadn't decided about "the act," however. Should she—no, could she—smother the convent and stalker voices in her head and give in to Scott? Spread her legs for him? *Stop it. That was the stalker talking.*

"Wait. Before we get caught up in that, tell me about the initiation for Raging Death."

A theatrical sigh. "If you insist. Urnu will have Ishtaria lead you on a short quest, to gain health and energy. When you're skilled with your crossbow, we'll battle as a pair, to get in sync."

"Tell me again why is this so special."

"Urnu's Clan is legendary, Giulia. Whatever he asks to join him, it's worth it. Fail any one of his trials, and we're out. No second chance."

"Will I have to eat a heart?"

He laughed. "Nah. That's Urnu's specialty. After we complete the quests and win the battles—and we will—the final step is a real-life initiation."

She leaned away and her sweater skimmed off one shoulder. "Real life?"

"Yeah. Kyle gave me the details." Scott closed the extra distance between them and stroked her bare shoulder.

"Tell me." Giulia's voice wasn't as strong as she'd like. His hair smelled of her shampoo. She'd forgotten they used the same brand.

"Urnu invites us to his house. He has a converted farmhouse out towards Coraopolis." His fingers unbuttoned another cleavage button on her sweater. "The rest of the Clan will be there, too." Another button. "Veiled Siduri, how did you know I prefer front-hook bras?"

Giulia couldn't take a full breath. Her head told her it was all pheromones. Her body told her nipples to harden.

"What happens at Urnu's house?" Another button. *Think, don't feel. Distract him.* "Does Urnu have a real name?"

Scott's voice, thicker than usual, said, "Dan, I think. Kyle mentioned it once." He unfastened the last button and the sweater fell away. "Who cares? It's Urnu the Snake everyone wants."

"So, what happens with the cult—sorry, clan—when we go to his house?" *If Scott's attitude is typical, they're more like a religious cult than a simple group of like-minded people . . .*

His hips moved and her thoughts frayed. The bulge in his pants pushed against her hand. She pushed back, gently.

"Oh, baby." Scott put his thigh between her legs and rubbed. "You're new at this, aren't you?"

"Yes." She should stay new. She should stop this. How? Her face radiated heat. Her hips started to move in rhythm with his thigh. *Stop.* She didn't want to sleep with Scott. She wanted love, not lust. She wanted—

"Gonna be real gentle with you, Giulia." He traced the lacy top edges of her bra. "Gonna show you how good it'll be at Urnu's."

He kissed her mouth, her neck, the curve of her breasts.

"Stop. What did you say? Stop, Scott."

"I want you, Giulia." He opened one hook. "Unzip my pants and I'll show you how much."

She put her hands on his face. "What do you mean about Urnu's? Tell me."

"The final ritual is complete obedience to Urnu. Game and body." Another kiss. "The Clan, all of them, Stoneblood and Nightclaw and Hrunting and the rest, surround us. Urnu sketches a tattoo of our character on us. We get a real tattoo later."

"Scott, I don't want a tattoo." She should stop him. She didn't want to stop him. Her fingers touched his zipper.

"Oh, yeah." Another hook. "Tattoos are cool. I know where I'd like you to get one." He fondled her. "We kneel to Urnu and promise complete obedience." Another hook, only one left. "Then we fulfill the promise."

"What, what does that mean?"

"Urnu has sex with us while they watch."

"What?" Giulia pushed herself backward and Scott's face smacked into the cushion. "Are you nuts?" She grabbed her sweater and shoved buttons through buttonholes. "Public sex? For a video game?"

"For Raging Death, Giulia. It's not just a game. It's another life. A thrilling life. Kyle said the sex was weird at first, but then it really turned him on." Scott's voice was back to normal. "You saw Urnu with Lugal and Ishtaria in the bar. Kyle's straight, but says Urnu gives head as good as any woman."

"He does what?" She left her bra as-is and buttoned all but the sweater's top button.

"Gives head. A blow job. You never heard that phrase?"

"I'm sorry I heard it now. Don't those people have any morals?"

"They don't sleep with each other after the initiation, only with Urnu as a reward for winning a battle. Urnu's steady partners are Lugal and Ishtaria, but he lets them play around with the groupies when they want. They always come back to him." Scott drank half of his open beer. "It's worth it, Giulia. You should hear Kyle. He says the sex bond is what makes Raging Death so powerful."

"Good God in Heaven. Scott, whatever made you think I'd agree to this?"

"I don't know. Maybe because you like me?"

"I do like you, but not enough to turn whore for you."

"No, no, babe, whores do it for money. This is for power and pleasure." He groped her thigh.

She tumbled over the arm of the couch. "Sex isn't supposed to be about power. It's supposed to be a means of expressing love."

"Sure, sometimes. You're a fun gal, Giulia, I'm a nice guy, and we want each other. That's all two consenting adults need, besides a condom." He dug in his jeans pocket. "I've got one all ready."

Giulia stood. This was possibly the most ludicrous situation she'd ever been in.

Scott jumped off the couch quicker than she expected and grabbed her butt. "Let's do it, baby. When you're loosened up, we'll talk some more about Urnu."

Giulia pried his hands away. "I never want to hear the name Urnu again." She snatched her purse off the kitchen table and stuffed her disk and résumés inside. "And I am not loose, Scott. I'm probably the most repressed adult you'll ever meet."

"Giulia, where are you going?"

"Home." She took the cooler off the counter.

"But—"

"Glad you liked the pizza. Keep the leftovers." She opened the door on a—thankfully—empty hall. "I hope you find another game and sex partner."

Don't slam his door. Don't give the neighbors a reason to see what the noise is about.

Giulia marched down the hall, down two flights of stairs, and out the front door. Scott didn't follow her.

235

THIRTY-THREE

Even the pay phone at the corner fast-food joint smelled of sausage grease. The disemboweled telephone book dangling from it still had the taxi company section of the yellow pages. Thank God for small favors.

"May I get a cab at the Bratmeister on the corner of Park and Pond Streets? . . . Ten minutes is great. Thanks."

Giulia hovered by the plate-glass window and checked her watch. Nearly six. Should she buy something because she used their phone? No, not on the jobless budget. Bad enough she was spending money to get home.

The taxi arrived and she escaped into the clear evening air. "2244 Pearl Street, please."

Ching. $1.25 just for pulling away from the curb.

She put the cooler on the seat next to her and leaned back. How fast those tenths of a mile racked up.

Ching. $1.35.

Public sex. Not even *Cosmo* pushed that.

The Music Man had two weeks left to run. Six more shows to try and ignore Frank and Scott. She'd bet that by Friday Scott would find a groupie willing to sleep with the Snake for the privilege of membership in Raging Death.

$2.75.

Frank thought she was a slut. Scott thought she was an idiot.

Uncle Vincenzo was right. Mom, Dad, if you're watching this farce up in Heaven, don't cry over me. I deserve everything I get.

$3.15.

She couldn't change it, so she would just move on. Stow the pepperoni and cheese in the fridge, be grateful she didn't give her virginity to that man, and hit the sack early. Set the alarm for 5:45, get caffeine in her system, impress her potential new boss with her alertness, eagerness, and impeccable manners.

Sounds like a plan.

$4.65.

Her neighborhood. Just a few more blocks.

$5.15.

"2244 Pearl. That'll be $5.35."

"Thank you. Keep the change." The price of escape and worth every dollar. One minute later, she leaned against the inside of the building's door. Safe.

She was an anal-retentive idiot, and she didn't care. Scott would flaunt his new "consort." Frank would probably sneer when he figured out Scott had dumped her, and so what. She'd be able to sleep without her conscience berating her.

Giulia walked through the lobby and past the rows of mailboxes. She was glad she had morals. Glad she had standards. Glad she had, well, virtue, darn it, and the only idiocy would be to throw away all of it out of fear.

A door banged. The aroma of frying hamburger drifted down from the second floor.

"Jerk!"

"Baby!"

"Am not!"

"Are too!"

Two sets of feet pounded down the stairs, and the prank-pulling twins from the second floor raced past Giulia, firing pressurized streams from humongous water cannons. The buzz-cut twin ducked behind her and soaked his brother's shoulder-length hair. "Gotcha!"

His brother shook water from his eyes, used the anemic ficus in the corner as cover, and returned fire. Giulia stepped aside, saying, "I'm not a shield," and got the full, ice-cold charge on her chest.

"Yow!" Goosebumps erupted all over her.

"Sorry, lady," Long-Hair said.

"Missed me, jerkwad!" Buzz-Cut stuck out his tongue and ran out the door, slamming it in his brother's face. Long-Hair pumped his gun and pulled open the door. "Chickenshit baby!" The door swung against the wall and bounced closed. From upstairs, she heard their mother yell, "Watch your mouth!"

Giulia leaned over the ficus and wrung most of the water into its cracked potting soil. Wouldn't Scott have something lecherous to say if he saw her now? Doubtless including hi-beams, clingy rayon, and his desire to help her out of her wet sweater before she caught pneumonia.

She walked down the empty hall to her apartment. Mmm. Old Mr. Colombo in 110 was cooking enchiladas. Giulia's stomach growled, ignoring the two pieces of pizza she'd fed it not so long ago. Her watch read 6:20. She could put together peppers and eggs. There should be brioches in the freezer, too.

She shivered. Her goosebumps didn't seem to care that it was . . . 73, according to the hall thermostat. She had to get into a dry shirt before her encounter with the squirt gun on steroids sabotaged her immune system. *Brats.*

When she inserted her key, the door swung open a few inches.

"You've got to be kidding. Giulia, you idiot." After the sticky problem yesterday and today she still didn't think to double-check it when she left for the theater. Well, after she talked to the doughnut shop tomorrow morning, she'd call the landlord. He might have a hangover if the Pirates won, but he could replace her lock despite that.

She twisted her key back and forth. Smooth to the left, a hitch to the right. At least the deadbolt worked. She shot it home and set her flute case and music on the counter.

Cold water soaked the front of her jeans, too. Giulia detoured from the kitchen to her bedroom: first, dry clothes. She pushed open the bedroom door and kicked off her shoes.

Blake Parker lay naked on her bed, hands and feet tied to the posts on the near side like a blond Slim Jim.

THIRTY-FOUR

THE GLOSSY BLACK ROPE tying Blake's wrists didn't look like rope. Neither did the crimson fabric around his ankles. *Ties? Bathrobe sashes?*

His dilated pupils hid much of his blue irises. Duct tape covered his mouth.

"Mr. Parker—" Giulia stepped toward him, hand out to remove the tape.

The door slammed behind her. She whipped around as a pair of hands jammed a metal-and-chain contraption into her doorjamb, locking her in her own bedroom.

A tall blonde put her back to the door. "Don't touch him."

At first, all Giulia saw was a gold satin push-up bra. Beneath it, a pierced navel with an emerald and gold charm. Beneath that, a matching satin thong above long, slim legs and manicured feet in lamé high-heeled sandals.

"Sandra Falke?" A dozen ignored clues collided in Giulia's head.

Now what? She had to think. What kind of psycho problems did Falke show in her interview? What was up with the slinky underwear?

"Why are you—what is Mr. Parker—"

"We're going to show you what a negligible piece of litter you are, sugar." Her eyebrows matched her lipstick matched her "outfit" matched her shoes. Her bellybutton charm winked in the sunshine as she brushed Giulia aside and stood by Blake's head. "And Blake will do it by showing me one of the ways I'm the perfect match for him." Sandra ripped the duct tape off his mouth.

Giulia flinched.

"Ow!" Blake's face contorted. Then he giggled. "Sandy, dolly, that hurt." He puckered glue-speckled lips. "Kiss it and make it better?"

Giulia's forehead wrinkled. That wasn't Blake's usual revolting style. "What's the matter with him?"

Sandra picked up a gold and green knife from the nightstand. "Just a little something we added to Blake's wine at supper." The knife handle caught the same ray of sunshine as the charm.

"Pretty," Blake said.

"Wait a minute." Giulia wanted to get in Falke's face, but the knife was still in her gold-manicured hand. "How did you get in? Ever hear of trespassing?"

"Like anyone would notice in this derelict neighborhood." Sandra came closer, towering over Giulia in those heels. "Were you in a wet T-shirt contest this afternoon? I gather the sweater was your concession to modesty." She laughed. High and tinkling, like tiny wind chimes.

"What I do is none of your business." Giulia kept an eye on the knife. "By the way, you drugged and kidnapped an innocent man.

That's illegal, last I checked. I don't think you'll like getting sent to jail. Gold underwear isn't state issue." *Keep her distracted. Let her think you're a clod. Get her to set down the knife.*

"What an innocent you are. The only justice Blake will be seeking with me is a justice of the peace." Another tinkling laugh. "Blake, you didn't know I added wit to my accomplishments, did you?"

"Huh-huh-huh, Sandy, you're funny." Blake squinted like he was trying to focus with those dilated pupils. "You look pretty. Just like a Barbie doll."

"I am not an empty-headed bimbo—" Sandra raised her hand.

Blake cringed. "No, Sandy, don't hurt me, I'll be good. I'll make you happy again."

Sandra sighed. "It's time for the pill to wear off. You're making me gag." She picked up Giulia's Bible from the nightstand. "That joke about a JP was just a joke, of course. We'll have a cathedral wedding attended by select business and society contacts." She flipped pages. "'Come out, you daughters of Zion, and look at King Solomon wearing the crown, the crown with which his mother crowned him on the day of his wedding, the day his heart rejoiced.' Blake's mother always liked me. She'll love putting a crown on you, won't she, Blake darling?"

"Prince Blake and Princess Sandy." Blake shook his head. "Ooh, dizzy." He shook his head again, and his eyes lost their glazed look for an instant. "Sandra?"

Giulia hoped she kept the relief out of her face. *Keep after her. Distract her till his circuit breakers reconnect.* "What's the idea behind the last message you slipped me, Falke? What makes me so important in your obsessive little universe?"

Sandra's eyes narrowed. "You need to learn some respect, little investigator wannabe. My family background puts you in the class of, oh, hired help. And when I marry Blake, you'll sink to the level of illegal-alien migrant worker."

Giulia aimed *wake up* thoughts at Blake and gave a deliberate laugh. "The mistress of the manor shops at Frederick's of Hollywood? If you can't keep a man without imitating one of your own Barbie-doll creations, you ought to look into self-esteem counseling."

Sandra slapped her. "Watch your mouth, she-camel! That was my favorite message to you, you know. After what you did with Blake, I wanted to rip your eyes out. But my teacher reminded me that you don't matter. You don't matter at all."

"Teacher?" *So Sandra wasn't in it alone and didn't take the photographs. Did a personal assistant qualify as a teacher? Who would Sandra trust enough to take their doctored photos as gospel?* "That explains it. Your fluffy blonde brain couldn't hold enough of the Bible to choose the appropriate verses."

Giulia expected another slap. Instead, Sandra crossed her arms and produced a game-show host smile. "Our Lady of Sorrows Boarding Academy for Young Women, eighth through twelfth grade. Bible study every morning and evening taught by dried-up old women in black serge. When I left there, I swore I'd never wear a plaid skirt or a Peter Pan collar again."

The verse came to Giulia's tongue. "'You have trusted in your wickedness and have said, "No one sees me."'" *Blast. What was the rest of it?*

Sandra closed her eyes just for a second, then opened them and said, "'I will pull up your skirts over your face that your shame may be seen.'" She threw the Bible across the room. It hit the mint and basil pots, knocking over the stand and scattering dirt and leaves on the rug. "It doesn't matter what happens to you, Miss

Wannabe, but Blake needs to be taught a lesson. My teacher told me the best way to make him obey was to make his latest piece of ass part of the lesson."

Scent from the bruised herbs filled the room. Giulia finally noticed the closed window.

"Ooh, Sandy, you said 'ass.' You never . . . What's wrong with . . ." Blake shook his head in repetitive bursts. "You never swear. Ooh . . . head stuck in maple syrup." A giggle, petering out.

Keep at her. He's almost back to normal. "News flash, Falke: Blake Parker doesn't care about anyone but himself. If you think humiliating me in front of him will show him what a powerful consort you are, it won't work." *Consort. Gross. I still have too much Scott on the brain.*

"Sex is power, little nun." Heels and all, Sandra climbed onto the bed and straddled Blake's legs. "You thought I've been acting in ignorance, didn't you? I researched you after your pathetic attempt to interview me. You're one of the frustrated bitches who hate real women. You have no life, no friends, no anything but your job and your bookshelf of fairy tales." Sandra cupped her hands beneath her push-up bra and jiggled. "This is real. This is power and pleasure, and those two things are all that's worth having."

Blake whistled. "Nice tits, Sandy."

"Thank you, dear. Ready for your lesson?"

Blake pouted. "Don't like school. Knife isn't pretty anymore." Another series of jerky headshakes. "Sandy? Where are we?"

"We're in bed, Blake dear. You're going to consummate our relationship again."

"Consumm . . . You wanna have sex?" Blake's eyebrows met. "We're not together anymore, Sandy. I promised Pammy I wouldn't."

"Forget that inbred, condescending bitch!" Sandra whisked the knife beneath Blake's chin.

Giulia held her breath as the tip sliced into Blake's neck. If Sandra was out of control already, Giulia had to tackle her for the knife. Then she realized Sandra's hand was rock-steady: Blake's chin was doing the quivering. Blood trickled down the side of his neck onto Giulia's bedspread. The haze vanished from his eyes as Sandra pressed the knife deeper.

"You are going to learn obedience. The nuns taught me that a lesson is infinitely more effective in front of witnesses." Sandra stroked the knife point across Blake's neck, but didn't cut him again. "I came back from summer vacation with cherry-red hair to start my junior year. I did it myself, of course, and cross-hatched the sides with a razor. Remember Cyndi Lauper? Everyone loved my daring new style, except the nuns. I was wicked, bound for Hell, and God told them to purge me."

Not good. Falke's working herself into retaliatory anger, and she's already got me pegged for vicarious revenge. Giulia aimed stronger *Wake up, pretty boy!* thoughts at Blake.

"They dragged me into the bathroom and shaved my head. The entire junior class got squeezed in with us to watch. I spent every lunch period for the next month saying the rosary on the chapel floor." Sandra stretched out one leg and ran a hand over her smooth knee. "The calluses didn't fade till spring."

"Look, Falke, I'm not a nun anymore. And I wasn't one of the nuns who shaved your head. I don't need to see you punish Blake." *Was that going too far? Will Sandra come after me with that tortoiseshell knife?*

"He's Mr. Parker to the hired help. Don't forget that." The knife left Blake's chin.

"Sandy, why can't I move? Where are my clothes?"

Giulia and Sandra looked. Blake's pupils retracted to near-normal, and he was frowning instead of giving Sandra a loopy smile.

Sandra put a finger on his lips. "I promised I'd make you forget what this cheap whore did with you in this bed. Now's the time to fulfill that promise."

Blake spoke around Sandra's finger. "Sandy, are you off your meds again? You know how you get—"

Her fingernail dug into Blake's lip, drawing blood. Blake stopped talking.

Giulia stepped forward. "You're not doing anything with him in my bed, Falke."

"You have nothing to say about it, little nun."

"Sandy, what'cha doing?" Blake's eyes tried to glaze over again. "Mmmm."

Argh. "How many times do I have to say this? Those photos are fakes."

"That you, sugar? You both gonna do me?" Blake's voice came thick, like Scott's when he was unbuttoning Giulia's sweater.

Sandra grasped Blake's face in both hands. "She'll never come near you again."

"I never came near him at all," Giulia said again. "We never had sex."

"You don't lie well, little nun."

"I am not a nun anymore!" Giulia grasped her own hair and just said it. "I'm still a virgin."

Blake's voice cleared. "You're a virgin? I could've had a virgin?" His weak laugh filled a momentary silence. "All I've ever had is used goods."

246

Sandra's quick breath frightened Giulia more than the screech that followed.

"You sexist piece of meat! If virginity is so important, why didn't you keep yours?" Sandra punched Blake's head. "You think I'm used?" She slapped his face. "You think an intact hymen is better than a killer blow job?" She punched the other side of his head. "I'll give you something—to forget you—ever—slept—with her!" Sandra's bony hand slapped him at every pause. Blake's lips split, and a welt appeared under one eye.

Only when Sandra stopped did he try to speak. "Sandy, doll, no one I've ever slept with comes close to you. You're one hot babe. You didn't have to drug me to get me close to you."

"Don't whine, Blake. It doesn't go with your manly image." Sandra wiped her blood-speckled hand on the bedspread. "I thought you might not have the spine to teach this cheap whore a lesson, so I took a few precautions."

Set down the knife, Falke. Giulia forced herself to look away from it, redirect Sandra. *Set it down. I'll grab it and call 911.*

"The pill my teacher slipped into your last glass of wine made you happily wasted. When we brought you here, you attracted exactly the kind of attention we planned. All the neighbors think the little nun's having a party." Sandra draped herself over Blake's prone body. "It's also an aphrodisiac. Now I'll show my teacher how well I've absorbed my lessons."

Show? Giulia tried to keep her face neutral. Had Sandra set up a video feed? Hidden a camera? That'd be evidence. Any kind of camera would give the police evidence. Where? Behind the clock radio? On the bookshelf? Giulia moved her eyes, not her head, in case Sandra was watching.

Sandra leaned forward and nipped his lower lip. "I'll put every woman but me out of your head, darling."

Blake's eyes rolled back in his head. "Oh, baby."

Giulia gave in to her growing disgust. She wasn't going to stand in her own bedroom and watch an actual incidence of a woman raping a man. In her own bed.

Sandra closed her eyes.

Giulia took one step closer to the knife.

THIRTY-FIVE

Someone grabbed Giulia from behind, and she hit the floor face first. A knee dug into her butt and a strong hand wrenched her right arm behind her back.

"You're a virgin. What an unexpected pleasure."

A man hiding in here. Where—must've been in the closet. No place else in her small room.

Wake up, moron! Get out from under him. She squirmed and bucked her hips, but she couldn't move.

"You're missing the show, Giulia. I staged this for you."

He yanked her up and left, releasing her twisted arm to jerk up her head by her hair. "Now watch." He wrapped muscled arms and legs around her and crushed her arms against her breasts.

Shock blew through Giulia's fear. "Urnu the Snake?" *Scott. He wanted to get me into Raging Death. Was he working for Urnu all along? To get me here? Oh, God.*

He smiled at her in his odd, teeth-baring way. "I enjoyed meeting you face to face after Friday's battle. Scott doesn't know that I used him solely to get you to my final initiation."

She tried to pull her trapped legs from between his scissor hold. He merely laughed.

"Sandra didn't take the pictures, you know," he whispered. His hand stroked up and down the row of buttons on her sweater. "I did. She wanted Blake's engagement broken. When you brought him here, I brought out my telephoto lens. I'm an expert at photographic manipulation. Sandra still believes Blake took you." He unbuttoned her top button, one-handed. "Shall I seduce you by opening one button at a time? Or shall I tear it off and expose your breasts to your client? In his current state, I'm sure he'd make some interesting comments."

Giulia's legs tingled. How would she escape if they went completely numb? *Help me, Jesus. Don't abandon me.*

She could head-butt him. She could claw him. Her fingernails needed cutting. She had a little ammunition. Could she get to his eyes?

"Sandra, come here. This is also what you wanted."

"Don—"

"I said come here." His voice stayed polite, yet Sandra at once peeled her body off Blake and stood in front of Giulia.

Don . . . her brother. God, I'm an idiot. She thrashed her already twisted upper body from side to side within his immovable grip. Giulia's almost-dead legs hampered her. She tried to hit his lips or nose with her head.

He must have signaled Sandra, because she leaned down and slapped Giulia. Once. Twice. Again. Again. Giulia's head snapped from side to side and tears filled her eyes.

"Thank you. Bring me the knife." He pushed Giulia onto her back, slammed her shoulders flat on the thin rug, and kicked her inert legs straight.

Sandra put the knife into his outstretched hand as he sat on Giulia's hips.

Giulia tried to build a coherent thought. *Move your legs. You can't stay in his power. He likes to—*

Urnu the Snake crooked a finger, and Sandra tick-tacked around to Giulia's feet in her stiletto heels.

Urnu ripped open Giulia's sweater and trapped her arms above her head with it. When she couldn't do more than squirm, he sliced through her bra.

"I will show you the power of pleasure and pain." He glanced backward. "Sandra."

Giulia's straightened legs gave a hint of life. She had a chance. Just a minute or two more and she could move them.

"Sandy, come back." Blake squirmed in his silk bonds. "Wanna make you scream, Sandy."

Sandra's pointed nails scratched Giulia's waist as she dragged off her jeans. "Hush, Blake. May I have the knife, Don?"

He looked over his shoulder at her. "It's not time for that yet."

"I want her naked and humiliated now."

He smiled. "If you wish."

Time for what? Giulia flexed her feet. Hundreds of little stabs. The knife snicked her skin as it slit her plain cotton underpants. Sandra tugged them off, and Giulia's naked butt touched the rug.

God, Jesus, stop her. Stop him. Giulia flexed her calves and stifled a gasp. Not that bad. She could deal with the pain. Urnu the Snake had her but she wasn't in his power. Not yet.

"Little virgin, let me whisper something in your ear." Urnu put his hands around Giulia's neck and breathed into her mouth. "I don't confine my victory ritual to Combat Realm triumphs."

Don't let him scare you.

Too late.

Shake it off. People don't carve out hearts in real life.

Sandra held Giulia's utilitarian panties next to her gold thong, and Urnu laughed.

Forget his hands on you. Forget your legs. Giulia bent her right elbow. With her eyes on Urnu watching Sandra, she slid her arm out of her sweater and bra strap by increments The moment it was free, she inched it back to a trapped-looking position under the sweater.

Sandra climbed over Blake and sat on her heels on the bed. "Now learn your lesson." Her gold-tipped fingers pushed his head sideways to face Giulia.

Urnu smiled. "Now I'll teach you what happens to bad girls who bite instead of suck."

Bite—when did—the rapist. In the park. Oh God. Oh no.

"Didn't I leave any marks on you?" He mashed her breasts up and sideways. "Ah. Healing nicely. Almost like a tattoo."

Sandra imitated Urnu's smile. "Thank you for letting us watch, Don. Public lessons are the ones that endure, Blake. Remember this."

"No!" Giulia threw off the sweater. The heel of her hand smashed Urnu's nose.

He yelled and slid backward. She made a fist and punched the bloody mess on his face. He screamed and clutched his nose, blood spurting on Giulia, on the rug, on his dead-black shirt and pants.

"Don!" Sandra leaped off the bed and crouched beside him. Urnu cursed and spat blood and cursed some more.

"You bitch!" Sandra crashed into Giulia, knocking her against the balsawood closet doors. They cracked inward as Giulia lost her footing. Sandra snatched the knife from the floor and swung it, but Giulia's backward stumble put her out of range.

Pound pound pound. A foot kicking the apartment door? A muffled voice. "Giulia!"

Giulia ran for the bedroom door. Urnu's slippery hand snatched her ankle. She pulled it free as Sandra slashed again. Flame seared her ribs. She clutched her left side and blood oozed through her fingers.

More pounding. A sharp crack. Another. The outer door slammed against the wall.

Sandra cursed. The knife came down. Giulia grabbed Sandra's wrist. They pushed against each other. Giulia's arms started to fold. Sandra pushed harder.

Bang. The bedroom door shook. A less-muffled voice yelled, "Giulia!" *Bang.* The door shook again. "Giulia!"

Giulia jumped backward. Sandra sprang forward and stabbed at her again. Giulia missed Sandra's wrist and caught the knife blade instead. She hissed from the pain and her hold slipped as blood ran down her arms.

The door hinges ripped out of the wall. Frank ran in, gun out. "Get off her or I'll fire."

Urnu grabbed Frank's ankle and yanked.

"What the—" Frank glanced down and kicked. Urnu's head hit the corner of the closet and he slumped onto the rug.

"Last chance, Falke. Get off her."

Sandra yanked the knife out of Giulia's hands and brought it down.

Frank fired.

THIRTY-SIX

SANDRA'S BODY JERKED. BLOOD gushed from her mouth. She dropped the knife and her hand clutched her throat. Her eyes dilated and she fell onto Giulia.

Frank holstered the gun.

"Get her off—get her off—" Giulia pushed at Sandra's body, but her hands kept slipping.

Frank heaved the body onto the rug. "Giulia, are you all right? Christ, what happened? Never mind. Where's the towels?"

"Um, kitchen drawer." Her ears rang from the shot.

Frank ran out. Giulia held her gashed ribs. *I'll never get all the blood out of the rug.*

Drawers opened and closed in the kitchen. "Which one? Wait, found them."

Her hands burned, too. How was she going to interview for the doughnut job with injured hands?

"Giulia, don't pass out on me. Here, give me your hands." Frank, muttering in Irish, wiped her left hand with a towel before wrapping it around her hand.

"Ribs . . ."

"What? Holy shit." Frank pressed towels to Giulia's side. "Here, lean against the bed."

Blake coughed and tried to spit. "Can one of you cut me loose?"

Frank stared for a long beat, then ran into the kitchen again. A moment later, he returned with a bread knife and sawed through the black sash. Blake sat up, rubbing his wrists.

Frank tossed his cell phone at him. "Call 911."

Frank shoved open Giulia's broken closet doors and pawed through her clothes. "Where's your bathrobe?"

"Hook on the bathroom door." Giulia didn't feel quite so woozy now that blood wasn't running down her arms and chest. *Good heavens, I'm still naked.*

Blake's voice above her. "Can I get an ambulance and police to—" Blake held the phone toward Giulia. "What's your address, sug—Ms. Falcone?"

"2244 Pearl Street, apartment 115." *Frank's seen me naked in person now. He'll probably have the snarkiest comment yet. No. No more. I can't take another insult from him. I should leave. I can't leave. The police are coming. I have to tell them what happened.*

Blake put the phone to his ear again. "We have one gunshot wound and one knife wound . . . Thanks." He snapped the phone closed and cut the cord around his feet. "What the hell did they do with my clothes?"

Frank came in and tossed them to him. "On the bathroom floor." He draped Giulia's bathrobe over her shoulders. "What happened?"

255

Why was he being polite? "They drugged Blake and broke in here. Tied him to the bed. Waited for me, I guess."

"They gave me something that acted like pot mixed with ecstasy." Blake already had on his boxers and socks and was stepping into his pants. "I remember them walking me down the hall. I think I was singing."

Frank pointed to the still-unconscious Urnu. "Who's he?"

Blake zipped his pants. "Sandra's brother Donald. Met him once, thought he was just another RPG geek."

Giulia shuddered. "Urnu the Snake." She backed away from him, but the bed stopped her. Her chest hurt when she moved. "Can you tie him up or something?"

Frank looked at Blake. "That bad?"

"I think he was behind Sandra stalking me." Blake glanced at the body, then away. "She's dead, isn't she?"

"I think so." Frank crouched to feel for a pulse, but Giulia could see Sandra's open, blank eyes.

A few moments later, Giulia heard running footsteps. Then a deep voice at the outer door: "Police."

"In here," Frank said.

"Who else would get me away from my air-conditioned office on a slow Sunday night?" Captain Hogarth stood in the bedroom doorway.

"Jimmy, where's the EMTs? Giulia's bleeding."

"They're right behind me. What did you—"

"Coming through. Excuse me." Paul Bunyan in uniform ducked the doorjamb and walked into the bedroom. He looked at Giulia, then Sandra's body, then Urnu still unconscious at Hogarth's feet. "Who's urgent?"

"Right here." Frank stepped aside. "I did what I could with towels."

"All right, miss, let's have a look." He untied Giulia's bathrobe and pulled away a bloody yellow-checked dishtowel from her ribs. "Doug, water and gauze."

Giulia hadn't noticed Little Richard behind Paul Bunyan. Rock stars didn't moonlight as EMTs. *I'm tired. How can I be tired? It's not even seven o'clock . . . is it?*

Water-soaked gauze squelched against her. "Whoa—cold."

Paul Bunyan pressed the bandage against the injury and wiped along its length. "Sorry, miss, gotta assess the damage." He removed it and wound fresh, damp gauze around her. "Not deep, just long. They'll glue you together at the ER in a snap."

He had the gentlest touch, even through the squeaky rubber gloves. She stopped tensing every muscle. "I did a number on my hands, too."

The smaller technician repeated the water-and-gauze treatment. "Stitches for these, miss. But they're not that bad. In a couple weeks you'll be playing the violin again."

Giulia blinked. "I play the flute."

The tall one laughed. "She got you, Doug! Miss, no one's ever called him on that lame joke. Congratulations."

"But I do play the flute."

Doug laughed, too. "Ted, I think the lady is still shook up. Come on, miss. Let's get you and your friend on the floor to the hospital."

Giulia drew back. "Not together."

Frank stopped talking to Hogarth. "Jimmy'll ride with you, Giulia. You'll be safe."

A uniformed cop rolled a groaning Urnu face up. The cop whistled. "Helluva nose job on this one. Rise and shine, emo-boy." He pushed Urnu into a sitting position and handcuffed him.

"Let's have a look." Ted squatted in front of him and probed his mashed face.

Urnu said, "Bitch broke my nose." He glared at Ted. "Get your hands off me, asshole."

Ted snapped a chemical cold pack into life. "She sure did. Bleeding's pretty much stopped, Russ. Just let me strap this on him and he's all yours." Doug handed Ted more gauze. Urnu yelled and cursed and tried to butt Ted with his shoulders.

"This is why I love my job." Ted stood and grinned. "Enjoy the trip, Russ."

The uniformed officer grinned back as he hauled Urnu to his feet. "Thanks for nothing, Ted. Let's go, emo-boy."

"Piss off." He spat blood at Giulia. "Gonna make you pay, bitch."

Giulia flinched and wanted to kick herself for it. Frank took a step after Urnu, but Hogarth's hand fell on his shoulder and he stopped.

The cop shoved Urnu's back. "Shut up." Urnu tripped over one of the broken door hinges and cursed again.

Doug put one arm around Giulia's shoulders and the other beneath her elbow. "Here we go, miss. Up on your feet. Dizzy?"

"No . . . no. I'm okay."

"Good. Let me help you with this bathrobe. There you go. I'll just tie it closed . . . Can your friend bring some clothes along for you?"

"Got it." Frank dug sweats and a T-shirt from Giulia's closet. "Where's your underwear, Giulia?"

She grimaced. So much for a woman's mystique. Like it mattered. Like she mattered. "Top dresser drawer."

Blake cleared his throat. "Excuse me."

Ted snapped on a fresh pair of gloves. "Sorry, sir, got caught up in all that blood. Let's have a look at your neck." Doug left Giulia's side to hand water and gauze to Ted, then went out.

"Not bad at all." Ted's cleaning sent a trail of water down Blake's shirt. "Just needs a stitch or two."

Doug returned with a stretcher. It wouldn't fit through the broken bedroom door, so he came into the room and grasped Giulia's elbow again. "I claim the privilege of escorting the lady to her conveyance."

"Wait a minute." Ted stood toe to toe with Doug and spoke to the tops of his cornrows. "You're barely as tall as the lady. I think height trumps first dibs."

Doug pushed Ted away with one finger. "I provide balance and security. Out of the way, overbearing one."

Giulia smiled. "Jack the giant-killer."

Doug laughed. Giulia avoided Frank's eyes as she passed him. Why hadn't he sneered at her yet?

"I feel like you're making too much of this—ow." Giulia clutched at her side as Doug eased her onto the stretcher.

"It's our job to get you to the hospital no worse than when you left here. Ever drive over the potholes on the east side? You don't want to bounce around the passenger seat of a car with that rib injury." He pushed the stretcher into the hall. "All right, folks, let us through here."

Blanket tucked around her, Giulia rode past two dozen whispering adults. The twins were there, too, mouths open and water cannons dripping. She closed her eyes. Urnu might not be her biggest problem after all. Mrs. Bleeker already had Mr. Colombo by the arm, talking faster than humans ought to be able to. By tonight the story would grow into a wilder tale than anything on primetime TV. Maybe she'd get evicted because of all the damage. *I'll lose my security deposit for sure when the landlord sees my bedroom.*

The stretcher bumped out the street door. She could ask Mingmei to get her clothes and books. That way she wouldn't have to face anyone here again. There were cheaper apartment buildings. Someplace anonymous, in a different part of town . . . Her ribs burned . . . Where was her friend with the marijuana stash when she needed him?

Ted appeared on her other side, and he and Doug lifted the stretcher into the ambulance.

"Well, well. I get to be near you again." Urnu's voice, twanging and muffled from the cold pack strapped to his face.

Giulia's eyes snapped open.

Captain Hogarth's arm slammed Urnu against the opposite wall of the ambulance. "Let's rehearse this again, Falke. You are under arrest. Anything you say can be used against you. That includes every word aimed at Ms. Falcone."

Urnu kept his green-gold eyes on Giulia. "All I have to do is wait, bitch. You won't have protection forever."

Hogarth pulled Urnu's head around by his long hair and put his nose right against Urnu's lumpy gauze. "You're only sitting up so you don't choke on your own blood and I don't have to fill out a pile of reports on why you died on the way to the hospital. If I had my way, you'd be cuffed facedown on this cot."

"I dare you, pig. I'll come after you for attempted murder."

"You don't have the balls, Falke. Listen up: if you say one more word to Ms. Falcone, our helpful EMTs can tape your mouth closed and you can figure out how to breathe through your ears. Or you can shut the hell up. Your choice."

Urnu flipped off Hogarth despite his manacled wrists and slumped against the wall.

Hogarth smiled at Giulia. She closed her eyes and tried to drift, but Ted and Doug turned on the siren and she understood why Quasimodo went deaf. When she opened her eyes, Urnu was still staring at her, so she focused on Hogarth's teddy-bear face.

"Where's Frank?" It hurt to yell.

"Behind us. Your client needs stitches, too. Frank's driving him." Hogarth's deep voice carried much easier than hers.

"Oh . . . I forgot about him." Self-pity tears formed in her eyes. "Not my client. Frank's looking for a new partner." *Grow up, Giulia. Tough broads take their severance pay and find a new job. They don't snivel over ex-bosses.*

Hogarth's eyebrows merged over his nose. "Frank didn't say anything about that."

Giulia tried to smile. "We had a disagreement. Parted ways and all those euphemisms."

The ambulance bumped over a pothole, then over several in a row. Giulia bounced and pressed her lips together. At least the siren was louder than her reflexive whimpers.

They slowed and turned left. Hogarth peered between Ted's and Doug's heads. "Just pulling in the emergency entrance."

The siren stopped. Giulia's ears rang from that aftermath now, rather than the gunshot.

"You're not—" Hogarth stopped and spoke at normal volume. "You're not working for Frank anymore? Really? Call me tomorrow and we'll schedule an interview. His loss is definitely Precinct 8's gain."

The back doors opened.

"Amazing, Ted. You still haven't killed a patient with your driving." Doug climbed in and unlocked Giulia's gurney. "Here we go, miss. Doctor's waiting inside."

Ted hefted the other end of the gurney. "Don't listen to him, miss. Everyone applauds my driving."

"Yeah, when you stop and they escape intact." Doug grinned upside-down at Giulia. "I'm the better driver, but he always beats me at arm wrestling. If I only had one of those robotic arms."

Over the hiss of the sliding glass doors into the emergency room, Giulia heard garbled PA announcements and a high female voice begging for another hit.

"Hey, cop, where's my sister?" Urnu kicked a green plastic chair the length of the room. "You arrest her, too?"

THIRTY-SEVEN

"Shut up, Falke." Hogarth wrestled Urnu into a pink plastic chair. "Doctor, please see to the lady first."

"Where's my sister, dammit?" Urnu struggled under Hogarth's grip.

"Honey, I wish I could say I was happy to see you again."

Giulia recognized the fuchsia-nailed hands picking up her bandaged ones. "I wish I could, too." She smiled. "First beer's on me when you get off shift."

"Gimme a hit, dammit! I'm gettin' the shakes. You gotta gimme some." Two male nurses wrestled a screeching woman past the admissions desk. Giulia smelled body odor and Tabu. Only the thought of how much vomiting would hurt kept her homemade pizza in her stomach.

The uniformed officer's—Russ's—voice reached her. "Ms. van Alstyne? This is Officer Colburn calling from Vandermark Memorial Hospital. Mr. Blake Parker . . . Please, ma'am, calm yourself. Mr. Parker is in no danger. He wondered if you'd be able to drive him home. He's with the doctor now . . . Just a few stitches, ma'am. Thank you. I'll tell—" A cell phone snapped shut. "She hung up, Mr. Parker. I bet she's going to run every red light between her place and here."

"Driscoll—" Urnu grunted and another chair hit the floor. "What'd you do with my sister?"

The nurse wheeled Giulia through the double doors into the exam room corridor.

"Dead? No! No, she's not! No!"

The doors closed and spared Giulia more of Urnu's hysteria.

"Doctor'll be here in a minute, honey. No, don't sit up. What happened to your side?"

"It's kind of complicated." Giulia gave her an arch look. "I refuse to say another word until I know your name. 'Nurse Smith' is too impersonal."

Nurse Smith laughed her warm belly laugh. "Mama named us all after operas. I have two sisters, Lucia and Norma. Me, I got Aida."

Giulia smiled. "I'm very pleased to meet you. I'm Giulia. My grandmother named her five children after the Mysteries of the Rosary." She started to shake Aida's hand. "Ow. Let's treat the handshake as already done."

The meticulous doctor pushed through double doors at the opposite end of the corridor.

"Room two," Aida called to him.

Giulia concentrated on his face as he cut through the crusty gauze on her ribs. One of her great-aunts had eyebrows that thin. Not by nature, either.

Aida passed him water, a sponge, and disinfectant.

Giulia hissed when the disinfectant touched her. More institutional smells. *Gack.*

"Looks clean, honey." Aida threw bloody gauze and sponges in the trash can behind her.

"Indeed. I am always pleased when that particular team of emergency medical technicians brings in a patient. They halve my work. Glue, please, nurse."

Aida twisted off the cap from a small tube and handed it to him.

Giulia raised her eyebrows. "That's not the glue you buy at the drugstore, right?"

"Everyone asks that, honey. This is the latest thing: surgical glue. Looks like that stuff the guy in the hard hat uses to hang from the girder, and applies the same way. But no stitches, and your body will absorb it in a few days."

"Steri-strips, nurse." The doctor taped over the gash in two-inch intervals. "Now the patient's hands, please."

He drenched the gauze on her right hand before removing it. "How did this injury occur?"

Giulia had managed to put it out of her conscious mind. Now it threatened to drown her again. Sandra's screaming face, Urnu's curses, her arms weaker than Sandra's, the knife closing in on her . . .

"Miss?"

She inhaled a long, shuddering breath. "Sorry. Um, a knife. Something like a switchblade."

"These require stitches." He swabbed her palm with disinfectant and injected something. "A clean knife? Did you see any rust?"

Oh, yes. Numb hand. Much better. "No, it was very shiny and scary sharp. After she got my ribs, she came at me from the front. She was a lot taller than me—ouch."

"I have only a few more stitches to complete, miss. However, if you desire more anesthetic I can accommodate you."

How could one simple sentence make her feel like such a wuss? "That's okay. Go ahead."

Aida's hand rested on Giulia's head. Giulia smiled up at her. "I guess I grabbed at my side when she cut it and got blood all over me. When she tried to stab me, I reached for her wrists but my hands slipped and caught the knife blade instead."

"Yes, that explains the angle of the injury." He walked around her to her other hand and poured water over that stiff gauze.

"How'd you stop her, honey?" Aida applied antibiotic ointment to Giulia's hand and wrapped the stitches in a thin layer of fresh gauze.

Giulia looked away from the tiny needle shooting chilled liquid into her sliced palm.

Her mother named her Aida? Well, better than my Aunt Crossifisa. That was some fast-acting anesthetic. She tried to ignore the weird curved needle and thread playing hide-and-seek with her skin.

"My boss—ex-boss—broke in the door and shot her." The needle hit the instrument tray, and Giulia stared at her stitched-up hands. "She fell on top of me. I couldn't get her off because of my hands."

"Okay, honey. It's okay. It's all over now."

The doctor peeled off his disposable gloves. "The stitches can be removed in approximately ten days. Your primary physician's office might be a shorter wait than returning here. If you see redness or pus on any of your injuries, return here or contact your primary immediately." He typed into his laptop as he pushed open the door with his shoulder.

Aida helped Giulia sit up. "How's the ribs, honey?"

"Ow. They burn a little, but it's much better. My hands look useless."

"Not at all. Go ahead and bend them. Not too much. See? Your fingers work fine."

"Good thing I take the bus to work." Giulia attempted a penitent expression. "I broke his nose. The guy they brought in with me."

Aida cocked her head. "You don't look like the violent type, honey."

"Remember why I was in here last time? The attempted rape in the park? That was him, too."

The bright fuchsia lips parted, then grinned. "Honey, I'd high-five you if your hands could take it. How'd you catch him?"

"Long story. That reminds me—I have to tell the police what happened." Giulia looked at her blue bathrobe, splattered with dried blood. "Not like this."

"Did your friend bring some clothes for you?"

"Oh—yes. Could I ask you to help me get dressed? I think my fine motor skills are on the fritz."

Frank opened the door but didn't look in. "Hey, Giulia, you done yet? Jimmy's got our statements, and he's ready for yours."

Giulia mouthed *Men!* to Aida. "If you could give Nurse Smith my clothes, Frank, I'll be out there in a few minutes."

Frank stuck his hands through the opening, Giulia's clothes and sneakers stacked on them.

Open cuts splashed with someone else's blood and they don't test her for HIV??

Aida waited until the door closed. "Here we go. Underwear first."

Perhaps it was Aida's soothing presence, but Giulia wasn't embarrassed about her nudity. She tried to help, but her awkward fingers only got in the way.

"No bra?"

"It's bad enough that my boss's hands were in my underwear drawer. I'd rather bounce a little than picture him holding my bras." It didn't matter, though. She didn't matter. *When Frank hears what Urnu did to me, he'll surpass himself. He'll ask me how much I enjoyed it. He'll . . .*

"Hey, honey. Hey, Giulia." Aida shook out Giulia's 5K Run For AIDS Research shirt. "I worked registration for this last year. That makes us old friends, right?"

Giulia suppressed visions of certain public embarrassment. "You bet it does." She was sure her smile didn't succeed. *What a weak, useless female I am. I can feel my lips quivering. Well, I'm not going to cry.*

"Hold up your arms, honey, and I'll slip this right over your head."

Giulia shook her tangled curls free from the neck opening. They acted stiff, like she'd doused them in hair spray. "What's wrong with my hair?"

"You got some blood on it, that's all. It'll wash right out." Aida tugged Giulia's socks over her blood-flecked feet and worked her sneakers over them. "You're not going to cry, honey. You're stronger than that."

Giulia made a laughter-like gurgle. "I was just trying to convince myself of that exact same thing."

"I thought so. Here, stand up."

Giulia wormed herself off the bed.

"Listen to me." Aida pulled the sweats over Giulia's hips and tied the drawstring. "You're going out into the hall and tell that wooly-bear police captain how you stopped that pig. You're going to say it proud, and you're going to look him in the eyes and you will see him respect you."

Respect. She missed that. The habit once gave her implicit respect. She deserved respect still. Could she look at Frank and still believe that? No . . . but she could look at Captain Hogarth. He knew she deserved it.

"All right."

"I knew it." Aida rolled a wheelchair away from the wall.

Giulia sat in it—which her stitched-up hands made more difficult than she'd expected. Aida wheeled her into the hallway and parked her next to Blake, also in a wheelchair. A gauze pad covered a few inches of his neck.

Captain Hogarth came out of the room facing Giulia and banged shut the door. "Ms. Falcone, I promise to look the other way if you'd like to punch Falke again." He blew out a long breath. "When he's not cursing you and Frank, he's demanding to take possession of his sister's body. Seems to think he's his own law."

"He's Urnu the Snake."

Frank propped himself against the wall. "You said that before. What's it mean?"

"Frank, wait your turn." Hogarth set his laptop on a supply cart beneath a sprinkler. "Ms. Falcone, can you start at the point where you entered your bedroom this evening?"

Giulia detailed Sandra's threats and Blake's incoherent words. Next to her, Blake started to blush, but the greenish walls and fluorescent lighting disguised it.

"When she got . . . into . . . seducing Mr. Parker, I thought I could get the knife away from her and get out to call for help. That's when Urnu the Snake grabbed me."

Hogarth held up one hand and typed a few more words with the other. "If it's an alias, it's not in our database. How is Donald Falke also Urnu—spelled U-r-n-u? How is he Urnu the Snake?"

"It's his Combat Realm character. He's the leader of the Raging Death Clan."

Frank laughed. "You're kidding. Raging Death? What is he, a teenager who never grew up?"

Blake said, "Sandra told me about it once. He started playing the game when their parents split. She thought it was just an outlet for his anger. He kept with it, though, and gathered a following. They used to meet in this old farmhouse he renovated. She never knew where he got the money for that."

"He controls them. Maybe he controls their money, too." Giulia started to wrap her arms around her waist. "Ow. Can't do that."

"Let's get back to this evening, Ms. Falcone. You said Donald Falke grabbed you? Where was he?"

"Hiding in my closet, I guess."

"Yes, he was." Blake's cell phone vibrated. "I'm supposed to turn that off in here, aren't I?" He opened it, hit *End* without checking the screen, and shut it down. "When they tied me to Ms. Falcone's bed, I was still high on whatever they gave me, so I didn't understand what they said to each other. But Don stuck this weird metal thing on the bedroom door, like an extra lock or something, and Sandy knelt down and kissed Don's snake tattoo. Then she gave him a blow job."

Giulia inhaled sharply. "Raging Death."

"Explain, please," Hogarth said, typing.

"Urnu uses sex for power in his game cult. I saw them in that Net bar on Quaker Circle. The cult likes to show off for their groupies. Scott told me about it."

"Scott?"

"I had a date Friday. He took me there."

Frank burst out, "And if you—"

"Frank." Hogarth's frown caused Frank to swallow whatever he'd started to say. "Mr. Parker, what did both Falkes do after that?"

"Don hid in the closet, and Sandy read a big book from the nightstand. When Ms. Falcone came home, Sandy hid behind the bedroom door and locked it as soon as Ms. Falcone came into the room."

"She read my Bible?"

"If that's what the big book is. Sandy always had this weird religious streak."

Giulia wondered what Blake would think of her religious background. Or if he even cared. He might not wonder anymore why she was still a virgin, if he knew. "Urnu threw me onto the floor and trapped me in a scissor hold. He pulled my hair so I had to look up and told me he'd staged this for me."

Aida came out from the exam room and piled ointment, gauze, and ibuprofen packets in Giulia's lap. "In case you don't have them at home, honey. Insurance covers these supplies anyway. Be back in a minute with a bag." She walked through the door at the far end of the hall.

Giulia's heart glitched. "I never thought about that. I don't have insurance any more. I can't pay for any of this."

Frank's frown rivaled one of Hogarth's. "What are you talking about? Of course you have insurance. I gave the receptionist all the information she needed."

"But we agreed."

"Don't be stupid."

Hogarth cleared his throat. "I knew it was too good to be true, Ms. Falcone. What happened after Donald had you on the floor?"

Giulia couldn't process it. Frank hated her. He thought she used sex as power, just like Urnu. Oh, God, no. She was the polar opposite of Urnu. But Frank didn't—

"Ms. Falcone?" Hogarth had his teddy-bear expression again.

Later. Think about it later. "Um . . . He said he took the photos and doctored them. He bragged about his computer skills. Do you know about the photos?"

"Frank told me. Go on."

She didn't want to describe this. Not in this public hall with janitors and doctors and nurses walking by every few minutes.

Blake said, "I can help."

Blake wanted to make things easy for her? Like she wasn't sub-human? Was Hell freezing over?

"Sandy climbed on top of me, but Don called her over and she went, just like a dog." Blake shrugged. "For a woman who liked to control, she sure knew who her master was. She slapped Ms. Falcone several times, and then the two of them took off her clothes."

"*Go dtachta an diabhal iad.*"

Hogarth stopped typing. "Frank, speak English."

"Never mind." Frank looked up as the opposite door opened.

Giulia took a steadying breath. "I can finish. Urnu told Sandra to have Mr. Parker watch and then said he was going to punish me for, for biting instead of sucking."

"Did he explain that? Frank, what's the problem now?"

Frank stared at Urnu being wheeled out of the room across from Giulia by a muscular male nurse. Handcuffs fastened Urnu's wrists to the arms of the wheelchair. His swollen face already had the beginnings of bruises, but they didn't affect his teeth-baring smile.

"Your little virgin looks good naked, Driscoll. Think of my hands on her if you ever get her into bed."

THIRTY-EIGHT

GIULIA NEVER SAW FRANK move. One moment he was leaning against the wall next to her. The next moment Captain Hogarth and Blake were dragging him off Urnu, and Urnu's mouth was gushing blood.

"Bastard! Let go, Jimmy—I'm gonna beat the shit out of him!"

Hogarth shoved Frank's shoulder against the wall. "Frank! Get a hold of yourself!"

"He's the bastard who tried to rape Giulia in the park. Let go of me, Jimmy!"

Blake put his weight against Frank's other shoulder. "You can't fight both of us at once. Back down."

Hogarth jerked his head at Urnu. "Nurse, get the prisoner out of here and tape his mouth shut, will you?"

Urnu spat, and a tooth clinked onto the floor. "Tell him, virgin—tell him how I'll mount you in front of Raging Death. Tell him how I'll cut out your heart and eat it—"

Hogarth kicked Urnu's wheelchair. "Shut up, freak, or we'll let Frank go and I won't officially see anything he does to you."

The nurse stopped gaping and wheeled Urnu backward into the exam room, as Pamela van Alstyne barreled through the double doors at the end of the hall.

"Blake! Blake, darling, are you all right?" She launched herself at him. "I got a speeding ticket because of you, you ridiculous man. What happened? Oh—your neck—is it serious? Do you need a transfusion? I don't know my blood type, but I'm sure our family doctor does." She clutched Blake and wept into his collar.

Blake looked over her head at Frank and Hogarth. He'd lost his grip on Frank when Pamela crashed into him, but both men were gawking at Pamela anyway.

"Pammy, it's not serious. The crazy stalker stabbed me, but I'm all stitched up now."

"Stabbed you? Oh, Blake, when the policeman called I thought you were going to die." She stopped sobbing and raised a beautiful, tear-streaked face to him. "I thought I was going to die. You're never leaving my side again, Blake Parker, do you hear me? Never."

Pamela extracted a lace-edged handkerchief from a minuscule evening bag and wiped her eyes. Then she held out her hand to Frank. "Mr. Driscoll, thank you so much for explaining those evil photographs to me. I was such a jealous fool."

She turned to Giulia. "Ms. Falcone, please accept my apologies. I allowed my emotions to override my common sense."

Giulia was sure she just heard Pamela say Frank had told her the photos were faked. She held up her bandaged hands. "I'm afraid I can't shake hands, but of course I accept your apology." It must have been a trick of her ears.

"Ms. Falcone, whatever happened to you?"

Blake put his arm around Pamela. "She's a hero, Pammy. Sandra and her brother kidnapped me. Ms. Falcone was injured trying to get a knife away from Sandra."

"Sandra Falke was stalking us?" Pamela's elegant nose wrinkled. "I should have known. Of all your dalliances, she was the only one without a pedigree."

A coughing fit struck Hogarth. Frank slapped Hogarth's back, and they both turned and faced the wall.

"Ms. Falcone, I don't know how to thank you. You'll come to our wedding, of course. And if there's ever anything we can do for you, don't hesitate to contact us." She touched her cheek to Giulia's and kissed the air near Giulia's ear. "Can we go home, Blake? I'll have Pilar make *gambas pil pil* just for the two of us. I know how much you like them."

Blake grinned. "Frank, you'll have a check tomorrow morning. A wedding invitation, too. Ms. Falcone, thank you." He leaned over her chair and spoke in Giulia's ear as Pamela replaced the handkerchief in her bag. "You're one helluva woman."

He kissed Pamela's hand before he returned to his wheelchair. "I'm all yours, Pammy."

Pamela didn't stoop to a girlish giggle, but Giulia detected a touch of foolishness in her smile. She pushed him into the reception area and the doors swung closed behind them.

Giulia blew out a breath. "Frank, I don't think all of Blake's drugs wore off yet. He just spoke to me as an equal."

Hogarth finally stopped choking. "Dalliances? Pedigree? Was the woman serious?"

Frank didn't smile. "Big of him, Giulia. Yes, Jimmy, she was. I'm amazed she condescended to talk to me this morning. Being the hired help and all."

Hogarth leaned on the supply cart and reread the last sentences on his laptop screen. "Ms. Falcone, you were finishing your report when that touching reunion happened. I'd like to get you and Frank out of here before I transport the snake to jail. What happened after you realized he was the one who attacked you in the park last week?"

Almost done. Then maybe she'd never have to think about Urnu again. "When he was watching his sister for a minute I worked my arm free—he'd tangled my sweater around my arms and they were stuck above my head—I hit his nose. I don't know how much force I put behind that one, but he lost his balance and then I punched his nose as hard as I could." She almost smiled. "Did I really break it?"

"You did. I'm sorry you didn't get a chance to do more. Then what happened?"

"His sister attacked me with her knife. That's when I fell into the closet doors and broke them. Urnu grabbed my ankle and Sandra slashed me. I heard Frank yelling in the hall and kicking my door, and I grabbed her wrists. Then Frank was at the bedroom door and I almost got away, but she came at me again and I missed my grip and grabbed the knife blade instead."

"When I busted in, Falke's brother grabbed my ankle and I kicked him." Frank took a tongue depressor from the supply cart and tapped it erratically on the cart's metal rim. "Knocked his head against the wall, I guess, because he stayed out for a while. I warned Falke to get off Giulia. Instead, she pulled the knife free and tried to plant it in Giulia's chest. That's when I shot her."

Hogarth typed for another minute and closed the laptop. "That should do it for tonight. Frank, I'll start the mountain of paperwork you'll need to fill out because of the shooting. You've got Parker and Ms. Falcone as witnesses, so it won't be much more than a giant pain in the ass. Stop in to the station tomorrow for all that. Call Parker and tell him to come down, too."

"Got it."

"Ms. Falcone, you're a strong lady. Make sure you tell Frank just how lucky he is to have you." He kissed Giulia's cheek. "And remember, if you ever want a better job—"

Frank pushed Giulia's wheelchair past Hogarth. "Good night, Jimmy. Thanks, Jimmy. See you tomorrow, Jimmy."

"Wait, Frank." Giulia twisted in the wheelchair. "Captain Hogarth, thank you for everything. And I really am unemployed—"

"No, you're not." Frank spun her chair around and backed her through the doors to the main entrance. "I'm just getting my car. Don't go anywhere."

Giulia stayed put because exhaustion had planted a sixteen-ton weight on her chest.

"You okay, honey?" Aida returned and scooped all the supplies into a blue plastic hospital bag.

"Just tired."

"The cops took the psycho out another door and off to jail, so you won't have to hear his foul mouth anymore."

That lifted half the weight. "Oh. Good." Giulia smiled up at her. "When's your next night off?"

"Wednesday, honey. Why?"

"I told you. Girls' night out. First drink's on me." Giulia stopped smiling. "That is, I mean, I'm not trying to push you, I just want to thank you for how kind you've been."

Aida stooped and hugged her—gently. "Honey, I can count on two fingers the patients who've ever looked at me like I was a human being and not a piece of hospital equipment." She chuckled. "Not including the unconscious ones, of course. I haven't had a girls' night out in ages. Where do you want to meet?"

"Have you been to the Mexican place downtown, Salsa Fresca? I heard they make a great margarita."

"If there's a margarita, I'm all for it. Seven okay with you?"

Giulia gave her a modified thumbs-up. "Fine. You'll be able to spot me. I'll be the one with the spiffy hand accessories."

Frank's Camry stopped before the sliding doors.

THIRTY-NINE

GIULIA LEANED AGAINST THE headrest and closed her eyes. This wasn't much different from her last strained car ride with Frank. Employment status in doubt, reputation still in shreds, silence the width of the Antarctic between them.

She didn't look like the loser in a cat fight that time. She glanced to her left. Frank had the same frown on his face, though. Well, she was tired and hurting and in no shape to battle her boss. Ex-boss.

"Frank, why did you tell Captain Hogarth I still work for you?"

"Not now. I'm driving."

At the next stoplight, she said to the dashboard, "Did I hear Pamela say you told her the photos were fakes?"

"I said, not now."

At least you listen to me, dashboard. You need dusting. Frank should take better care of you. I need more than dusting. I should take better care of me. Let's weep on each other's shoulders. You don't have shoulders. Sorry.

"Giulia, wake up. We're here."

White light from tall metal halide lamps illuminated the inside of the car. A breeze with the scent of running water blew against her face. Frank had opened the windows. Nice smell.

She yawned. "Sorry. Didn't mean to crash." She looked through the windshield at the spotlit sign of some hotel or other. "Why are we here?"

"Your apartment is a crime scene. You can't go back there for a few days."

"What? All my stuff is in there. My purse—"

"Your purse is in the back seat. I took it off the counter when I left with Blake."

"Didn't you break the front door? It won't lock. I'm not sure all my neighbors are trustworthy."

"Jimmy's guys took care of it. He sent for your landlord and a locksmith while they were loading you onto the stretcher."

That made sense. She guessed. Muscles ached in places she didn't even know had muscles. They didn't make thinking easy. The ibuprofen packets in the bag on her lap looked good. She could probably swallow two pills dry. She ran her tongue over her teeth.

"Frank, I don't have anything with me. I need the basics: Toothbrush, toothpaste, deodorant."

Giulia looked again at the inn's carved and painted sign.

"We're at the Creekside? I can't afford this place." She sat up straight and grimaced. "All right, if I can't go home, could you please drive me to someplace cheaper? The Sleep Cheap Inn is only a couple of miles from here. I can swing a night in there. Two if I have to."

Frank switched off the engine and finally faced her. "You seriously want me to dump you in that cockroach haven? How do you plan to sleep? Or do nonstop eighteen-wheelers rattling the windows soothe your nerves?"

There. He dropped the polite mask. Dealing with a sarcastic Frank was cake when compared with two crazed Falkes.

"I sleep better when I'm not spending money I don't have. In case you've forgotten, Mr. Driscoll, I have no job. Tonight's events will prevent me from interviewing for a doughnut-maker position tomorrow morning. My landlord will probably evict me because of the damage to my apartment, and I'll lose my security deposit on top of that. Ten days from now, when the stitches come out of my hands, the dollar store might have an opening for a cashier. What part of this scenario leads you to think I have money to waste at a three-star hotel?"

He slammed his hand on the gearshift. "How many times do I have to say it? You are not unemployed. You are Driscoll Investigations' partner-in-training."

"Since when? Yesterday afternoon I learned that I'm a bad influence on Sidney. That my skills are nonessential. That my boss is incapable of adjusting his initial conclusions no matter how wrong they are. Forget the facts, everyone. If it's on paper, it must be true." She bent over her aching, glued torso.

"Giulia, what hurts? Can I help?"

"Everything hurts. You weren't there. You didn't see it. He lied to her, and she believed him. Of course she did—he's Urnu the Snake. He mesmerizes people. He has sex with new cult members in front of the rest of the cult. He told me that he wanted Scott in the cult only to get me in that bed."

"Wait. I'm not following all of this. Falke's brother wanted to have sex with the Second Violin and with you?"

"Yes, Frank, wake up. Have you missed the theme of this investigation? He tried to rape me and Pamela in the same night. Blake used all the exes for what he could get from them. Urnu convinced Sandra that sex is power. She wanted Mr. Perfect so bad that she made herself into Urnu's slave. Didn't you hear Blake in the hospital? Urnu snapped his fingers and Sandra got on her knees and—" She choked on the phrase. Every cell in her body had had enough of words about sex, watching sex, being forced into sex.

"And gave him a blow job." Frank lowered his voice. "Yes, I heard him."

Two boys and a girl on skateboards zipped past the windshield. The girl performed a kick flip and laughed as one of the boys tried and failed.

Giulia watched them rather than look at Frank. "You don't understand the extent of their violation. She had sex with her brother in my room. She nearly had sex with Blake in my bed. She helped Urnu cut off my clothes with a knife that matched his weird-colored eyes."

"Giulia—"

"Funny, isn't it? I once thought what a perfect sitcom Blake in my apartment would make. It turned out to be porn theater of the absurd. Sandra must've been Urnu's prize pupil—she graduated from dressing up Barbies to undressing me in two short weeks." *Shut up, Giulia. Frank doesn't care. Go live under a bridge so you'll bother no one but the rats. You don't matter.* "Forget it. I don't know why I'm explaining all this to you. You told me more than once what you think of me. Look, if you could just drive me to the Sleep

283

Cheap, the last words you'll ever have to hear from me are 'Thanks for the ride.'"

"I don't . . . I mean . . . *hifreann is damnú*. Giulia, before I drive you anywhere, don't you want to know how I showed up at your door just in time to be the hero?"

She moved her eyes to Frank's face. "That's right. You did."

"Where is an appreciative audience when I need one?" He formed a tentative smile. "You gave me the idea, you know. I went back to the office this afternoon to see what you'd worked on. I read your notes about an accomplice and I threw them away."

"You what?"

"I know, I know. I was mad. Don't say anything yet. Why didn't you open the overnight delivery?"

She rolled her eyes. "Because I never open mail not addressed to me."

"Thought so. You should've broken that rule for once. It came from my friend in D.C. who did the fingerprint check."

"The pomegranates. Of course."

"My friend e-mailed me on Friday to tell me it was coming. That's why I went to the office Saturday. When I didn't see it on the door, I assumed he didn't make the Saturday delivery cut-off. Not till this morning did it occur to me that you might've picked it up and brought it to my desk. I didn't have time before orchestra call to go to the office, but I dashed there as soon as the show was over. I found a charming photo of one Sandra Falke with spiky hair and too much makeup holding a row of numbers across her chest."

Giulia's brain went from "standby" to "on."

"Sandra was arrested once?"

"Yup. In college, for possession. Half an ounce of pot. Only an overnight jail stay, but her fingerprints are on record." Frank's smile changed from amused to exasperated. "I picked up the phone to call you and remembered you were out with the Second Violin. I called Blake. No answer. I wonder if that's when Sandra and Don were following him, waiting for the right moment to slip him their combo drug."

"Did you go after Sandra?"

"No, I decided to park in Blake's driveway and wait for him. I didn't want to deal with more of his 'I need that promotion' whining. I wanted his express permission to take this to the police. I would've gone anyway if he said no. As I crossed the threshold, I stepped on one of those six-by-nine envelopes."

"Oh, God."

"It was a note like the others. Part of it read, 'It's time for you to be punished,' and another part said, 'Your friends have turned into your enemies.' Or something like that. There was a photo of you on your bed, too."

"I don't want to know, Frank."

"Yes, you do. You were naked—"

"I said—"

"Shut up, Giulia. You were naked and your chest was cut open and your heart was missing. For one second, I thought she'd already killed you. But she wrote a time and date in the corner: 'Midnight, Monday, June eighteenth.' Ten minutes from now."

Giulia saw herself on her rug, on her bed, Urnu and Sandra keeping her alive from six until midnight raping her and cutting her until the Snake chose to finish his battle ritual. She remembered now: when Sandra had asked for the knife to take Giulia's underwear, Urnu said something like, "Not time for it yet." The image of herself, filleted, expanded in her head until she saw nothing else. *What else would they have done? Would they have violated me together? Would they have forced Blake to assist? Would they have forced that drug into me so I couldn't stop myself from enjoying—*

"Giulia. Giulia, stop shaking. You're safe now. She's dead. He's in jail. You're with me. You're okay." Frank pushed the hospital supplies onto the floor mat and contorted his body until his left leg straddled the shift and he balanced half on Giulia's seat and half on the hard plastic catchall between the seats. Then he put his arms around her, and with a light touch rested her head on his chest. "Does that hurt anything?"

"No."

"Okay, now just listen for a minute. That photo looked just as real as the other ones. I turned on all the lights and got the loupe and studied them. I looked at the one you said showed the rug instead of the sheet. I looked at shadows and angles of light." He swallowed and her head moved with his Adam's apple. "I realized that if one photo was faked, then all of them could be faked."

Giulia shouldered herself out of Frank's embrace. "I told you that from the moment she taped them to the door."

"I was furious, Giulia. All the bragging Blake's done over the years rushed into my head, and I jumped to conclusions. You don't want to know how many women he's slept with. The last time a girl said no to him, he was a senior and she was a Bible-thumping freshman. She actually lectured him on purity. He repeated most of it to me and got ticked off when I laughed."

"So you decided to un-fire me." Anger—good, clean, righteous—filled her with a hit of energy. "Rather, you decided to overlook the fact that I quit yesterday."

"I'm sorry. I'll say it as often as you want. I was a pig-headed idiot who didn't know enough to analyze the facts without emotion."

"That's a start. So tell me why I should keep working for you."

"Because you're talented. Because you'll be wasted stocking cheap shampoo and stale candy at the dollar store." He rested his hand on her shoulder, but without the protective embrace. "Because you're not a pig-headed idiot who digs in her heels and won't accept an apology."

A man and woman parked two spaces over, their car swathed in white paper streamers and finger-painted everywhere with phrases like *Just Married*, *Congratulations*, and *Honk and they'll kiss*. They walked to the inn's front door, kissing, and half a dozen people appeared at the entrance, throwing rice and blowing bubbles.

Giulia stared at Frank's dashboard, looking for a cosmic answer in its dust patterns. Frank had been a first-class worm for days, but he'd just saved her from a terrifying death. And she wouldn't be the Franciscan she still was inside if she refused to forgive him.

"Sandra sent me the same note."

Frank's arm twitched. "What?"

"The one you said she attached to the last photo. She broke into my apartment Saturday and hid it in my flute case." How calm she sounded. "I don't know which Prophet said it, but she found an effective closing line: 'You are fallen, never to rise again.'"

Frank snatched away his arm. "She broke into your place yesterday? Why didn't you tell me? I would've—"

"You would've what?" Giulia bounced against the seat when he moved, and her glued skin stretched. "Told me to ask Scott for protection? Told me how appropriate it was that my apartment was open to all, just like I spread my legs for anyone who asked?"

Her desire to forgive evaporated. "I tried to tell you before and after the show. You turned your back on me both times."

Frank deflated. "I said I was sorry." His forehead-puckering frown reappeared. "What more do you want?"

"I want my reputation back. I want to be innocent again." She needed another rush of purifying anger. "A hundred *I'm sorry*s can't give that to me. God doesn't want me. No man would want me."

Frank kissed her.

FORTY

Surprise wiped everything else from Giulia's head.

Frank broke the kiss and took her face in his hands. "You are innocent. Evil tried to touch you but it failed." He kissed her again, his lips soft, gentle.

Giulia had the awful impression she looked like a deer in the headlights. Where was the angry Frank? The smug Frank? The pig-headed Frank?

"I don't know much about God's omniscience, omnipresence, all the other omnis the priests tell us He's supposed to be." Frank kept hold of her face. "But if I'm made in His image—I am, right?" He nodded her head for her. "Then I'm going to risk lightning striking out of a cloudless sky and speak for Him. God still wants you. But I'm glad you divorced Him, because flesh-and-blood men have a chance now."

This time when he kissed her, her lips gave him a fragile response.

He released her head, and his grin challenged her. "That means I have a chance now." A pause. "Right?"

"I, I . . ." She gulped. "Maybe. Right."

He pocketed his keys. "Then that's settled. Can you pick up that bag?"

She bent halfway and stopped. "I'd rather not."

"Thought so. All right, sit there a sec. I'll help you out of the car and grab everything." He untwisted himself from the gearshift and took a plastic grocery bag from the floor in the back.

While she leaned against the back passenger side of the two-door Camry, Frank piled everything into the hospital bag, then took her arm and led her into the inn.

"I called for a reservation when I got the car from the emergency-room lot. It's on the first floor, so you don't have to deal with stairs."

"I don't have any luggage."

Frank laughed. "I shall give a censored explanation to the desk clerk. He or she will have no cause to raise an eyebrow at you."

———

"Blast." Giulia fished the new toothbrush out of the sink for the third time.

"Need help?" Frank's voice reached her over the soccer game on the room's TV.

"Gotta learn how to brush my teeth sometime." If she held it with her thumb and last two fingers, the stitches bent only a little. She tried squeezing the travel-sized toothpaste tube using the same three fingers on her left hand, and it worked.

She wanted a shower, but not with Frank here. Besides, her head still hadn't quite wrapped around that kiss.

Except "Ten Minutes Ago" from Rodgers and Hammerstein's *Cinderella* was running through her mind.

Shelve it. You're on overload. Give it a day or two.

Frank patted the other cushion of the loveseat when she came into the bedroom. "Come here, Ms. Falcone, and I will wrap up this case for you. After which I will tuck you into bed and you will sleep the sleep of the righteous."

Giulia laughed. "Frank, since when do you speak like Philo Vance?"

He grinned wider than before. "Since that's what finally got you to laugh again. Want me to brew you some pre-measured, weak, bitter coffee?"

"I think I'll pass."

"Smart woman." He turned off the soccer game. "Okay, after the angels sang over the photo revelation, I headed for Blake's. While I waited in his driveway, I called Pamela and made the angels sing for her over the photos, too." He put his arm around her.

She started to relax. *Don't be a marshmallow. Don't give in.*

Their reflections in the TV screen started to merge. Despite all her aches, she did not sink against him like a spineless B-movie heroine. The Giulia who'd survived the past two weeks intact mentally patted herself on the back.

Frank said, "When I hung up, I reread the last note and I swear something invisible punched me in the gut. At first read, the note was just another rant from Ms. Falke."

Giulia tilted her head toward him. "I thought the same thing, except for that last sentence. It creeped me out."

"But when I put the note with the photo, I realized it wasn't a threat. It was a description." He tried to put his other arm around her. "She—well, her brother—created the photo of you, dead, and put the Bible verses as your epitaph."

Giulia drew away just enough to emphasize the tiny space between them. "I'm missing something. Why did he create a photo? Why not just take a picture of me, um, afterward, and send you that?" She shivered, and Frank rubbed her arms without taking advantage of her moment of remembered fear.

"I think brother Falke is smarter than anyone expected. They planned to kill you and frighten Blake into silence. If the police ever suspected them, all the photo would prove is that he's a sick puppy who creates digital snuff pictures, not that he killed you and memorialized it. A clever lawyer could twist that into an insanity plea."

"You mean he'd get away with it? What about now? What about everything he and Sandra did?"

"Jimmy has him for kidnapping, sexual assault, and possession of controlled substances. He had a gonzo stash of pot in his car inside a winter emergency kit. We'll both have to testify against him, but he'll serve time."

"I have to face him in court?" Giulia drooped.

"Pamela probably can't identify him for certain—the parking garage was dark. Blake will tell about the bedroom incidents, but you can testify to both. You want him to get away with it?"

"No. Absolutely not."

"All right. You're a strong woman. You can do it."

He shifted position and Giulia made another move away, but he pulled her closer.

"You're not leaving me just yet, Ms. Falcone. The idea that the photo was a prediction scared the hell out of me. I peeled out of Blake's driveway and went straight to your place. Did you know that your neighbor across the hall watches everything through her peephole?"

"It's her hobby."

"When I knocked on your door, she stuck out her head and said your party started an hour ago. I asked her what she meant, and she had a lot to say about the lovely blonde and the man in black holding up the singing drunk." He snorted. "She was still passing judgment on them when I pulled out my gun and started kicking the door."

"Your timing was impeccable, Mr. Driscoll."

"Naturally. That's what makes Driscoll Investigations top of the line." He gave up trying to get her to snuggle and stood, stretching his back. "Time for you to get some sleep. I fully expect you to be at work in the morning. And I don't want to hear any excuses about overtime on a Sunday. You don't punch a clock."

"I know. Assuming I still work for you. I put in as many hours as necessary to get the job done." Giulia stuck out her tongue. "That's what I told Sidney Saturday night."

Frank moved to the bed and folded the comforter down to its foot. "I saw her in the audience with a tall black man. Is that the hunky boyfriend? Did you talk afterward?"

"It is. Olivier and Sidney and I had an in-depth discussion over dessert. You may have some explaining to do."

"What? Why?"

"I told her I quit and that you'd probably promote her. I gave her a summary of the case as it stood last night."

"Giulia, Sidney is not my kind of partner. Bubbly and eager are good qualities, but she'd drive me to violence in a month."

Giulia stood in increments. "But think how healthy you'd be. She actually ate frozen tofu at the Garden."

Frank shuddered. "The thought makes my tongue curl." He pulled back the sheet and balanced Giulia's elbow as she creaked into bed.

"Ohhh, that's comfortable."

Franked tucked the sheet under her chin and paused before opening the door. "I'll be back tomorrow morning. You're safe now, *a ghrá*. Sleep tight."

———

Giulia jerked awake at the knocking on her door.

Kick harder—she has a knife—

"Wake up, lazybones." Frank's voice through the closed door. "All good employees are halfway to the office by now."

She breathed again. Just a nightmare. "Be right there." Off with the sheet. Ouch. She was stiff.

Frank barged in as soon as she turned the handle. "Move back. I have to drop this."

Giulia's ancient black overnight bag hit the floor. Frank walked straight to the circular table beneath the window and set a loaded tray on it.

"That was heavier than I expected." He poured coffee from a chrome carafe into a real china cup and handed it to her. "Sit. You take it straight, right?" He sat in the opposite chair and poured a cup for himself. "The sign of a class hotel: real cream for the coffee." He added a generous amount and drank half the cup. "Don't stand there; come and eat. We've got Belgian waffles, fresh strawberries, and whipped cream—the real stuff, too. I tasted it."

"Frank, what is all this? Where did my bag come from?" She looked like a refugee in her slept-in sweats and T-shirt. Frank looked impeccable—a modified Philo Vance. She couldn't change without help, though. And she was certainly not asking Frank for help. Maybe Sidney . . .

"Giulia, you're zoning. Drink that coffee. You need the caffeine. All this is breakfast. And your suitcase came from your apartment. After I left here last night, I called Jimmy and he sent someone over to watch me as I packed some clothes and stuff for you. Lest I abscond with the silver and the rare tomato plants."

He was so sweet again. After all the foul things they'd said to each other the past week, the real Frank had returned. And she hadn't even thanked him for saving her life.

"Good Lord, Giulia, why are you crying?" He stopped a forkful of waffle halfway to his mouth. "You're not in that much pain, are you? Should I get something for it?"

"I'm sorry. I'm a wreck." She blew her nose on a cloth napkin. "I just realized I never thanked you for yesterday. You saved my life and killed the bad guy—no, bad girl—just like in the movies." She flexed her hands a little. "Can I take you up on the painkillers? They're in the bathroom where you left them."

After she swallowed two ibuprofen, she said to the worried look on Frank's face, "By the way, I'm also upset because you went through my underwear drawer again, Mr. Driscoll. Is there nothing sacred left between men and women?"

Frank laughed. "I swear on my mother's grave that I kept my eyes closed the entire time."

"Frank, your mother's not dead."

"Okay, on my pet hamster's grave. We buried him in the backyard when I was seven."

Giulia gave a theatrical sigh. "I liked this conversation better when your mouth was full of waffle."

Sidney ran down the office stairs so fast she slipped, and only the handrail saved her.

"Ms. Falcone! You're really okay! Hi, Mr. Driscoll. Ms. Falcone, you're so pale. Mr. Driscoll told me what happened, sort of, but he woke me up and I didn't get all of it. He just said to open the office and be careful not to touch the paint and that you'd be late because the police sealed your apartment." She sucked in a huge breath. "I told you it would work out. I'm so happy—" She flung her arms around Giulia.

Giulia gasped. "Sidney, let go."

Sidney jumped back and tripped on her floor-length broomstick dress. "Oh, I'm so sorry, I should've thought about your injuries. Who did it, Ms. Falcone? Which girlfriend?"

"Sandra Falke. Her brother was involved, too."

Sidney closed her eyes and pointed her fingers into the air between her and Giulia like she was running down an invisible list. When her eyes opened, she said, "The one who matched everything to everything else?"

"You could describe her like that. Yes. That one."

"Olivier didn't think it was her. I am going to rag on him so bad for that." Sidney clapped her hands together.

"Sidney, I think Giulia wants to get off her feet." Frank gave a pointed look up the stairs.

"Oh, that's right. I'm sorry, Ms. Falcone, I already forgot you're all glued up." Sidney's hands covered her mouth, but only for an instant. "Oh, my gosh, think of the toxins. Have you ever seen the list of ingredients in disinfectants? And glue is nothing but chemicals. I bet you're on synthetic pain meds, too. Mr. Driscoll, everything's all set upstairs. Ms. Falcone, I'm going online right now to look for whole-herb alternatives for pain. I know you want chamomile and meadowsweet tea, and aloe as a topical healer. You'll need a detox flush, too. Just give me a few minutes." She ran upstairs, tie-dyed gauze fluttering around her ankles. "Wait'll you see the flowers Mr. Parker sent you!" She darted inside, saying, "A messenger delivered them along with a big, fancy envelope for you, Mr. Driscoll."

"You'll have to drink that tea, you know." Frank grinned. "Be grateful she didn't mention tofu."

"I'll offer it up."

He laughed. "Spoken like a true Catholic."

She walked upstairs, Frank hovering at her elbow.

"Frank, I'm not going to break. I'm just stiff and a little sore . . ." Giulia's voice faded as they reached the office.

The lettering on the frosted glass was different. DRISCOLL INVESTIGATIONS still covered the center. But now the bottom left read FRANK DRISCOLL, and the bottom right, GIULIA FALCONE.

"It's a little premature, because you won't get your license for three years. But I called the sign painter at six a.m. and paid him an extra fifty bucks to finish by eight." Frank shifted from one foot to the other. "You're staying, right?"

Giulia reached out to touch her name.

Frank caught her arm. "I'm not sure it's dry yet." He waited. "Well?"

Giulia bit her lip. How could she convey her unexpected, amazing sense of belonging?

Silly—it's a job, not your life. Keep some perspective.

Frank cleared his throat. "Giulia?"

He wasn't perfect. So what? Neither was she. All the ugly things they'd said to each other still festered, but they could get past them. Besides, she wouldn't discourage a little groveling from this restored Frank.

Giulia raised one eyebrow. "I'm certainly not going to make you throw away good money. Think what it would cost to redo the lettering again."

Frank started to pick her up, but her startled "My glue—" stopped him. He nodded and said, "So tell me how to erase everything we said to each other last week."

She pictured a date—a real date with the Frank she thought had changed for good. *I could beg Mingmei to help me find a silk blouse to go with his Philo Vance suit.*

"Giulia?" Frank's confident voice wavered.

"Dinner would be a start."

"Great. Takeout in your hotel room it is."

She spluttered, and he laughed.

"I'm just yanking your chain, partner." Frank sketched a bow. "May I have the pleasure of your company for dinner this evening at . . . at . . ."

She grinned. "The Japanese place on Maple? I hear their wasabi is like a miniature flamethrower to the sinuses."

His eyes widened. "You can eat that? All right, you're on. I want to see you beg for water."

"If I do, Sidney can feed me tofu for a week."

The office door opened and papers rustled. "Of course you should be eating tofu, Ms. Falcone. You'll need to replenish your antioxidants, too. I printed out these recipes—"

Giulia tried to scowl. "Sidney, if you don't start calling me Giulia, I'll replace your whole-wheat bagel and green tea with Twinkies and beer."

Sidney's mouth hung open for five full seconds. "Ms. Fal—Giulia, you don't mean that!"

Then she ruined it by laughing. That pulled at her ribs. "Ow. Don't make me laugh."

"I didn't—oh. Joke." Sidney scowled at the printouts. "Giulia, you can't cook with your hands all stitched up. Oh, this is great!"

Frank laughed.

"No, no, I didn't mean it like that." Sidney tossed the papers on her desk and picked up her purse. "I'll run to the co-op and pick up some silken tofu. Mingmei will let me use the blender to make you a chamomile smoothie." She bounced down the stairs.

"You'll love it!"

THE END

ACKNOWLEDGMENTS

Writing may be a solitary occupation, but this book had help from many people. At the top of the list, my agent, Kent D. Wolf, whose skill and experience made years of hard work pay off in the best possible way. Hard on his heels is my wonderful editor, Terri Bischoff, whose e-mails always make me smile. And Brett Fechheimer, my production editor, whose brain works eerily in the same ways as mine. Thank you for adding Giulia and Frank to Midnight Ink's team of sleuths.

I'm also grateful to the people who made me much smarter than before: Susan Owens for her medical knowledge, Bryan Koczur for his MMORPG expertise, and Mary Kinahan and Danielle Greene for fixing my Irish. Marguerite Butler, Marge Fotheringham, and Jay Young, my beta readers. My husband, Phil, for support, encouragement, and helping me block the fight scenes. (Marry an actor! It has all kinds of benefits.)

And of course, Purgatory. *vamp dust* for all of you and a huge /bootay shake. You've been there through years of ups, downs, vents, and celebrations. You—and Absolute Write—helped *Force of Habit* find its place on bookshelves. I love you all. Especially those of you who agreed to "become" nuns in the next book. Mwahahaha!

© D. Steven Hodge

ABOUT THE AUTHOR

Alice Loweecey is a former nun who went from the convent to playing prostitutes on stage to accepting her husband's marriage proposal on the second date. A contributor to BuddyHollywood.com, she is a member of Mystery Writers of America and Sisters in Crime. She lives with her family in Western New York. *Force of Habit* is her first novel.

Please visit Alice's website, at www.aliceloweecey.com.